HARRY'S WORLD

A NOVEL in FIVE PARTS

[signature]

A. B. PATTERSON

Enjoy Harry.

Cheers

ABP

Second Printing 2016

Published by A. B. Patterson 2015
PO Box A1364
Sydney South
NSW 1235
Australia

First Printing 2015

Cover design by Luke Beeton at Sailor Studio
www.sailorstudio.com.au

Back cover photographs from iStock
Logo design by Stephen Hill at Dylunio

National Library of Australia Cataloguing-in-Publication entry:

Patterson, A. B. (Andrew Bruce), 1965- author.
Harry's world / A. B. Patterson.
9780992327309 (paperback)
A823.4

Also available as an ebook:
ISBN: 978-0-9923273-1-6

Published with assistance of Publicious P/L
www.publicious.com.au

To ethics ...
And all those prepared to
stand up for them.

Contents

Contents

About the Author

A. B. Patterson is an Australian writer who knows first-hand about corruption, power, crime and sex. He was a Detective Sergeant in the WA Police, working in paedophilia and vice, and later was a Chief Investigator with the NSW Independent Commission Against Corruption.

Born in Sydney, he grew up in England and France, returning to Australia when eighteen and soon commencing his career in law enforcement, and other government agencies.

He now lives in Sydney and loves to holiday in France. *Harry's World* is his first book.

www.abpatterson.com.au

PART 1

HARRY'S TRIBULATIONS

Slim, dark and lovely and smiling. Reeking with sex. Utterly beyond the moral laws of this or any world I could imagine.
She was one for the book all right.

> - Raymond Chandler

The house, like all brothels at dawn, was the closest thing to paradise.

> - Gabriel Garcia Marquez

– 1 –

The sparkling Christmas tree. The lovingly wrapped presents.
The gleeful smiles and shrieks of joy. The happy family, the three of them.
Sunny summer holiday time in Sydney ten years ago.

The frantic phone calls a fortnight later.
The police search for days. No answers, no leads.
His colleagues' awkward reassurances.
The interminable agony of waiting.

A shallow grave in the Royal National Park a month later.
Her little body, brutally raped and butchered.
Left for animals, by animals.
The horror of identifying Orla at the morgue.
No arrest. Months passing. No arrest.

The meaninglessness and depression of the days. His wife leaving. With another bloke. The bitter divorce.
His descent through the bottom of the bottle and out the other side to hell.
The incident in the charge-room. The mouthy jibe from an arrested child molester.
The crack of the sex offender's jaw as his fist smashed it into silence.

3

The media furore. His 'medical discharge' from the police.

Losing his badge. Losing his mind. Losing himself. Losing …

Harry's attempt at a decent night's sleep was its usual nightmarish ride through the sewer of his subconscious. As he tossed and turned, his somnolent thoughts returned to his latest case and, as it so often happened, his most recent episode of gratuitous dissipation.

He'd been working on the missing girl case for weeks. He generally tried to avoid missing kid cases, but business was slim at the moment and the bills didn't stop. He'd had weeks of tearful, pleading phone calls from Tanya's mother, desperately seeking progress. Weeks of meetings with her and the girl's stepfather, an unctuous man who wouldn't look Harry in the eye, not once. A man whose handshake was like grasping a soggy condom, and about as dignified. Parents clutching their memories whilst longing for more, and trusting unquestioningly his expertise to bring Tanya home.

She was young and beautiful, efflorescent in the framed mantelpiece photograph of her and her identical twin, Sasha. They had lost Sasha. Apparently she'd gone overseas last year and they had only had some secondhand messages via her friends. Harry had been quite taken by the twins, but fought down his reaction with self-flagellation about appropriateness. Tanya was just eighteen. She was studious, hard-working, and clean living, according to her parents. But then all parents he'd met gave the same blinkered synopsis of their beloved offspring. All his years, first in the cops and now as a private detective, had taught him to the contrary. But he never shattered illusions; that wasn't his business and it wasn't good for business.

– 2 –

He'd been working long, late hours trawling through the seedier avenues of enquiry, and this had proved a catalyst to the urges he routinely ran into, in his forty-something, bachelor and loner lifestyle. Tonight his reserves of self-sufficiency had capitulated and he slunk into the Scarlet Boudoir, an establishment in Surry Hills he remembered from his days as a detective.

He sat in the booth and was greeted by a procession of amiable girls ready to please, all pretty though none exceptional, with the usual repertoire of working names: Brandy, Candy, Paris, Roxanne. And then the fifth girl, drop-dead gorgeous, walked in. He choked on his breath as though he had been hit with a particularly dire question in the witness box. Petra introduced herself with a warm, working smile and a handshake of similar sincerity. She was a dead ringer for the twins. She exited as nonchalantly as she had entered. Then the manager arrived, like a waitress ready to take his dinner order.

'Petra', said Harry, as he put down his drink. He was still dazed when Petra returned, smiling affectedly, and took him by the hand.

She left him showering whilst she fetched drinks. He needed a cold shower, but that was the last thing he wanted. Half of him was telling him to take what he was paying for. The other, always the sleuth, was urging him to find some way of perusing Petra's posterior; there was a tattooed scorpion above Tanya's left buttock. He was standing naked and refreshed by the bed, admiring a large vase of purple and white orchids on the dresser, when Petra returned. She said nothing as she placed the cheap wine on the bedside stand. Then she dropped her negligée. She stood there facing him in her magnificence. She had curves that would have made a monk tumescent. She took him by the hands and ushered him onto the sensuously soft sheets. Internal conflict was rapidly vanquished by a tidal wave of primal desire. He closed his eyes and inhaled the unmistakeable scent of Gaultier Classique. He took a deep breath and opened his eyes.

N. R. Peterson

– 3 –

Sasha arrived for her shift at the Scarlet Boudoir, twenty minutes late thanks to the ever-efficient Sydney trains. Mary, the receptionist, grinned and told her not to worry, the boss was out. Sasha went out back and greeted the other girls in their lounge-cum-dressing room. She joined them doing her make-up and sorting out her tussled hair, disentangling the long natural blonde tresses from the chain around her neck, a gold chain upon which swung a delicate heart-shaped gold locket, coming to rest between her full and pert breasts.

She'd got used to the work, and the good money – seriously good money – particularly for an eighteen-year-old. She generally liked the other girls, kindred spirits in many ways, once she got to know them. They all had their stories and tragedies. The clients varied a lot, some more tolerable than others. A couple of her regulars were even pleasant and fun. No doubt a lot of the men had their stories, too. But, in the contrived exchanges that passed for conversation up in the rooms, you'd never discern fact from bullshit. As for the mechanical sex part, well, nothing new there. Sasha had started that many years before. Both her and her twin, Tanya, had learnt all about it before they were twelve, courtesy of their stepfather.

It was a quiet afternoon, no customers yet, just coffee,

cards and gossip in the girls' lounge. The receptionist's buzzer got the girls to their feet and the meat parade began. Sasha sauntered indolently through the guest lounge last and introduced herself to a middle-aged guy with a bit of middle-age weight starting, but still not short of some rugged good looks.

'Hi, I'm Petra,' she smiled coyly. He was Harry, apparently. Some punters gave their real names, some didn't. The girls didn't care.

She could smell copper, or a private-eye maybe. Always something about cops' eyes and the way they looked around. Whatever, it wouldn't be the first client with a badge. Just as long as he didn't want to live the cliché with the bloody handcuffs.

Harry had picked her, and she put on her most enticing smile as she led him upstairs. The usual preliminaries, including his three hundred bucks, done with, she pulled him onto the apricot satin sheets and started the games. He wanted her from behind. She saucily complied. He took a while, probably poor condition from a lifestyle of grog, smokes, and fast food. But at least he was gentle and didn't want to talk dirty; she hated the guys who insisted on spitting the word 'slut' in her ear as they neared climax. As Harry lay back, spent, she lit them both a cigarette.

'Don't mind if I do. There's nowhere left you can smoke these days,' said Harry as he took the lit smoke and drew back hard.

'The boss lets us as long as we freshen up the room before the next customer. Lots of guys seem to want a cigarette afterwards, even those who don't really smoke.'

'Suits me, Petra.'

They exchanged some friendly small-talk for the next

twenty minutes. When the hour was up, she relieved him of the fifty buck tip he proffered, gave him a lingering peck on the cheek and bade him farewell.

— 4 —

– 4 –

Harry had retreated to the most wretched and degenerate place he knew, his own soul. He still had nights like these from time to time. Working on missing child cases brought out the black dogs, which is why he only took them as a last resort. He sat in the beer garden of the deserted Emerald Bar in Glebe, anaesthetizing himself with shots of Irish whiskey and drawing long and hard on his Marlboro reds. His exhaled smoke rolled languorously across the metal table like the creeping mist of a B-grade horror movie. He had put his credit card behind the bar for a tab tonight, so avoiding having to open his wallet every drink and see the fading photograph in the plastic pouch. It still hurt whenever he looked at her, but he couldn't bring himself to remove the picture; moving on wasn't as easy as the counsellor had tried to convince him. He hadn't bothered with any counsellors since. He was getting himself sorted out, he knew that, but there were maudlin lapses. And this bloody case had brought on another one. At least they were getting a lot less frequent in the last couple of years.

It was dark outside now and had started raining heavily, suiting his mood and legitimizing his desire to stay put at the pub. He went back inside to the bar to escape the shower and plonked himself on a bar stool.

His tortured thoughts alternately mulled over and darted around his evening's debauchery. He had certainly enjoyed what he'd paid for, and when he'd told her to get on all fours he'd seen there was no rear-end scorpion.

So, he'd just screwed Sasha, Tanya was still missing, and Harry, through the Jameson-induced haze, wondered what the hell to do next. His self-absorbed gaze wandered to his left hand resting on the polished mahogany bar. Even after all these years, there was still an annular blemish around his ring finger. He winced inwardly before dragging his thoughts back from that particular precipice.

Back to work. Well, this was the only lead he had. Only one answer, he'd have to follow it. Given his earlier capitulation to his libido, there would be complications. Still, way too late to worry about professional ethics now. He may as well go back, follow the lead, and enjoy the fringe benefits of this assignment. Anyway, who was he trying to kid? Any pretence at social respectability, or any vestige of it, had evaporated years ago as he had abandoned himself to his profligate lifestyle. His plan forward sorted, Harry fed the cigarette machine, ordered another double, and settled in for the evening.

— 5 —

Harry awoke surprisingly early given the previous evening's marathon at the bar. His ability to sleep in, irrespective of alcoholic marination, had deserted him as middle age set in. He swung out of bed, tried to avoid looking at his increasingly rotund gut, and ambled through to the kitchen. He swallowed some Panadol with a black coffee and headed for the bathroom. He looked at his own reflection for a moment, but didn't linger. Better to shave than ponder. After brunch at the local café, Harry phoned the brothel to see when Petra was next on shift. This afternoon. He was in luck.

'Well, you're a keen boy then,' Sasha teased as she led him upstairs again.

Harry looked a bit sheepish, 'You're worth it.'

Sasha made sure the lameness of that retort didn't dent her wanton smile. Once in bed it seemed that Harry wasn't a man who wanted variety. Still, he was paying, so she got on all fours again.

Afterwards, Harry lay there with Sasha, having a smoke and feeling most comfortable in his nakedness. The sex had again been worth every single cent, and ethics hadn't even bothered with a cameo appearance today. Well, time to mix some business into the pleasure. He dropped his bombshell.

'You've got a twin sister, haven't you?'

12

Sasha leapt off the bed as if she'd seen a snake and hissed at him. 'What the fuck? I knew you were a copper! Get the fuck out of here.'

'Relax, cool it, I'm not a cop, just a PI, a private investigator. Your parents hired me to find Tanya. They're worried about her.' He spoke gently as a grandfather would, holding up his open palms in a pacifist gesture.

Sasha snorted. Like hell they were worried. That kiddy-fiddling bastard couldn't keep his hands off them, and she'd turned a blind eye for years. Wilful ignorance of the desecration of their innocence, and a pathetic parody of maternal instinct. Their sisterly bond was the only worthy remnant of their childhood. The rest was better suited to a police charge sheet. The parents from hell, and that's where they belonged.

Sasha started thinking fast. If this wasn't handled just right, the nightmare for her and Tanya would resume and the struggle so far would all be wasted. They'd got their jobs in the brothel the week after they'd turned eighteen and worked hard for weeks to get the money together for their first apartment, as shitty as it was. Leaving home one at a time had been part of the plan. Sasha's street cunning kicked in and an idea started to crystallize.

'I need to think about this, Mr PI,' she said, reverting to her sultry tone. 'Come back tomorrow and we'll talk. I'll be here in the evening, after six.' She smiled at him, her best effort, and stroked his face. 'And it'll cost extra.' She enjoyed watching his face as she told him just how much.

Years of practice with the most volatile types had given Harry a most soothing persona when he needed it, and he felt he had defused this minefield artfully. She said she wanted some time. Fair enough. He agreed to the extortion. The deal made, he shrewdly gave her another tip, got dressed and headed off feeling pretty satisfied all round. Sasha, meanwhile, got straight on the phone to Tanya.

– 6 –

Sasha smiled at him the next evening as he climbed naked onto the silky red bed. She dropped her negligée and strutted towards him, all the time wearing that temptress's smile and the gold locket nestled between her perfect breasts. He was definitely looking forward to more of this. As she got to him and placed her arms around his neck, he picked up a fruitier floral fragrance.

'New perfume, babe? That's not Gaultier.'

'Well, who would have thought? Mr PI knows his perfumes. So guess this one, big boy.'

'Not one I know, but I do like it. It suits you.'

'Yeah, of course.'

Harry tried to look convincing. 'No, really it does. So what is it?'

'Insolence. Guerlain.'

Harry laughed. 'They do come up with some great names.'

Sasha smiled and put her lips just in front of his. 'Yes, they do. And I like to mix them around a bit. Keeps you blokes guessing.'

He was a little surprised when she got on to his lap and pushed him down onto his back, but he was so entranced by this point that he was reduced to a quivering pile of grinning obedience.

'Okay, Mr PI, time for some variety; I'm on top. Attitude to match my perfume. Any problem with that?'

'Let me see … Nope, I can't think of the slightest problem in the world right now.'

At this moment, problems were further from Harry's mind than the public interest was from Parliament.

He compliantly laid on his back in the middle of the bed and let insolence rule the roost.

– 7 –

Sasha loitered in the shadows across the street from the parlour until she saw Harry walk in the door. She slid into the premises through a side door reserved for the girls. Once inside, she used a back staircase to avoid anyone else.

She could hear Harry's grunting through the door. The stifled finale arrived, followed by the clicking of a cigarette lighter twice. She lit one of her own and waited. No one was around to see her smoking in the hallway, and she needed one to settle her nerves. It had been a good script, she thought, drawing in the smoke, and so far perfectly executed. But this guy was a PI, so they had to be on their toes. Now just the climax to go. Well, hers at least. She stubbed the cigarette out in a pot plant and waited. She fiddled with her chain and locket, pausing as she rubbed it between her slender fingers. She looked down at it, flicked it open, and managed a wistful smile at the man looking back at her. Their dad had given them matching lockets the day he left eight years ago for some 'undisclosed destination' with the army: a destination from which he had never returned. Sasha kissed the photo and closed the locket. She put her ear to the door.

− 8 −

Lying there smoking, Harry felt a most contented man. Sasha wasn't as talkative today, but he was happy in his post-coital reverie. Sasha finished her cigarette and got up onto her knees next to him. She gave him a peck on the cheek and then twisted around to get up. She passed her exquisite butt about half a metre from his face. Harry choked on his smoke and felt his heart miss a beat. From that paragon of female posteriors, a large black and red scorpion gave him a cold arachnid stare.

'Oh, fuck!' he thought, but he actually heard his own voice almost shout it.

To Sasha outside, Harry's startled expletive came with some considerable volume. Her cue. She quietly opened the door and stepped into the scene. Harry was sitting up, still naked, on the bed, and looking ghostly pale. Tanya was also naked, perched on the edge of the dresser next to the vase of Singapore orchids, calmly dragging on another smoke. Harry's drained look turned to something approaching despair when he saw Sasha.

'Oh, fuck,' he repeated. He started to look more resigned than shocked now. Reality was dawning.

'Hi, Harry.' Sasha's voice was hard and business-like. She walked over to the dresser, reached behind a carefully arranged pile of clean linen and retrieved a small digital camcorder. She was smiling, as was Tanya.

Harry groaned and hung his head. He knew he'd been out-foxed and done over. These girls were good, he thought, half lamentingly, half admiringly.

'Okay, Harry, this is how it's going to be. The money first.'

'Girls, can't we talk about this?'

'Hey, big boy, who likes his entertainment horizontal and naked. What is there to talk about?'

Harry reached towards his wallet, which was on his pile of clothes on a chair near the bed. Tanya moved to it, picked it up and stepped over to the bed, sitting down next to Harry. He took the wallet, opened it and pulled out a thick wad of cash, handing it to the naked goddess sitting beside him. Tanya pointed to the photo inside his wallet.

'That your daughter?'

'Yes,' mumbled Harry.

'So how come you're not at home with her?' asked Tanya accusingly.

'She's dead.'

Tanya touched his forearm. 'I'm sorry.'

'Come on, sis, back to business,' intervened Sasha. 'And a business card, please, Mr PI.'

Harry pulled one from his wallet and Tanya added it to the pile of banknotes. She got up and went back to stand next to Sasha.

Harry listened dutifully to the twins' terms, almost mesmerized by two golden metallic hearts languishing between four perfect breasts. When he could lift his gaze he was transfixed by two pairs of pale blue eyes, as crystal clear as aquamarine.

Sasha resumed. 'Now, you will report back to our useless mother and kiddy-fiddling stepfather like this. You tracked down Tanya as far as her leaving the country. All her friends you interviewed said she'd gone to Europe to join her sister. And then you give them your bill, even bigger now, and close the case. If you don't, this video goes straight on to YouPorn.'

Harry didn't know what YouPorn was, but it didn't sound like the sort of media he wanted.

'But girls, this is blackmail. You don't need to do this,' pleaded Harry, still naked.

Tanya spoke softly, 'Do you want me to tell you what he did to us?'

Sasha's eyes dropped to the floor.

Harry didn't need to resist any more. 'No, I don't.'

Sasha looked back at him. 'So, you do as we say, or this gets uploaded and we'll arrange to link it to every PI search Google can do.'

'So every time a potential client does a search, up you come, Harry,' said Tanya.

'In more ways than one, Mr PI,' added Sasha.

Harry didn't have a clue how the hell you'd do what they were saying, but he didn't fancy the prospect. He also had no doubt these youngsters could pull it off.

Sasha continued, 'You'll be finished, Mr PI. Understand?'

Harry's resigned eyes indicated that he clearly did. He slowly started to get dressed.

'One question, girls, out of curiosity.'

'Go on,' said Sasha.

'Given what your mother has let you go through, why would she want you back? Surely there's a risk of you reporting him to the cops?'

'Good question, Mr PI. We put it down to her narcissism,' responded Sasha.

Harry frowned.

Tanya interjected. 'She's so self-absorbed that she feels she's lost the daughters she wants there to pander to her emotional needs.'

'That's pretty twisted,' said Harry.

'Twisted, but true,' said Tanya.

'And there's plenty of narcissistic mothers out there, Harry, believe us,' added Sasha.

Harry nodded and headed for the door.

Tanya spoke as he reached for the door handle. 'Hey, Harry? No hard feelings, okay? We can't go back there, you do know that?'

Harry turned and looked at the two utterly gorgeous girls, so wise before their time, and shuddered inside at the thought of what had been stolen from them years before.

'Yeah, I know, I know. Take care you two.' He managed a sad smile at them.

And with that he was gone, leaving the twins to hug each other ever so tightly, reflect on a close call, and divide up the money.

'Some serious shopping this weekend, sis,' said Sasha.

'Yeah, but let's not forget we want that new place in Surry Hills. We both want out of the Rockdale dump soon as.'

'Hell, yes.'

'So we can do the bond out of this, too. Let's stick to the plan, sis.'

Sasha hugged Tanya and kissed her. 'I love you so much.'

'I love you, too.' Tanya returned the kiss.

— 9 —

The jacarandas in Kelly Street were in full bloom as Harry wandered along, pub-bound. A light rain moistened his balding head. In the gentle early evening November breeze there was a steady cascade of purple flowers descending onto the ground. Harry loved this time of year in these streets and he stopped to watch for a few minutes, lighting himself a Marlboro.

At least now he knew why the stepfather wouldn't look him in the eye all those weeks ago, that piece of sanctimonious shit. In a way he was going to enjoy lying his arse off to the parents. When he had wished the twins well as he left, he had meant it, despite them outwitting him. He allowed himself a grin. Done over by a couple of eighteen-year-old sirens. Who would have thought?

The lavender rainfall and lilac carpet on the mishmash of bitumen and concrete was almost enough to teleport Harry to an alternative, and much improved, universe. He emerged from his floral reverie and lurched determinedly towards his favourite watering hole. The rain started belting down. What a day, what a week.

Shaking off the rain, he perched himself at his usual spot at the mahogany bar. Shaun, the Irish bar manager, leant over, grinned and shook his hand.

'Old Harry, good to see you. The usual?'

'Are the Kennedys gun-shy?'

'First one's on the house, Harry.' Shaun poured a generous double and slid it across the gleaming timber. Harry smiled and took a good slug. The music in the bar was subdued, as always, but unmistakably Peggy Lee started singing 'I'll Be Seeing You'. Harry winced and disappeared into his drink. It'd be a long sojourn at the Emerald Bar tonight. Another night staring into the bottom of a glass, desperately trying to stay clear of his private wasteland. Another night gazing through the stained-glass window into his dissolute soul.

Another night of losing ...

PART 2

HARRY'S NEMESIS

Whatever her business was, there had to be sex in it. She was as full of sex as a grape is full of juice, and so young that it hadn't begun to sour.

— Ross Macdonald

With the exception of the sexual act, there are few moments in life in which the body exults in the simple pleasure of being alive, fills with joy at the simple fact of its presence in the world.

— Michel Houellebecq

— 1 —

The torrential February rain drops gusted against the old sash window, with two of its four panes cracked right across and gaps in the putty like a dero's jawline. And the window was about the least shabby feature of the one-room office above an adult store, the Divine Rod, at the less salubrious end of George Street.

Harry was firmly planted in his third-hand, claret coloured leather office chair, its cracks giving it the appearance of a dried creek bed. The chair would have once been described as 'executive', but now 'retro' would be the kindest homage, although op-shop chic could equally apply. Harry was labouring, frustratedly, but doggedly, over his computer keyboard, gripping the mouse like it was a disobedient child. He was valiantly toiling at coming to grips with his latest technological office addition, social media on the Internet. The whole Facebook thing left him feeling like the meteor was about to hit, but business associates had assured him that if he didn't move with the times then his already scant business would become scarcer than a virgin at a bikies' barbeque.

A chunky cobalt blue glass ashtray lay nearly overflowing to his right, just past the mouse, and a Marlboro red clung to his pursed lips, a downward plume of smoke seeping from his nostrils. An Irish Cavan crystal tumbler, two sad chips interrupting the once pristine rim, sat to his left, a generous slug of Jameson lending its deep amber hue to the glass, still a work of immense beauty despite its added flaws. Well, Harry had thought, it was almost midday and the bloody technology drove one to drink anyway. He took a sip and leant back in his chair.

He picked up his iPhone and flicked to his messages. He treated himself to another look at those sexy twins, Tanya and Sasha. The cheeky buggers had sent him a photo of the pair of them modelling some skimpy lingerie with a message that this was some of the results of his cash, they hoped he was well, and 'XXX Mr PI'. It had been a couple of months since he last saw them in the flesh, but his memories were far from fading. Looking at them made him feel good to be alive.

The door bell buzzed and Harry almost jumped. It wasn't an overly regular sound.

'Come in, it's open,' he intoned at the inside of the frosted glass office door, layered as it was with enough dust to qualify for a place in a cleaning product commercial. The old tarnished brass handle rotated gently, but firmly, and an apparition flowed sensuously into the room. She had legs all the way up to heaven, but Harry's gut instinct told him she'd take him all the way to hell. Damn you, Satan, and on such a bleak, rainy day.

The apparition held Harry's stare as she advanced catwalk-style to the chair in front of Harry's desk. The client's chair was the only piece of furniture that didn't immediately qualify for the tip or the kerbside rubbish collection. Harry figured it was wiser to spend a little extra so the clients, occasional as they were, wouldn't be distracted by laundry thoughts when they sat down. The rest of the office he was happy to justify in professional character terms.

The apparition slinkily manoeuvred her delectable posterior into the chair, crossed her divine legs under her short skirt, and placed her Prada handbag on her lap. Her jade green eyes focused on Harry's burning cigarette, now in the fingers of his right hand, then meandered to meet his gaze.

'Smoking in the office? Don't you know it's the 21st century?'

He absorbed the accent suggestive of Catherine Deneuve in a playful mood and detected the slightest hint of a smirk at the corners of her sensuous mouth. His eyes met hers. He paused and then gently grated, 'Sue me.'

There was an almost imperceptible increase in the smirk on her face. She delved into her Prada bag, retrieving a slim packet of Vogue Menthols. Her long fingers, clearly designed by Nature for classical piano, slowly slid one of the slender white cigarettes out of their packet and placed it between her suggestive lips. A little too sensuously, Harry thought, but still, a client was always right – well at least at the first encounter, anyway. Besides, he was enjoying the view. With the other hand she flourished a Zippo lighter embossed with a French tricolour. Her smoke rolled across the divide towards Harry and mingled ethereally with his.

She looked down at the brimming ashtray. 'Are we going to share that, or would you prefer me to improve the pattern on your carpet?' The smirk remained, and a damned attractive smirk it was, too.

Harry smiled broadly and sincerely. He liked her style. He upended the ashtray into the wastepaper basket with a degree of ceremony like he was emptying the urn containing the remains of a distant aunt. The apparition's smirk blossomed into a full and lovely smile.

'You could burn the place down,' she said in mock chastisement.

Harry was still smiling; the day was becoming less bleak by the second, and he had a flash thought about spanking. He met her eyes again and put on his most professionally sincere voice.

'Well, firstly, that would represent significant civic progress at this end of the city. Secondly, if this flea-pit burnt down, the only person who would ever come under any suspicion from the cops would be the tight-arsed landlord for doing an insurance job.'

She laughed, with an undertone of huskiness, and stretched her right arm over the desk.

'Sandrine Gazeau, I'm pleased to meet you ... Harry Kenmare,' adding his name as she took in the chunky, carved ebony name board, perched on his desk. It was from a drinking trip to Bali many years previously and was looking rather battered and dated.

Harry took her proffered hand with a tingle of tantalizing trepidation.

'Pleased to meet you Ms Gazeau. French, I assume?'

'French Tunisian, actually. My father was with the French gendarmerie in Tunis and took my mother back with him to France when they pulled out in '56. Got her out of the kasbah, anyway. And it's Sandrine. In my professional life it's Madame Méchante.'

'Sweet, and very *méchante*, I'm sure. Well, I'm always just Harry. Fifth generation Australian, of Irish heritage, obviously.'

'Irish tastebuds, too,' she winked, looking back from the Jameson.

'Medicinal, not gastronomic,' Harry fired back, with a teasing smile.

'So are the ashtray and the charming repartee all you're going to share this morning?'

Harry chuckled. 'Sorry, my manners were stuck in traffic on fascination street, waiting to turn right into awe avenue. Plus, the people I meet who share a taste for grog before lunch don't present anything quite like you, Sandrine.'

Her eyes and slight pout said she enjoyed the way he added her name. She smiled as he dug another similarly weary crystal tumbler from the underworld of his bottom desk drawer. He poured her a decent measure.

'Straight, neat, or *au naturel?*'

'You are smooth, aren't you?' She locked eyes with him and smiled with just a hint of a pout again. 'All three, *merci.*'

'Smooth, crinkled, rough … texturally sensitive is how I like to look at myself, if at all.'

Sandrine kept smiling and gazing at Harry. No staring this one down, he thought, and he liked that. He looked at her classically beautiful face with its lustrous olive skin, and the long black hair, Cleopatra-style. He mused that she could have been Miss Carthage for eternity. He found himself transfixed by her glowing green eyes, and decided that the pause, whilst delectable, had been longer than was probably professional.

He held her stare, and lit another Marlboro.

'Okay, Sandrine. A lady of your style walks in here and I'm assuming you're not looking for a date with a dissipated detective. So, what business has graced me with your loveliness?'

'I'm told you're an ex-cop, Harry. An ex-detective, yes?'

Harry nodded, 'Yeah.'

'You are dressed quite casually, I'm a little surprised.'

Harry frowned.

'I thought detectives wore suits and ties?'

'I don't like things around my neck. Unless it's the limbs of a beautiful woman, and then preferably her thighs.'

She laughed and blew him a kiss.

'Smoother than the finest silk, I like that.'

Harry nodded in acknowledgement of the compliment.

'You spent a lot of years in the police?'

'More than I care to remember. I was a detective sergeant when I left.'

'So, you know what some of them are like, then, the corruption and all that?'

'Do I ever, and it's more than some, I can assure you of that, sugar,' grated Harry as he dropped his eyes to his desk.

'*D'accord, très bien.* So my story shouldn't sound incredible to you then.'

As Harry refilled their glasses, generously, Sandrine began her tale.

— 2 —

It was dusk when Harry finally pulled himself out of his chair. Two hours and half a bottle of Jameson had passed since Sandrine had kissed him on both cheeks, slid a fat envelope across his desk, and glided out of his office. In Harry's world, up front serious cash tended to make the client right as well. The mesmerizing note of Dior's J'adore lingered, despite half a packet of Marlboros having been inhaled along with the whiskey. It had been an emotional couple of hours for Harry, a circumstance he usually found most palatable when well lubricated. Sandrine's story, her problem requiring his professional assistance, had been simultaneously fascinating and disturbing for Harry. It involved the cops all right, and no love lost there, but more particularly it centred on a very senior cop, and Harry's nemesis.

Harry had always had distinctly uncomfortable, albeit intangible, feelings around Detective Commander Mervyn Lowe. He would have liked to have thought he always suspected he was a rock spider. But he was honest enough with himself to know he would probably be reframing his memory after Lowe had destroyed his police career. Anyway, he'd settle for always having been innately suspicious about Lowe, and just be satisfied with today's revelations confirming his gut feeling. The smile on his creased face was a wry one, albeit a bit indulgent.

Sandrine ran a solid and highly profitable establishment in Surry Hills, An Oasis of Sirens. Her girls were top shelf in the sex industry and they catered, very discreetly, for a considerable number of highly-placed and high-paying clients. Harry knew of the place, but his familiarity wasn't on the intimate level of the Scarlet Boudoir; it was well out of his price bracket when he had that craving for intimacy.

According to Sandrine, Lowe had discovered the identity of a couple of her loftiest, most respectable, and therefore most vulnerable, clients. Initially, through some deviant go-between, he had put the hard word on Sandrine for some younger flesh. Harry had to slap himself whenever he thought of the eighteen-year-old twins, but they were legal. What Lowe wanted was most definitely not. Sandrine had been left in no doubt that if she failed to deliver, or if she ran scared to anyone, Lowe would out her clients and her business would be finished, along with her industry reputation and her life. Harry reflected on her final words on the subject, a couple of hours previously.

'The bastard called me a "French slut" and that he would piss on me as I was lying rotting in the gutter.'

'That would be Lowe, all right. His soul is pure dog shit,' Harry had replied.

Virulent disgust and bloodlust hatred were inadequate terms to describe how Harry felt about Lowe. But he was going to channel it all into this assignment. Way before, a rather condescending counsellor had tried to talk to him about 'channelling', and had learnt the hard way about 'five knuckle scrotal channelling'. That one wasn't even covered in the Master of Psychology degree. But Harry had delivered the extra postgraduate module free of charge.

Sandrine's industry contacts had advised her not to

bother with Police Internal Affairs or the Police Integrity Commission – they'd treat her and her story like a cheap whore – a bit of salacious pretend interest and then discard her into the gutter. Despite the advice, Sandrine had vainly tried both avenues, and been seen off both premises like a diseased slattern from a Sunday school.

At this point in her story, Harry had cemented her recent experiences by summing up both IA and PIC as bunches of career-obsessed wankers who wouldn't even be able to find their own arseholes in a dysentery outbreak.

A friend had then suggested getting some evidence together herself, and when discussing this with some girls one had mentioned Harry. So, she had wafted into Harry's drab, drunken life, not to mention his office whilst he was uncharacteristically and relatively sober, and paid him ten grand, in used notes, as an advance. She needed evidence to deflect Lowe and save her business.

Well, Harry, you fucking owe yourself some fun on this one – satisfy your client and shaft that prick Lowe. Karma today was so sweet that Harry would have considered converting to Buddhism. This job was shaping up to be as much fun as a hot tub full of Swedish backpackers with large breasts and low self-esteem. O, Harry, yes.

— 3 —

Detective Commander Mervyn Lowe wasn't a career policeman, rather a career-maximizing policeman. He was just Merv to his peers, and 'Merv the Perv' occasionally out of earshot. He didn't believe in mates, nor did he have any. If someone was useful, then they were an associate, nothing closer. All he wanted was what he was – rank. Because rank meant power – the power over others for its own venal self, not for any noble motive. To Merv, serving and protecting the public revolved around just one member of the public – himself.

He epitomized the way public service worked nowadays. He had made himself an expert at talking the talk and playing the game. He had recognized long ago, courtesy of a rat cunning that left the rodent world in awe, the way things were going. Merit and experience had died like sad, forgotten battlefield heroes, to be usurped by technocracy, bureaucracy, and sheer self-interest, all dressed up respectably in the language of managerial weasel words and political spin, with a liberal dose of corruption thrown in. For sure, Merv wasn't an architect of this social regression, but now it was his religion, and no faith had ever attracted a convert as dedicated and loyal as Merv. And as with any religious fanatic, if you stood in his righteous way you paid the price of the heretic. He exemplified the credo that you got ahead by destroying others, mercilessly. And to really add to his potency in the game, he genuinely thrived on it; it was his amphetamine in life. Every time he crushed someone he experienced an ecstatic high, an orgasmic joy in the sadistic subjugation of others.

It was already late when Merv got home to his town house unit in the quiet, leafy complex in Artarmon. The neighbours, who all kept to themselves in the typical Anglo-suburban way, were respectfully and unobtrusively happy to be neighbours of Merv – that traditional comfort in having a policeman living next door.

Merv parked the unmarked senior officer's car in the carport, grabbed his briefcase and headed inside. His return home had had more urgency than normal, due to the illicit delicacies secreted in his briefcase. No Internet café visit tonight. Other greater pleasures awaited. That afternoon he'd done the quarterly audit of the exhibit room at the Child Exploitation Squad. He'd been absolutely ecstatic to find that the detectives had been particularly productive in their recent raids on sex offenders. Not because he had either respect or admiration for what the Squad was doing – apprehending the purveyors and possessors of child pornography – but rather because their efforts resulted in such a ready stash. During the audit, nobody would have picked his muted happiness, so accomplished was he at a vast array of façades. But he had been smiling to himself like a lottery winner. He was so late home because he'd had to wait for the detectives at the Squad to well and truly finish for the day. He'd banned overtime a while ago, to financially ingratiate himself with Command following the usual budget directives, but the detectives had an irritating habit of working back on their child abuse cases irrespective of whether they were getting paid overtime or not. He quietly cursed their damned dedication. And even when they had done with their casework, they were just as much in the habit of lingering in the Squad office over a carton of beer. Anyway, tonight he knew they had planned a send-off for one of their team, at the local pub, and he knew they were passionately serious about their drinking functions, so he'd been ultimately confident their office would be deserted by a semi-reasonable hour.

He hadn't been disappointed. He'd slunk back there shortly after six and, sure enough, upon using his all-areas access pass to enter the Squad office, the place had been deserted. He'd taken a Ministerial file marked 'URGENT' with him anyway, just in case he needed to justify his late presence, but it turned out to be superfluous. Once he'd ensured the place was genuinely empty, he'd gone straight to the exhibit room and employed the extra key he'd had made – the one made in the interests of police management taking a more proactive approach in holding the detectives accountable, an anti-corruption initiative Merv had volubly supported at the Command meetings.

Courtesy of the official audit earlier in the day, he knew exactly which shelf and which exhibit container he was interested in. He opened his briefcase, delving beneath the chunky Ministerial file and pulled out two VHS tapes with recently written labels. They were close enough replicas of two of the videos in the exhibit box, and he deftly did the swap. He decamped the building in a manner suitably official to any possible eyewitnesses, got into his car, and headed over the Harbour Bridge and up the Pacific Highway.

At last he was at home. Tonight was not an evening

to waste time on dinner, so he grabbed a can of VB from the fridge and headed for the lounge room, shedding his uniform onto the carpet along the way. Stooping salaciously in his underwear, he opened his briefcase like Pandora's box. He slipped one of the tapes into the video recorder and switched on the television set. He pressed play hungrily and was rewarded with the most delicious scene. There was an angelic little girl, nine or ten years old and anxiously naked, standing in front of this man, an example of ageing Eurotrash, also naked and with his hand on the back of the girl's head, forcing her face into his crotch. The man looked like he was enjoying a truly blissful moment. Merv, too, was truly in his element. Despite being alone, or perhaps precisely because he was alone, a smile spread across his face as his hand slid down the front of his jocks, already bulging with his excitement. It was going to be a great night.

As he watched his pre-pubescent porn tape, he reflected on his promotional path thus far. Apart from the usual politicking, back-stabbing, and general disregard of actual police work, it very much came down to aligning yourself with the right group. And now, there was a new and very publicly pious Commissioner, the first female to hold the post in the history of NSW. For Merv, that would mean joining the senior officers' bible workshop that a number of his more ambitious and canny peers had formed, the new Commish just having taken delivery of several hundred leather-bound bibles embossed with the police badge in glorious gold. The previous Commissioner had been a Freemason and Merv hadn't got on board with that faction, which is probably why he hadn't made Assistant Commissioner yet. It was something he'd heard about goats and rituals that had turned him off.

Disgusting, really. Who knew if it was actually true, but he hadn't been game to chance it. He had a tinge of bitterness every time he saw goats cheese on a menu. So his concentration turned back to the screen just in time to see a young altar boy kneel in front of a priest who then parted his cassock. Well, thought Merv, maybe bible class held some promise after all.

4

Harry closed up the office and grabbed a cab down to the Emerald Bar for a very fine steak, naturally *bleu, aujourd'hui,* with *frites* and *Béarnaise* sauce. Well, he wasn't actually sure what they'd eat in Tunis. He suspected couscous of some sort, but he wanted a good slab of red meat, so Paris would have to do. As he savoured his eye fillet and bottle of Beaujolais, he began to draw up his plan of attack.

His delectable fillet and bottle of red lodged warmly in his belly, Harry retired to the beer garden with a large Jameson. The earlier tropical rain had cleared completely, and it was now one of those intensely balmy summer evenings in Sydney, the air as still as a possum caught in the spotlight, and warm enough to have your head seeping moisture without even a hint of physical exertion. Harry's smoke hung in the sultry air as if Nature itself had disavowed movement.

He was ravenous for a plan, but had to keep reminding himself that he had to temper his deep, visceral loathing of Lowe for what he had done to him. After that calamitous night in the charge-room, when Harry had lost it and belted an offender being bailed for child sex offences, he had received several calls from senior colleagues expressing understanding and telling him just to stay on leave, see the counsellor, and it would all get sorted. At first, Harry had innately accepted that the Force would look after him; after all, he had been a good cop and made just one mistake after he had been pushed too far – way too far for any reasonable human being.

But then Mervyn Lowe had taken over as the head of Professional Standards, and Harry just knew it was all over. Lowe had fronted the media, following the launch of the civil case by the belted sex offender, to piously orate his views on 'dinosaur detectives who watched too many Hollywood cop films'. He had told the viewing public, numbly receptive as usual, that he would ensure that the 'disgraced Detective Sergeant Harry Kenmare' would face the full consequences of his 'disgusting actions'. After that evening newscast, Harry knew he was fucked. Despite certain senior colleagues trying to help him, the sanctimonious Lowe won over the Commissioner, and even the Minister, a good family man more used to covertly skulking around the gay bath-houses of Sydney than attending to real affairs of state. Even Harry's most ardent supporter, his mentor as a young detective and now an Assistant Commissioner, Bill Griffiths, had been limited in helping Harry to secure his medical discharge, rather than the ignominy of a dismissal. Harry reflected that if one looked up the word 'cunt' in the more progressive illustrated dictionaries, one would be greeted by a mug shot of Detective Commander Mervyn Lowe.

Harry walked along Kelly Street from the pub and turned left into Wattle Street. He had toyed with various ideas after dinner, but had settled on nothing. Lowe was as cunning as a shit-house rat, so any plan to trap him was going to have to be a hell of a lot more than basic. Harry couldn't be seen anywhere in the vicinity, or the game would be up, and Lowe would no doubt orchestrate some trumped up stalking charge against him. Lowe was the sort of man who never tired of twisting the knife: in fact, the more and the deeper, the better.

As Harry approached a row of somewhat dilapidated colonial terraced houses on Wattle Street, he caught that unmistakeable summertime scent: the languorous and heady fragrance of night jessamine that had been one of the greatest olfactory pleasures in his life. It seeped into his nasal lining as he closed his eyes and sucked a lungful of air through his nose. He spotted a scraggly example of the species growing in a soil-filled washing machine tub, on an otherwise barren concrete porch sucking up four lanes of vehicle exhaust fumes. Harry had seen much healthier looking specimens, but the aroma was such to match any of the finest French perfumes. Last time he'd walked past this house, there had been no flower buds on the struggling shrub, but tonight they were out to play. He stopped at the porch and put his face against one of the spindly branches. He breathed in slowly and voluptuously, bathing in sensual luxury. Just how did such a nondescript flower give rise to such a wondrous fragrance?

His reverie was broken by some bogan sounding his horn and yelling something alluding to Harry's apparent sexuality. Harry fought down his instinctive reaction to stick his middle finger up at the fading tail-lights of the bogan-mobile. It was too damned dangerous in Sydney these days. What used to be handled as a bit of sledging and maybe biffo now usually resulted in someone being stabbed or shot. The city had gone to shit, that was for sure. Harry usually packed a snub-nosed Smith & Wesson .38 special, the weapon's possession courtesy of his security guard license, although he stretched the permit conditions carrying it as much as he did. Still, so what? If it came to it he could account for himself most capably, and his life might depend on it. But right now the only hassles that Harry was prepared to get embroiled in were the ones he was getting paid for; cold, hard cash was his favourite mistress, on most occasions, anyway. And, alas, *mademoiselle* night jessamine, whilst redolent with aromatic perfection, wasn't porting any currency. Harry returned for one last luxurious inhalation, and walked on. He was still savouring the lingering residue in his nostrils when an idea dawned on him. He paused in his stride and let his mind take over. Perhaps all his hours struggling to come to grips with the Internet, as well as the sites he had inadvertently happened upon, had not been such a frustrating and frivolous waste of time after all.

– 5 –

Harry reckoned there was a better than even chance that Lowe, like most peds these days, cyber-loitered in the Internet's innumerable cesspits, and that was the best way to get him. But this was a world which Harry was only coming slowly and reluctantly to grips with. Harry had always been an ardent subscriber to the classic line drawled between the clenched teeth of Clint Eastwood's Inspector Callahan, 'Man's got to know his limitations'. Harry knew his own only too well, so he knew he needed expert help for his plan. He picked up the phone and dialled a contact from a job last year when he had needed an email account hacked.

'Yuri? It's Harry Kenmare.'

The heavy Russian accent responded, 'Ah, *privyet* Harry. Good to hear you. How is life? You want to drink vodka with Yuri, or you have another computer problem?'

Harry could hear Yuri chuckling on the other end.

'Funny, Yuri, don't give up your day job, mate. I'm well, yourself?'

'Always good in this beautiful country, my friend. What can I do for you?'

'Mate, I need to try and track down a paedophile on the Internet. And I wouldn't know where to start.'

'It is not my area, Harry. In Moscow I worked on

encryption systems and breaking them. But I do know someone here in Sydney. In my world you meet all sorts of people.'

'Yeah, mine, too, Yuri, although I suspect rather different people.'

Yuri laughed. 'Maybe sometime I can meet some of the lady friends in your world?'

'We can arrange that, mate. Meantime, where do I find your man?'

'Not much more than a boy, actually, but a computer genius. Goes by the name of Benji and hangs out at an Internet café on George Street, just near your office, I think. He is a bit of a dark fringe dweller in our business, but absolutely brilliant.'

'So will he do some work for me, do you think?'

'I think yes, for the right price. He's always after money for new gadgets. Also he has a reputation for revealing paedophiles online. I think he may have had some problems like that as a child. But he hates cops, too, so approach carefully.'

'Thanks, Yuri, I'll owe you one for this.'

'No problems, Harry. We must drink soon, my friend.'

'Definitely, mate. *Poka.*'

'*Poka,* Harry.'

Harry wandered into the Net Warrior Cybercafé mid-afternoon, looking as out of place as a double-ended dildo being unwrapped at a baby shower. There were numerous geeks hunched in front of screens, almost all with headphones on and their faces illuminated by the electronic glow. Harry had been given a close description of Benji, but the artificial lighting that ruled this grotto wasn't going to help in the slightest. However, as he walked the aisles between the booths, Harry didn't miss the red

Spiderman backpack slung over a chair that he'd been told was Benji's motif.

Benji was fixated on the screen in front of him and the fingers of his right hand were operating the keyboard and the mouse with a speed that Harry had trouble even focusing on. At the same time with his left hand he was texting on his iPhone, seamlessly and almost imperceptibly shifting his gaze between the large and small screens. Harry shook his head; he simply didn't get this Gen-Y shit.

Harry pulled up the chair from the next booth and parked himself to the left of Benji, who had an earpiece in his right ear. Harry spoke to the left ear, since the face hadn't shifted by so much as one degree since his sudden arrival.

'Are you Benji?'

'I don't know you. Go away and leave me alone,' came the reply aimed at the large screen. Benji then paused the computer to concentrate on his iPhone.

'Mate, I want to talk some business. Good business. I was told that you're the person who can help me. I'm told you're amongst the best.'

'I smell bacon. Fuck off,' this time directed at the iPhone screen.

Harry wasn't remotely in his comfort zone in this dingy, screen-illuminated semi-world, and patience wasn't his greatest asset. Right now he was through with niceties. In another milieu he would have thought to show a hint of Smith & Wesson gunmetal to get himself heard, but in this phosphorescent hell a good old fashioned .38 calibre equalizer probably wouldn't have the slightest cachet. He decided to keep his diplomacy purely verbal.

'Mate, by the time I've shoved that fucking iPhone where it belongs, your haemorrhoids will be setting up their own fucking Facebook page.'

Benji's fingers stopped their tapping action and his anaemic face, lent a greenish hue from the large screen, turned towards Harry, who could see the apprehension dawning in the eyes and, now that he had his attention, wanted to calm him. He foisted a tightly-rolled wad of fifties onto the desk as he spoke again.

'Listen, Benji. I need some work done and there's a very good cash payment in it. Do I have your interest now?'

'Yeah, but I still don't like the pork stench.'

'I'm not a cop, Benji. I'm a private investigator. And I'm working on a cop, a very senior cop, who likes kids, in all the wrong ways. Happy to keep listening?'

Harry detected the faintest flicker of anxiety in Benji's watery grey eyes, or maybe they were pale blue. It was hard to tell in this grotto. But the wariness was blended subtly with a trace of excitement. Benji swung his chair around so he was facing Harry, looking him directly and piercingly in the eye.

'You've got my undivided attention. Just keep it to a whisper.'

'Harry,' as he extended his hand. Benji's hand was delicate with long, surgery-suited fingers, and was a tad moist to shake. He was distinctly uncomfortable with the traditional handshake.

'So what's the story, Mr Private Dick?' said Benji, relaxing somewhat. He slid his tapered fingers along the desk and rested his fingerprints on the wad of notes.

'Not so fast, tiger. You'll need to do more than just listen if you want to earn that bunch of pineapples.'

Benji smiled and slid his fingers off the delicious yellow wad.

Harry proceeded to tell him the main parts of the

story, leaving out any names, but stressing the seniority of Lowe and not disguising his utter contempt for the man. Ten minutes later, story and nascent plan recounted, Benji's visage wore a sneer of contempt. He declined Harry's hand, but offered the bro grip instead.

'You have a deal, man. But there's more low-down I need before I can start hunting.'

Harry listened intently, jotting notes in his black Moleskin notebook. Some of the jargon he needed explained, some more than once, but he had grasped it by the time Benji had finished. Harry unwrapped the wad and split it in two as deftly as a Monte Carlo croupier.

'Half now, one grand, yours to keep regardless, and just to show I want us to trust each other. The other half when the trap is set. Cool?'

'Very cool, man,' said Benji, as his hungry fingers gathered the score of fifties up. 'I'm here most afternoons and evenings, so cruise back in when you're ready.'

With that Harry left, entirely unnoticed by any of the screen-glued patrons. As he emerged back onto bustling George Street, the glare of daylight made his eyes wince after the cavern-like, greenish dimness of the nether world he'd just trespassed into. With a renewed gusto in his usually languid stride, Harry headed for his office to get on with his work, not to mention a stiff Jameson or three.

— 6 —

Harry sat at his desk, sipping Irish nectar and slowly
refilling the cobalt blue ashtray. Whilst enjoying the
intoxicant pleasures as always, and periodically drifting
off to some very carnal thoughts about a Mediterranean
maiden, he hadn't neglected the tasks he needed to
complete to progress his plan. First and foremost had been
to contact a business associate to shadow Lowe. Harry
had worked out for himself that Lowe would almost
certainly loiter, with the most evil of designs, in the cyber
world's sewers. And as a cop and a senior one, he certainly
wouldn't risk having his predatory presence linked to his
home or work computers. So, he would probably have
to frequent Internet cafés, or maybe public libraries –
somewhere he could log on anonymously.

Clearly Harry couldn't dog Lowe himself, as tempting
as it was, so Harry had called a close contact and mate,
Trevor Matson.

Trev also worked for himself now, since being quietly
discharged five years ago from the Queensland Police
for publicising that year's actual crime statistics, in stark
contrast to the version released by the Police Minister. Trev
had met Harry on a joint cross-border task force whilst
they were both still detectives. He vividly remembered and
despised Lowe from all his sanctimonious media posturing

as he was skewering Harry, the news of which made interstate headlines. This, along with the generous terms, had led him to readily accept the assignment to tail Lowe, as risky as it would be.

Harry needed to know what Lowe did online, and he trusted Trev completely. Plus he was paying damned well, or at least Sandrine was. Harry's thoughts again drifted off to reminiscing about the aroma of J'adore and that tantalizing Tunisian temptress.

He slowly pulled himself back to earth and tidied his desk to leave for the day. All round a decent day's progress, although he'd had to venture well outside his traditional comfort zone. But every day was a learning day, he always told himself. He closed the office door, double-checking it was locked, and sauntered out onto George Street, entering the throng of city workers rushing home, or to the bar, or somewhere. Everyone rushed in this joint, he pondered.

He jumped on a bus down to Broadway and ambled along Bay Street, heading for his beloved Emerald Bar. He stopped to admire a cascade of magenta bougainvillea spilling down the wall of an apartment complex. Then he crossed the street and marched into his second home.

— 7 —

A week later Harry was sitting in his office in the late morning, his mind alternating between thoughts of Sandrine, the sexy twins, and his first Jameson for the day. Then the phone rang; it was Trev calling in with the payload. He relayed it all to Harry.

Trev had dogged Lowe for several days running and got him to an Internet café in Crows Nest, every evening in fact for about an hour. Trev had done a whole lot better than just this. He'd worked out after the first three visits that Lowe had a preferred terminal at the back of the café, the one which was positioned so the screen could not possibly be seen from any of the other cubicles. On the second evening when Lowe had gone in the sacred terminal was occupied, so Lowe had gone away only to return later when it was free. After the third visit, Trev had gone back after Lowe's departure from the area and booked a session on the same terminal. He then installed some illegal keystroke software along with a remote transmitting dongle at the back of the dusty PC box beneath the cubicle desktop.

Then, on evening number four, Lowe had happily, and depravedly, typed and mouse-clicked away for over an hour whilst Trev sat in one of his Volkswagen vans, an old Caravelle, amongst the rubbish bins in the car park behind the café. He was only actually about physically ten metres from Lowe, but he was, thanks to his illicit technology, invisibly monitoring every single keystroke Lowe was making, as well as mirroring every screen he looked at. He was on every practical level for that sordid soirée Lowe's deviant doppelganger.

So, now Harry knew what sites Lowe frequented, who he sought conversation with, what his interests were, all disgusting, and, most importantly, his various cyber identities and code words. It was time for stage two of the plan.

– 8 –

Harry ambled along George Street, mulling over the various bits of information about Lowe's chat-room persona and behaviour. Lowe seemed sickeningly confident in his anonymity and totally secure in his revolting, not to mention highly illegal, conduct. The last couple of weeks had been a mind-blowingly rapid learning curve for Harry, so much so he had even ceased to think of himself as a techno dinosaur. Mind you, he wasn't about to put himself out there to do cybercrime investigations; that's why one had mates like Trev and Yuri.

He couldn't help conjuring up images of the filthy hollows Lowe, and his ilk, crawled around in. Trev had described some and offered to show Harry, but he had been content to take Trev's word for it. Whatever Harry's limitations and failings, a lack of a vivid imagination wasn't one of them. For a fleeting, misguided moment in his disgust, he thought that maybe the government's proposal to censor the Internet might have some merit. He almost immediately returned to reality, which was the censorship proposal, despite the populist propaganda being used to garner community support, not only wasn't going to stop peds and child porn, but it wasn't even technically capable of doing so. The government had done well with their spin doctors to hide what it was really about: delivering a further increase in control over ordinary citizens and their free speech. Harry scowled as he considered the politicians: fucking lying bastards. They don't change, nor do they vary between the different governments. Harry spat into a pavement rubbish bin, to the disapproving glare of a pair of clean-cut, white-shirted young men. Harry glared back and scratched his nose with an outstretched middle finger. The bible-bashers stopped looking and went off to harass some passer-by; another bunch of fucking self-righteous liars, thought Harry as he walked past them, the word 'wankers' rolling off his tongue as if he had Tourette's.

Harry had half an hour before meeting Benji, so he wandered into a Stunning Beans café to get a much-needed caffeine hit. The young guy behind the counter looked at him vacantly.

'What's your order?'

'Flat white with a double shot, please'

'Okay, that's four-fifty. Your name?'

Harry looked at him, at once detesting both the bovine adolescent expression and the facile commercial model it represented.

'Why do you need my name, mate?'

The dull eyes looked at him, finding the question incomprehensible, ''Cos that's how it works.'

'Listen son, I want a coffee, not a fucking introduction.'

The mooing monotone continued, 'I can't process your order without your name.'

Harry wanted to grasp the scrawny pimple-landscaped kid by the throat and tell him about an altogether different type of process, something involving testicles and the large commercial coffee grinder behind the kid's shoulder. Instead Harry took a deep breath and gritted his teeth.

And when did it become all right for the little shits to stop saying 'Sir' or 'Madam'? The acned youth waited blankly. Harry unclenched his jaw and looked the kid in the eye.

'Cunnilingus.'

Needless to say, Harry had to spell it for the kid, clearly the State's next Rhodes Scholar in the making. He then followed the direction to wait at the other end of the counter for his personal coffee.

Harry sat at the only vacant seat and glanced at the newspaper. A few minutes passed and then a similarly calf-like teenager, only female this time and doing her best to look like Britney Spears, called out in a slow, halting voice.

'Kun-y-ling-gus.'

Harry smiled discreetly to himself and didn't move. One or two people raised their faces up from their beverages and conversations to look at the girl. The blonde ingénue repeated her call, this time more fluently and with greater volume.

'Kunny-lingus!'

Now the whole café stopped in their tracks and looked agape at the girl. Harry smiled openly this time, thought about having a pang of guilt for his little game, and then reminded himself life was short and he owed himself any fun he could find these days. A pregnant pause had descended on the shop, like a scene in one of those films where everyone except the protagonist is silently frozen in time. Harry stood up, moved to the counter and smiled at the girl.

'Yes, please. That'd be mine.'

The girl, still none the wiser, but perplexed by the sudden hush and various glaring customers, directed him to the sugar. He stirred in two, then smiled and winked at the patrons looking at him, still silent, and walked out with just a hint of a swagger. Ah, yes, it was good to be alive.

Harry went into the Cobweb Cybercafé to drink his coffee and do a little web job himself. He emerged a short time later, the owner of an email address of convenience courtesy of gmail, with the user name 'cunningcouscous@'. Time to meet Benji with the extra information.

– 9 –

It only took three days for Benji to get back in touch. Harry thought it a bit rude when Benji's first utterance over the phone after their second meeting wasn't even 'g'day', rather that he was ready for the rest of his cash payment. Harry lamented that that was probably just Gen-Y for you. Benji did follow up the fiscal small-talk by telling Harry he was all done, proud of his own handiwork, and the trap was set. And he didn't want to meet 'later on some time', he wanted to meet up now. Apparently there was some special deal going at Computer Gear City which expired that afternoon, so Benji needed his cash pronto. The cheeky prick had even suggested a bonus.

Harry pocketed some extra notes from his safe. After all, he did believe in rewarding good work, so if Benji had done as well as he had trumpeted on the phone, then a bonus wasn't unreasonable. Harry stubbed out his Marlboro, sculled the remnants in his crystal tumbler, and threw his jacket on as he closed up his office. He felt a tingle of genuine excitement now, sensing just the faintest sniff of delicious revenge for all those years of bitterness at Lowe.

Harry pulled up a chair next to Benji in the green-hued dinginess.

'Got my cash, Harry?'

'Yep, but I want the results first, tiger. Need to know just what I'm paying for.'

Benji chuckled. 'Chill out, dude, Benji has done very well.'

Harry loathed people talking about themselves in the third person, even more than he hated being called 'dude'. But he fought down his reaction. If the kid really had done the job, then he could talk about himself in the fucking subjunctive for all Harry cared.

'Lean in, dude. Let me show you.'

Ten minutes later Harry was both entirely disgusted and utterly impressed. His revulsion was almost at vomitous stage. He obviously felt innate nausea for peds, but he hadn't been ready for the filthy detail in Benji's 'chat' with Lowe online, contained in several cyber-conversations between them. However, his admiration for what Benji had achieved left him gobsmacked. Not only had Lowe swallowed that Benji was really a thirteen-year-old girl, 'Sunflower', who skankily suggested that she wanted an 'uncle' to shower her with gifts in return for her being a 'naughty niece', there was even a meeting set up for the next evening. Benji had evidently managed to get Lowe to expedite the grooming process.

'Benji, I did fucking say just to initiate contact. Now I've only got one fucking day to organize everything.'

'Dude, cool it, I know. But when the chat rolls you gotta go with the flow. When these scum are teased on to the hook, you have to reel them in fast. People spook easy in here. He was eager and gagging for it, so I had to go for it.'

'Yeah, okay, I take your point. Good work, Benji. Or is it 'fully sick, bro'!'

Benji laughed. 'Fuck, Harry, that's so not cool coming from you.'

'Yeah, okay. I'll cop that.'

Harry handed Benji a roll of cash.

'I've slipped some extra in, Benji. I love your work. See you round.'

'Happy to help hunt down this scum. Will I see it on the news?'

'If we're lucky. But don't get your hopes up too high. Justice is often a no show in this life.'

'Yeah, don't I fucking know it.'

'Mate, whatever has happened to you, at least you're getting some satisfaction now.'

Benji looked at Harry with a trace of disdain.

'What would you know about what happened to me?'

'I lost a daughter to these fucking scum. My Orla was just nine, and she'll never turn ten. So I don't ... I can't know exactly what you went through. But I do know something, mate.'

The disdain dissolved from Benji's face.

'Sorry, Harry. It's just always hard. People make judgements.'

'Yeah, I know that. So we're all good? All set and cool?'

'Yeah, cool. See ya, dude.'

Harry guessed that real 'dudes' didn't shake hands after a deal, so he just salutingly ticked his forehead with his finger and headed out into the daylight on George Street. The clouds rolling in from the south were gunmetal grey and the air had gone completely still. A Sydney storm was imminent and Harry didn't have a minute to spare.

– 10 –

Harry's options were limited. There was definitely no point in going to NSW Police Internal Affairs, half of whom couldn't be trusted, and the other half of whom were incompetent, overly ambitious climbers who had gone there looking for early promotions. Both IA and the PIC had already tossed Sandrine and her story out of their respective offices. Further, the PIC wasn't a good option given Harry's 'departure' from the Force years earlier, compounded by Lowe's rapidly rising star in the police hierarchy as well as political circles. Harry shook his head as he pondered just how bent NSW was. It was going to have to be the Feds. Not that they were exactly 100% pure, but compared to the NSW Police they were infinitely preferable. In Harry's view, it was like comparing a fine filet mignon to a can of Pal.

His mobile bleeped with a message. He listened to the voicemail from Sandrine, saying that Lowe had got a message to her that he expected to hear from her by the end of the week. She sounded stressed, so Harry called her. Nothing to do with the memory of J'adore, of course. It had been several days since he had last spoken to Miss Carthage, and the sensuous accent, despite the evident stress in her voice, drove him to reverie. He hauled himself back and assured her that things were in place, and that

Lowe would not be a problem for much longer. Well, he thought to himself, he might be jumping the gun just a tad, but he was quietly confident. Then he called up a contact in the Feds and secured an urgent meeting. With that he quickened his gait and headed to the AFP building in Goulburn Street.

Once through security, Harry was met by Federal Agent Tom Strong, another jaded detective like Harry, but one still hanging in there for his pension. Tom took Harry up to his office, offered him a seat and made a pointed reminder about not smoking, indicating the large red signs on the walls.

'So, Harry, my old mate, how's life and where's the fire? Not like you to be so fucking pushy for a meet.'

'And I really could do with a smoke right now, Tom. No? Okay. Here's what I've got.'

And Harry proceeded to give Tom an edited version of his case, leaving out Benji's name and Sandrine's entire role. When he had finished, Tom, who had silently soaked up the story, could only manage, 'Fuck me drunk!' He swivelled in his desk chair, pausing momentarily to look out the window, and then came back to face Harry.

'Mate, this is seriously heavy shit. Happy to tell it all again to the cybercrime boys downstairs? They'll be the ones who'll have to take this one on.'

'No worries, Tom. So long as they are actually going to do something. I didn't come here to have this buried. I think better of you guys than that.'

'Oh, don't worry. Our boys will be fucking over the moon with this opportunity. They still haven't forgotten the last time the bent locals fucked them over on a task force. All the front money for that drug buy, 100K, just vanished into thin air.'

'Yeah, NSW still has the best police force money can buy. And they've even found God, too, apparently.'

Tom grimaced. 'Didn't touch you though, Harry. One of the reasons I've always liked you, mate.'

'Tom, mate, that's why I'm out, and on the bones of my arse. And the only place I'd be seen fucking dead on a Sunday is my local pub.'

The pair laughed, shook hands – no 'dudes' here – and went downstairs.

The AFP's Sydney cybercrime unit was fledgling, and the office fit-out looked it. Lots of sparkling veneer furniture, masses of computer gear, even framed prints on the walls. A lot of budget had gone into this, and the successes had been reasonable. Tom introduced Harry to the OIC, Phil Greene. Federal Agent Greene just didn't look anything like a detective. He had greasy black ringleted hair down to his collar, thick Coke bottle glasses, and the anaemic complexion of a cave-dwelling hobbit. However, the chocolate brown eyes behind those chunky lenses were as sharp as a pair of Gordon Ramsey's kitchen knives, not to mention his tongue. And Phil's desk – presumably there was one somewhere under the accumulated piles of chaos – looked like a nuns' dormitory after the visitation of a particularly horny Viking raiding party, only minus the shagged out sisters.

Phil called his offsiders over. When they were all seated, Harry told them exactly what he'd told Tom an hour earlier. Phil whistled softly and rubbed his hands together.

'I do like this one, Harry, but can't we get your geek boy to actually go to the meet and wear a wire? Would make things a whole lot easier.'

'Phil, firstly can I remind you he's supposed to be a thirteen-year-old girl. He sure won't pass for it. Secondly,

I'm not getting him involved in any of this side of things. He's done his work and besides, he hates cops.'

'Well, just who is he anyway?'

'My contact. My confidential contact.'

Phil looked like he was going to get testy when Tom interjected.

'Listen, Phil, the meet's arranged and we've got the printouts of all the chat in the online forums. There's enough there to prove that Lowe has groomed this 'girl' over numerous conversations, and that he intends to meet with 'her' for sexual purposes. If Lowe shows up for the meet and does everything 'Sunflower' has told him to, then that's enough to well and truly nail him for procuring a child for sex, at the very least. That'll do the job. We can leave Harry's contact out of it.'

'Yeah, all right,' replied a reluctant Phil. 'But, Harry, your geek boy is sailing close to the wind himself with this chat stuff. A zealous Crown prosecutor could go after him for incitement, not to mention a defence barrister for Lowe.'

Harry snorted. 'Mate, good fucking luck finding a jury that would convict geek boy. You'd have a better chance of getting a gut-full of piss and a stray root at the Christian Democrats' Christmas party.'

Phil chuckled, pulled off his chunky specs, gave them a wipe on his shirt front, and plonked them back on his nose.

'Okay, Harry. We'll work out the details for the operation. I'll even let you sit in the backup car, as long as you just sit there and watch. Understood? We have a deal?'

'Yep. I can watch you guys work. I'll enjoy the show. I might even learn some new tricks.' Harry neglected to reveal to Phil his personal history with Lowe, although Tom knew of it. And Tom hadn't seen any reason to tell Phil and his team either.

– 11 –

The next evening, suitably before six o'clock, the AFP backup teams were discreetly in place around Victoria Park off Broadway. Benji, aka the thirteen-year-old 'Sunflower', had arranged to meet Lowe at 6 p.m. near the public swimming pool, so it would look like a male relative picking her up from the afternoon swim. Harry was sitting in the back of one of the sedans, parked on the roadway below the university library, looking directly over the pool area. The AFP's snatch team were convincingly sweating away as Metropolitan Council gardeners in the park, complete with a ride-on mower and a mini rubbish truck. Harry couldn't help but be impressed at the effort Phil and his team had gone to, not to mention how quickly they had put it together.

Perhaps it was all the pent up hatred that Harry had for Lowe, exacerbated tenfold now that he knew about Lowe's predilection for jailbait, but Harry spotted Lowe before any of the Feds. Lowe was walking up the main path from the City Road entrance, and looking damned casual about it as he crossed the wooden bridge over the pond. The Feds with Harry alerted their colleagues and the tension began to mount.

'Sunflower' had told Lowe to drop a Coke can in the bin nearest the swimming pool entrance and then walk over towards the entrance, so she would know it was him. Sure enough, Lowe was sipping a Coke as he meandered up the path.

Now he was only about thirty metres from the bin and he had a couple of furtive glances around him. He'd taken no notice of the gardeners, despite there being six of them all working hard after 5.30 in the afternoon. He had taken a good look at a couple of young girls leaving the pool compound, but they'd wandered off down the path towards Broadway. Phil's voice came over the radio, reminding the tense teams that no one was to move until the Coke can had been dropped in the bin and Lowe had moved to the prearranged meeting spot.

Thirty seconds later, with Lowe only metres from the bin, all hell broke loose. Harry could only watch in utter disbelief.

An immaculately dressed woman, in her forties and carrying a large, flashy Christian Dior handbag, had just come down the steps from the university direction and was walking along the main path. A clearly drug-addicted desperado, who had been lolling about under a fig tree, ran to the woman and grabbed her handbag, shouting at her to let go of it. He followed the grab with a half-baked punch to her face. Whilst the woman reeled, she clung on to the bag and a struggle ensued as she screamed for help. The two nearest gardeners, as yet unidentified, were running towards the woman and her assailant, yelling at the mugger to let go of her. As they were almost upon him, the mugger pulled a syringe out of his dirty khaki army surplus jacket and put it to his victim's throat. He screamed at the gardeners, 'Fuck off or I'll stab the bitch!' The woman was becoming hysterical.

And so the die was cast. Both gardeners instinctively

drew their Glock automatics and their badges. Suddenly two gleaming gun barrels were levelled at the mugger's head, only a couple of metres away, and the balance of power had changed. From where he was Harry couldn't be sure exactly what order the shouted words came in, but somewhere in the chaos the mugger learnt two things quite clearly: one, he was facing, via their gun barrels, a pair of Federal Agents, and, two, unless he dropped the syringe and got on the ground 'real fucking fast', his brains were going to be 'spread all over the fucking park'. It was no contest. So, whilst a lady and her Dior were saved, Detective Commander Mervyn Lowe turned heel and headed back down the path towards City Road, somewhat more purposeful in his stride this time. Harry lost sight of him as he disappeared over the pond.

Harry sat in the Feds' car, stunned and lost for words at how the cards had played out. Meanwhile, Phil was going ballistic over the radio and was sure to get reprimanded about the stream of on-air expletives.

The Feds headed back to their office for their debrief, and Phil dropped Harry outside his office on George Street. They looked ruefully at each other, but both well knew that sometimes shit just happened.

'He'll lie low, excuse the pun, for a while, Harry. But we'll be looking out for him from now on. He's on our radar.'

'Thanks for all your effort, Phil. No bloody cigar this time, alas, but you guys are a solid professional outfit. I've been impressed. See you round.'

Phil waved and drove off towards Goulburn Street.

Harry couldn't get to his bottom drawer fast enough, having already jammed a lit Marlboro into his lips on the way up the old staircase. The first very large Jameson didn't even touch the sides of his parched throat. He poured himself another immediately, lit his third consecutive cigarette, and gazed into the Cavan crystal. He still had his jacket on.

'Lowe, you cunt, I'm not finished with you yet. Every dirty dog has its day, and yours will come.'

Harry swallowed a third whiskey without any further words. Then he got up, closed the office, and headed over the road for the Internet café.

– 12 –

Later that evening, Mervyn Lowe slipped into the Internet café in Crows Nest. If anyone had looked at him they would have noticed he was exceedingly pale and there was a patina of moisture on his forehead and face. But no one took any interest in him as he sat himself at his usual terminal near the back of the shop. Despite his anxiety from the events a couple of hours previously, Lowe was fuming inside. Someone had tricked him and no one was allowed to get the better of him. He always prevailed. 'I'm going to find you and destroy you, whoever you are,' he said under his breath as he logged on to the computer.

Lowe opened his email account to find a message from someone he'd never heard of, 'Cunningcouscous@gmail. com'. The message was profoundly clear.

> 'Lowe you rock spider cunt. Nearly had you today. Next time, and there will be a next time, I won't miss. Your arse will be the shower-time prize at Long Bay. And if you ever again go near my friend Madame Méchante, you're fucking dead meat. Cops don't scare me, you piece of shit. And as you can see I know where you live. Remember 3 words, Lowe, FUCKING DEAD MEAT.'

He looked beneath the email text to see a close up photograph of the front of his town house in Artarmon.

Lowe shivered, despite the sweat now starting to run down his forehead, and stared at the message and photo. 'Who the fuck are you? How dare you threaten me,' he whispered to himself. He deleted the message. He was normally an insidiously cool customer, but he was rattled now. And still bloody angry. He had to have vengeance on this upstart pretender.

He leant back in the chair and took several slow, deep breaths to settle himself. He needed to calm down and get back to rational planning. It had been too close for comfort today, far too close. He'd allowed his hormones to take control after all the online dirty talk with 'Sunflower'. He'd got carried away with himself and his rampant desires. It was time to restrain himself, at least for a while.

Certainly Madame Méchante was off limits now; she seemed rather better connected than he had thought. He couldn't figure out how, but today was clear evidence she could pull strings with the Feds. To have got the Plastic Fantastics off their fat arses and out doing actual police work took some doing. No, definitely no way to keep pressuring her for some fresh young meat. He'd need to devise a new strategy and remind himself to temper his libido with more caution. Meanwhile, in the background, he'd find out who this 'cunningcouscous' was, and then arrange a 'next time' on his own terms.

Right now, Lowe needed to de-stress with some more urgent release, so he left the café and headed home to crack a beer and pleasure himself.

– 13 –

Harry had tried to tidy up his office a little, although it didn't really show. Not normally one to give 'a flying rat's arse', as he liked to put it, about his desk, the impending arrival of Miss Carthage in perpetuity had impelled Harry to act a little out of character. He'd even washed, not just rinsed, the Cavan crystal tumblers.

Five minutes before the appointed time, and Harry liked the before factor, Sandrine wafted into his office on a delicious cloud of J'adore and with only the merest of playful knocks on his door. She was smiling knowingly, teasing Harry as she sat down, accepting a Jameson as she did so. She took his offer of a light for her cigarette, and he lit up another Marlboro. Even the cobalt blue ashtray had been scrubbed for the occasion. Sandrine noticed, too, running a slender finger along the gleaming glass rim.

'Well, Harry Kenmare, I don't know what you did, and I probably don't want to know, let alone need to, but Mr Lowe doesn't want anything at all to do with me. Ever. He was most adamant about the 'ever' bit before he hung up the phone.'

'That's great news. Job done, I would say.' Harry smiled.

'*Merci*, Harry. *Vraiment, merci infiniment.*'

Harry started to melt in his loins. Instead of dribbling

71

something inane, he took his own wise counsel, kept silent, smiled and nodded, doing his best Bogart impersonation.

Sandrine delved gracefully into her Prada bag and slid an obese envelope across the desk.

'It's more than agreed, Harry, but worth every cent. I'll keep you in mind for any future problems I have. I like your style.'

She winked at him and he shifted uncomfortably in his chair to reposition his swelling groin.

'A real pleasure, Sandrine. And I haven't finished with Commander Lowe. There's an element of personal pleasure in taking him down.'

'Tsk, tsk, Harry. Mixing business and pleasure?'

'Sandrine, I learnt a long time ago that that's an artificial line drawn by those who have the means and the position to enjoy the distinction. I have neither, and I wouldn't even want to live in that world.'

'Well, Harry, anytime you feel like some VIP treatment, of the pleasure variety, you know where my establishment is.'

Harry swallowed hard. Two exhaled clouds of smoke came together and mingled in the tension over the desk, like two vaporized copulating lovers.

'*Merci*, Sandrine. Noted, gratefully.'

Sandrine smiled, stubbed out her cigarette, blew Harry the most delicate and suggestive of kisses.

'Well, *à bientôt*, Harry. I think we will meet again, non?'

'Oui, Sandrine, somehow I think we will.'

Sandrine got up from the chair and started for the door. She stopped in front of some framed certificates hanging on the wall. She pointed at one of them and looked over at Harry.

'A Master of Arts, Harry?'

'Yes, believe it or not. In English and history.'

'Well, there is some serious smart under that smooth. Now I definitely like that.'

And with that the apparition twirled and walked out of Harry's office. But Harry's gut told him it wasn't out of his life. He would certainly take up on the offer of an evening at An Oasis of Sirens; he'd often wondered what a visit there would be like, apart from out of his normal price range. And maybe Sandrine would like to peruse his bookcase sometime? Well, dreams were one of the things that made life worth living.

He smiled to himself and poured another Jameson. One more, he thought, and then it would be off for a well-earned feed at the Emerald Bar. After that, he figured he deserved a couple of hours with the girls at Puss in Boots, around the çorner from the pub. Tonight, being rather loaded with extra cash and feeling pretty pleased with himself, he'd enjoy a special and rather expensive treat. The crowning item on the parlour's menu, at $1,500, was listed as 'Double Trouble in Pussy Valley'. Harry felt some movement in his loins just at the thought of a double length session with two of the girls together. Better ease off on the wine over dinner, mate. Wonder if they do each other as well? Ah, life was good right now.

PART 3

HARRY'S RATES

She was as beautiful as the devil, and twice as dangerous.

- Dashiell Hammett

At nine in the morning the strip-tease clubs were all closed and only the delicatessens of his memory were open.

- Graham Greene

— 1 —

The surrounds were warm, moist, gently fragrant, and deliciously familiar to Harry. Whilst the twins' naked bodies were dancing in his mind, Harry was enjoying the post dinner phase in the secluded, walled beer garden of the Emerald Bar. He was settling in to a large Jameson, naturally to help with the digestion of his Moroccan lamb shanks and a bottle of Beaujolais, and drawing hard on a chunky Monte Christo cigar. With the recent successful, at least financially, job for Sandrine, he'd decided to treat himself. The Cuban smoke seeped out from his lips. So good, so very good.

His thoughts had drifted back to those naughty twins owing to a text message from Tanya before dinner telling him to look at today's Sydney Morning Herald. Now that his gut was deliciously full, he moved the Jameson and the ashtray to the side of the wrought metal table and opened the paper. The article was on page three with a large photo of the Premier. At first glance it appeared to be just another story about how the new State government spouting rhetoric about 'family values', and urged on by the upper house fundamentalist Christians, was going to clean up the sex industry. Harry had seen several such articles in recent months since the change of government, but nothing seemed to have changed so far. He had dismissed it as the usual hypocritical hot air from the hogs at the golden trough on Macquarie Street; many of them had rather more than political interest in prostitution. However, as he read on his interest was piqued. Brothels had long been the regulatory concern of local councils, partly the reason the new State government had left them alone so far. But the tide was now turning. Harry shook his head as he reflected on how there always seemed to be sanctimonious wankers queuing to screw things up for others. Not only was Harry a damned good customer of the industry of intimacy, but he was also a staunch advocate of civil liberties, especially in the bedroom department. His many years in the cops had left him entirely cynical about any form of social control of human urges, at least between consenting adults. And so the story as it went on started to alarm him.

Up until now, the Sydney Metropolitan Council hadn't shown any inclination to hop on the right-wing bus and attack the sex industry, but it now seemed a most unholy and unforeseen alliance was fermenting. The long-standing City Mayor, Roger Bottomley, was a political independent, with some lurid green tinges. He was certainly no friend of the State government.

Mayor Bottomley had spent his years in command at City Hall progressively constructing a chaotic matrix of pedestrian malls and cycle ways throughout the city. The desirable jewel in Bottomley's crown was a final series of bike lanes in the CBD, providing the culminating links to his fantastical matrix. This ultimate prize was supposed to render the existing chaos obsolete, at least for cyclists. But it would require the closing of several more road lanes, thus rendering central Sydney's public transport system even more hopeless. Hence successive State governments had stood resolutely in his way.

The new State government, also at loggerheads thus far with the Mayor over the roads and the bike lanes, had suddenly seen an irresistible opportunity. Conveniently forgetting their pre-election promises about public transport in Sydney, they would give Bottomley the bike lanes he wanted in return for his acquiescence to a right-wing assault against the city's brothels, a righteous and holy cleansing which, when complete, would have been the envy of the Crusaders. The government had used one of their Party's Councillors at City Hall, Stanislav 'Slim' Kasun, to quietly broker the deal. Bottomley had swallowed the bait as eagerly as a Mormon trying on their new undergarment. So the battlelines were drawn. Harry looked at the photos accompanying the article. Bottomley he was well used to, although he didn't usually take much notice of him. But Slim was a new face to him, and a new Councillor from the last election. If the photo was even half realistic, Slim's epithet was well-earned.

Harry folded the paper and put it down. He picked up his fat brown tube of joy and drew in a delicious mouthful. He wondered if it really had been rolled on the thighs of a virgin. As he was beginning to drift off into lascivious thoughts, a stocky man in his fifties, clutching a fresh pint of Guinness, pulled out the chair opposite and sat down.

'Old Harry, me mate! I take it this seat isn't taken by some divine wench who's just ducked off to powder her nose?'

Harry grinned and enveloped the newcomer in a cloud of Cuban fog.

'Your Eminence! Bloody good to see you. It's been at least a couple of months.'

'His Eminence' was the colloquial address the locals

used for Liam Doolan, actually nicknamed 'The Emerald Eminence', due to his daily, and nightly, sojourns at the pub providing copious quantities of philosophical discourse and social criticism to anyone who would listen. Plenty actually did, as Liam was a very bright man, a PhD from Trinity College, and hardly blunted by the years on the daily sauce. He was also wildly entertaining when well lubricated, and had become the most famous item of furniture in the Emerald Bar.

'Been back in the old Erin. Me ma finally passed on, so it was a sudden trip.

'Shit, sorry to hear that, Liam.'

'Thanks, Harry. I spent a few weeks after the funeral catching up with folks. And drinking, naturally. The Guinness anywhere else just isn't quite the same.'

'I must get there one day to test that theory.'

'Indeed, Harry. Well, with me ma, ninety-seven is a more than fair innings, and she was crystal clear right to the end. Can't ask for more.'

'True enough. I can't bear the idea of lying in a nursing home for years, dribbling uncontrollably and shitting my pants.'

'Damn right there, Harry. Mind you, blokes like us won't need to worry. Our wonderful lifestyle will make sure we exit early and in a happy state.'

With that the pair lifted glasses, chinked their respective Irish beverages, and toasted life. Liam looked at the Monte Christo as he was pulling a packet of duty free Rothmans International out of the pocket of his light grey linen jacket.

'Are we celebrating, Harry?' Liam jutted his angular chin at the cigar in Harry's left hand.

'Just finished a job, which paid well.'

'So are *we* celebrating then?' Liam still hadn't taken a cigarette out of his packet.

Harry grinned and pulled another Cuban cigar from his jacket hanging on the back of the chair.

'Of course, your Eminence.'

'Good man. One shouldn't celebrate alone, after all. Next round's on me.'

Harry smiled. 'Damn right.'

Liam held the cigar in the flame from a match and sucked back several times, kindling the glowing tip of tobacco.

'Oh, that is truly beautiful,' he said, as he exhaled slowly and thoughtfully.

'So, tell me about the job, Harry. I trust it was your usual Pandora's box of vice.'

'You could certainly say that, Liam.'

As Harry told his story, Liam proved a remarkably attentive listener, given he was invariably the one on the soapbox. Maybe it was the jetlag thought Harry.

As Harry was finishing his recount, he pushed the folded *SMH* towards Liam, with the brothel story uppermost. Liam read the article, cigar smoke rolling from the corner of his mouth. When he had finished, he looked up at Harry, over the dregs of his pint, and said, 'It's definitely my round before we continue this. I suspect we're going to be here a while.'

'Your Eminence, no argument from me.'

Liam got up and headed for the bar, whilst Harry toyed with the newspaper, rereading the article. Liam returned with four drinks and a big smile.

'Saves effort, Harry.'

'No complaint here, Liam.'

Harry relit his cigar, as well as Liam's, both having gone out in the hiatus of storytelling.

'So, your Eminence, what do you think about this most vexed subject?' tapping the paper article.

'It's all about power. For a lot of people, that's what sex is actually about, too. But not the likes of us. We like sex for what it is, utterly gorgeous moments and the epitome of freedom. No religious or moralizing bullshit attached to it. Just fantastic, wild sex, Harry. You know, the 'devil rides tonight' stuff. Can you think of any greater moments of liberty and self-expression?'

'Nope. And certainly not with the women I get into bed with.'

'Exactly. As that great man Orwell said, the sex instinct creates a world outside of the Establishment's control. So of course the religious right-wing are going to clamp down on the sex industry. Individual freedom is anathema to the controlling Establishment.'

'Hell, Liam, I wish I could sum things up as beautifully as you.'

Liam laughed. 'Harry, I don't want that day to come, because then you won't be prepared to sit here and listen to me. And I would really miss you.'

They chinked glasses as they laughed and two clouds of cigar smoke mingled over the table.

– 2 –

Councillor Stanislav 'Slim' Kasun was walking up to the front door of his semi-detached house in Erskineville. The front path was overhung by two frangipani trees in full bloom, one white and the other pink, leaving a beautiful scattering of petals on the ground. It was a particularly lovely autumn day in Sydney and the red-painted concrete of the path was bathed in the dappled late afternoon sunshine. Slim paused when he spotted a large ant meandering across the hard surface.

An impulse to stomp on it flashed through his toxic mind, almost instinctively: the overwhelming desire to crush, to assert his righteous and rightful dominance. But no, stomping was too quick, the ant needed to suffer. Why? Because he had the opportunity and the ability to inflict misery, purely for its own sake, and he simply couldn't neglect the application of his predominant talent. He picked up a blunt stick in his porcine fingers and crushed the ant's abdomen, slowly, gratuitously, sexually, feeling a visceral tremor of pleasure. As he watched the mortally crippled ant writhe around, glued to the spot by its own sticky innards, an insidious grin slithered onto Slim's despicable face. Satisfied, he headed into his house.

Slim Kasun was a truly splendid specimen from that most fetid and odious of breeding grounds, Australian politics. And he was rapidly lubricating his way up the slimy pole of NSW local government politics. He managed to lumber over 140kg on his 150cm frame, a remarkable achievement anatomically. Every part of him wobbled as he walked. A few more years on from his current thirty-nine and he would be wheezing impressively, too. Jowls dangled from the bottom of his face, which surprisingly was long rather than round. The top was an expanding vista of pallid forehead surrounded by receding blond, almost albino, hair. He kept it cut military short, a small tribute to an uncle who had been a Serbian commander during the Balkans war. The facial middle ground was occupied by constantly pursed lips, reminiscent of a warthog's anus, a fleshy nose with a hairy mole astride it, and beady, slightly bulbous eyes, a weak grey in colour and most definitely inherited from a fine line of large bacon pigs. He had endured the 'piggy' taunts all his childhood. Upon reading *Animal Farm* as a teenager he had begun to picture himself as Napoleon, knowing in his already vicious mind that one day he would have the power to avenge himself upon the world, to make his tormentors pay. His righteous and superior view of himself was doggedly reinforced by his Serbian family, all good adherents of the extreme Catholic religious group The Brotherhood of the Horsemen. In particular, his beloved Aunty Dragana, now a rising star and junior minister in the Federal government in Canberra, was his most ardent mentor. Despite his physical unattractiveness to potential voters, Slim had been able to progress politically, courtesy of a razor-sharp mind and sheer rat cunning, which had combined with his innate desire to dominate and crush as comfortably as a North Korean leader sending family members to the gallows.

Slim settled into his desk chair in front of his computer in his home office. He was reflecting on his successful campaign to woo the Mayor, ghastly greenie arsehole that he was, to his anti-brothel program. Party head office was delighted with him, and Aunty Dragana – God how he fantasized about her comforting bosom – had called him earlier in the day to say that the Premier, no less, was already talking about Slim as a pre-selection frontrunner for the next State election. It was over three years away, but Slim was very contented with his ambitious progress to date.

He began work on some new Notices of Motion for the next Council meeting, but interspersed his political cookery with pleasant and panting breaks looking at images on his favourite website, oedipusfeeding.com. Photos of men sucking the swollen breasts of big fat mammas adorned the site's pages, and clicking on a chosen one would take Slim to a video clip of the live action, culminating in a spray of breast milk onto the camera lens. He put aside the draft motion about recycling e-waste, and concentrated on a far more urgent motion. He pulled his flaccid, although arising, fleshy member out of his pants.

Harry was back at the Emerald Bar the next evening, minus his Eminence this time. He was relaxing over a post-dinner Jameson at the bar, firmly ensconced on a stool and eyelids half down in quiet contemplation. His reverie was disturbed by a lady, almost around his age, but in decidedly better shape, parking her well-shaped arse, snugly outlined by a skin-tight black cocktail dress, on the neighbouring stool, sliding it 15cm closer to his as she glided her buttocks onto the leather cushion. She had a full glass of white wine, a good sign in Harry's eyes that she wasn't just a desperado after a free refill. Then she put her Gucci purse on the bar. Looking at her, Harry suspected it was a genuine rather than a Phuket special. She exhaled class, this one.

Ms Style took a sip of wine, turned forty-five degrees towards Harry – he was already inclined towards her – and looked into his eyes.

'I've seen you down here before. They tell me you're called Harry.'

'Well, Harry it is then.'

Her treacle coloured eyes narrowed noticeably.

'No, really, it is Harry, no shit,' he said.

And with that Harry extended his hand. She took the proffered palm and Harry enjoyed her firm yet feminine handshake, something he liked in a lady.

'I'm Tessa.'

Harry picked up on a definite English lilt, of the upper class variety, and he inhaled her classy floral scent.

'I know that perfume and it suits you perfectly. It's on the tip of my tongue, a Dior ...'

'Very good. Poison, but only in name.'

She had refined features, simultaneously beautiful and handsome, with high cheekbones. She had that pale, smooth and perfect skin that English women do so well, as if they are carved out of fine alabaster. Looking into her delicate, sultry visage with its pale brown eyes was like gazing into a fondue pot of liquid amber. Harry felt some distinct movement in his boxer shorts. Tessa was tall, imposing and graceful, like the Statue of Liberty, and Harry wanted to partake of hers. She looked at Harry's nearly empty tumbler.

'Can I get you another one?'

Harry thought he was dreaming. Like a butterfly emerging from its chrysalis, she was getting more beautiful by the second.

'Absolutely, thank you. This feels like my birthday again, but that was last month.'

'An Aquarian?'

'Indeed, the eighth of Feb.'

'So, independent, principled, stubborn, and needing lots of space. Close?'

'Absolutely. We must have met in a previous life. Except of course I'd remember that.'

'Somehow I think I would, too.'

She ordered a double Jameson and another sauvignon blanc. Harry looked at her quizzically.

'I observe things, Harry. Especially when I'm intrigued.'

'Intrigued? By me?' He must have been dreaming. Women like this didn't exist, let alone crack on to Harry at the bar.

'I hear you do some most interesting work. I've always wanted to meet a real life Sam Spade.'

Harry did his best Bogart expression.

Tessa laughed. 'Tell me some stories, Sam!'

So Harry took a sip of his new Jameson and began telling an edited version of his recent job, for the second time in as many evenings. He'd just got to the bit about setting the trap for Lowe when his phone rang. As he reached for it on his belt, Tessa glared at his hand now grabbing the iPhone.

'Are you really going to answer that?'

'It'll be business.'

'It might be personal at this time of the evening,' she fished.

'Not me. It'll be business all right, and that means income. Without that I can't indulge in good food, fine wine, and gorgeous women.'

Tessa smiled and nodded her head gently.

Harry answered the phone, listened to a female voice, and said, 'I'll be there in twenty minutes.' He hung up and put the phone back on his belt.

'Definitely business, my English rose, and you have no idea how hard it's going to be to step out that door right now.'

'Many girls would leave it at that, Harry. But you owe me the rest of the story, not to mention a drink. Hell, for running off on a girl like this, you can make it dinner.'

'Deal. And soon.'

'The sooner the better, Mr Spade. A hot iron and all that.'

'Consider me the speediest blacksmith in history.'

With that Harry downed his whiskey, stood up, took hold of Tessa's hand from the bar, kissed the back of her fingers lightly, and bowed his head in mock chivalry. He pulled a card out of his inside jacket pocket and handed it to her.

'If you text me your number I can call and arrange to regale you with my anvil-beating prowess.'

Tessa nodded and took the card.

'Will do, Mr Spade.'

Harry turned and headed out the door into the darkness of Glebe.

— 4 —

After a short cab ride from Broadway, Harry arrived at a rather upmarket looking establishment in Surry Hills, The Holy Garter. He knew of the place, but hadn't been inside, either as a customer or in his former detective days. Nor had he met the Madam, Miss Andromeda, although he had read that she was one of the industry's heavyweights. Not, however, physically, as it turned out. After walking in and convincing the front-of-house lady that he didn't want a root, and did actually have an appointment with the boss, Harry was shown through a door off to the side of the main lounge. A young blonde with breasts like rockmelons took him by the elbow and led him towards a solid jarrah door at the end of a short hall.

'This way, Mr Kenmare,' she offered, as she ran her tongue along her upper teeth. Harry looked down at her magnificent breasts, a gaze she followed, and then back into her eyes. Damn there were moments of his job he just loved.

'Anywhere you want to lead me, baby.'

She grinned. 'The only place you're going, under strict orders, is the boss's office. At least this time, sugar.' Touché, thought Harry.

With that she opened the deep red timber door, after one seemingly expected knock, and ushered Harry in.

Just as smoothly, the junior Kate Upton lookalike was gone, and Harry was left standing looking at a lady seated behind a large, leather-inlaid, French walnut desk. A heavy crystal vase held a large bunch of orange tiger lilies. His host radiated elegance, wearing a low-cut crimson evening dress with a string of black pearls hugging her throat. Her collar length auburn hair was immaculately coiffed, and her make-up was both flawless and subtle.

A pair of piercing blue eyes locked onto him and 160cm of petite, wonderfully well-cared for feminine physique stood up and came around the desk, hand outstretched. Harry thought he remembered reading Miss Andromeda was in her fifties, but if she'd introduced herself as forty he'd have thought she looked damned good for that.

'Harry Kenmare, so good to finally meet a man I hear such good things about. Especially given your not-so-attractive background.'

'Miss Andromeda, likewise a pleasure. Your reputation does precede you, and all good in my book. And I have learnt a lot along the way. Please call me Harry.'

'I will then. Drink?'

'Irish whiskey, if it's on offer.'

'Of course.'

She went to a generously proportioned drinks cabinet, also French walnut, against the wall and pulled a bottle of Bushmills from its armoury. She poured a hefty dose into a tumbler, threw in some ice cubes from a silver bucket, and handed it to Harry. She pulled a bottle of Krug, already opened, out of another gleaming bucket and refilled a tall crystal champagne flute.

'Come and sit over here, Harry. As you know, I want to talk business. Mine, and yours, potentially.'

She led him over to a pair of red leather armchairs by an original colonial fireplace. As Harry lowered himself and his glass into the chair, he was entirely captivated by a large stained glass window, carefully backlit to maximum effect and without being a window to anything in reality. It took up the entire wall to the left of the fireplace. At first glance it was wholly religious, depicting some Nativity-type scene, and Harry was initially confused. But after a moment it was clear there was rather more to it. The Virgin Mary was there, for sure, as was a veritable queue of wise men. The first wise man was handing a bag of gold coins to Mary, whilst she was on her knees pulling his sacred member from his robe and towards her open mouth beneath eager eyes. The other wise men in the line all had similar bags of gold in their left hands, whilst their right hands were clutching their groins. Harry laughed out loud.

'Miss Andromeda, that is truly awesome!'

'Ah, yes. I hate the sanctimonious Christians, and I love Raymond Chandler. Do you read Chandler, Harry?'

'All of them, and more than once.'

'Well, I was inspired by my favourite of his lines, the one about buying some "sweetness and light, and not the kind that comes through the east window of a church". So that masterpiece, Harry, is my tribute to Chandler and my take on Christians.' She waved ceremoniously towards the bright multi-colours of the stained glass.

Harry dragged his gaze away from the deliciously blasphemous glass scenario and met Andromeda's azure stare.

'I have, or I should say "we" have, a business proposition for you, Harry.'

'I'm all ears.' Harry waved his cigarette packet

questioningly, and Andromeda's delicate fingers pointed towards a stand-alone chromium ash tray, like a prop from a 1930s film noir set. Harry lit a smoke and drew back hard.

'Are you aware of the latest political push against us?'

'Actually, I was just reading about it yesterday.'

'Okay, I won't worry about all the background then. I'll concentrate on the hypocrites involved, especially at the Metropolitan Council.'

'Hypocrisy from our glorious elected representatives shouldn't come as anything unusual, Andromeda.'

She snorted. 'Of course not, Harry, and usually I wouldn't give a damn, let alone a second thought, but this time the hypocrisy directly impacts on us, our industry, our livelihoods.'

Harry was starting to meander in to the same chapter, even if not yet the same page.

'So some of the key characters involved politically are clients, perhaps?'

Harry pictured the City Mayor naked, on all fours, and chained up in some gay orgy chamber, complete with gimp mask. He shuddered and mentally disinfected his frontal lobes.

'What do you know about the main right-wing Councillor, Stanislav Kasun?'

'To be honest, I hadn't even heard of him until yesterday when I read the article in the paper.'

'Well, Kasun is pivotal to all this. He has brokered the deal with the City Mayor, and any changes in Council's stance will need his vote, and his cronies, combined with the Mayor and his bunch.'

'Okay, a story in the paper that this Kasun has been in a brothel might cause a minor ripple, better still if he used a Council credit card. But even so, the public is getting pretty used to politicians bedding prostitutes.'

'Harry, "sex workers", please.'

'Sorry, Andromeda, my mistake.'

'Yes, you are right, of course. And if he was a client here, for example, I'd tend to agree with you. But Kasun has a very, very particular interest. One which will, I think, sufficiently disgust the public and will leave his Party bosses no option, but to ditch him, along with the reforms he has been championing on their behalf.'

Harry was intrigued, knowing a lot about all sorts of vice, and wondering what was so 'particular' about Kasun.

'Well, try me, Andromeda, there's not too much I haven't seen in this game.'

She smiled. 'We'll see, Harry. Let's go online and I'll introduce you to some new worlds, perhaps.'

She beckoned him to follow her to the desk where a widescreen iMac was giving off a colourful glow.

'Have you heard of erotic lactation, Harry?'

'What?'

'Sometimes called adult suckling.'

'Okay, I'm starting to get a picture, and it's not real attractive. Guys wanting to be breastfed? Are you serious?'

'Oh, yes. And Councillor Kasun is a very fine specimen of suckling pig.'

'Bloody hell. Now that would make a media splash.'

'Exactly. Here's one of the favourite websites for this fetish.'

She clicked on the mouse and up came a site called oedipusfeeding.com. Harry was stunned; yes, this was one type of vice he'd never encountered before. A few more mouse clicks and Harry retreated back to his chair for a much needed smoke and drink. Well, each to their own, but it sure as hell wasn't on his bucket list. Unlike the breasts who had shown him in, of course, which had gone straight into the top five.

Andromeda floated back to her chair, refilling Harry's now drained glass on her way.

'So, Harry, this is where we need your expertise. We need evidence, and good quality evidence, before any journo will go near this.'

'No shit, you bet you do. Needs to be overwhelming and compelling, or the government puppet-masters will go you for a defamation suit faster than a rat up a drainpipe.'

'So we need you, Harry. Your skills, your hard work and the best plan you can come up with.'

'Okay, I'm in. But it'll take me a while to learn the scene. It's not exactly my usual hangout.'

'We can help there.' She handed him an envelope, clearly bulked out with banknotes.

'That's just a taster, and for expenses. Five grand, until we meet again to discuss your plan. There's also a plain card inside with a phone number. It's the private number for Mama Jocasta. She runs a very discreet establishment for this particular interest.'

'What? There's a bloody joint here in Sydney where you can pay to do this?'

'Harry, you know as well as I do that where there's demand, there will always be supply. This one's called Club Mammary. Strictly unlisted, and by word of mouth only.'

Harry shook his head, momentarily speechless. He resorted to his whiskey.

'I've already spoken to Mama, and she will be expecting your call.'

Harry looked up at her, a touch of surprise in his eyes.

'From what I'd heard about you, Harry, I knew you

would take the assignment. Now when you speak to Mama, be careful not to seem judgemental to her. I know you're a bit stunned yourself right now, but don't forget it takes all sorts. And Mama is a great, warm-hearted lady once you get to know her.'

Harry had a flash of a pulsating heart beneath a massive milk-covered bosom.

'Okay. I'll make sure I compose myself before I speak to her.'

'Good, because you'll need her for your plan, that's for sure.'

'Yeah, I can see that. You are certainly on the ball, Andromeda.'

She laughed. 'My days on the balls are well and truly over, Harry. Strictly managerial these days. All right, business is done, I feel. Let's have one or three for the road and you can enthral me with tales about corruption.'

Harry shoved the fat envelope into his inside jacket pocket, without opening it, which would be crass in his view, and held out his glass as Andromeda came over with the bottle of Bushmills.

'Which type of corruption would you like to start on? I've got a wide repertoire.'

'Yes, I'm sure you have. Police, politicians, priests – I'm good for any or all.'

Drinks refilled, Andromeda sat down, and Harry started on his recent war stories.

— 5 —

Harry was ensconced in his leather office chair the next afternoon, smoking heavily and sipping on the Irish nectar. He'd had a particularly broken night's sleep, interspersed with dark thoughts about breast feeding and then arousing thoughts about Tessa from the pub. When he'd finally properly woken up at about nine, he felt distinctly dusty. He'd slowly got into the day, cooking himself a large greasy breakfast including four rashers of bacon and a generous hunk of black pudding, and finally limped his way in to the office.

Several smokes and a few sips of Jameson started to put his day back on track. He'd put the envelope of cash from Andromeda in the safe, slipping five hundred of it into his wallet for any imminent expenses, and removing the card with the phone number. He'd then got onto the Net and immediately regretted visiting the oedipusfeeding. com site; it was not good viewing on a stomach full of greasy breakfast. Harry was generally a laissez faire type of guy, and not averse to a few kinky forays himself, but this adult suckling stuff was just way too bizarre for him. He'd choked on his whiskey when the milk had squirted on the camera lens, a whitish opaque film running down the glass like a dairy curtain call. He hadn't been ready for that screen gem.

Okay, back to work, Harry. He needed to put his disquiet aside and come up with a plan. He reached for the card Andromeda had given him and looked at the number for this Mama Jocasta. He pondered and smoked a whole cigarette just looking at the card. This was going to be an absolutely weird assignment, but he knew how damned well it was likely to pay. Andromeda had hinted at a hundred plus if he was successful. This was a game-changer for Harry, so he'd have to learn to swallow the milk of his pride on this one to pull it off.

He gulped his glass empty, gritted his teeth and picked up the desk phone. The card in front of him, he punched in the eight numbers slowly and with trepidation, as if he was entering the access code to some unknown form of depraved hell. The line connected and was picked up after the third ring.

'Yes?' came a deep, but definitely female, voice. Harry detected a distinct West Indian lilt, Jamaican he reckoned.

'I'm after Mama Jocasta, please.'

'And who be you?'

'My name's Harry Kenmare. Mama Jocasta is expecting my call.'

'Is that so? And what be your business?'

'Miss Andromeda's business, that's my business. She gave me the number and said Mama Jocasta would be expecting me to call.'

'Well, Mr Harry, sometimes we get what we expect and sometimes we don't. That is the way of the world. So looks like Mama got what she expected.'

Harry wasn't sure what the hell he was expecting, let alone what he would actually get, but the cryptic Caribbean voice was making him feel like he had stepped onto the set of a third-rate voodoo horror flick. He swallowed hard and focused, remembering his promise to Andromeda to get himself composed.

'Yeah, I guess she has. So can I speak to her please?'

'You got to do that in person, man.'

'Okay, so where do I find her "in person" then?'

'You be calling Miss Andromeda at precisely four o'clock today. If you check out with her, then she will give you the details.'

Before Harry could even acknowledge this latest riddle, the phone clicked and the line went dead.

This was turning into a game of smoke and mirrors, more befitting a Cold War spy thriller than an attempt to gain admission to a fetish club.

Harry looked at his watch. Half past three. He decided to kill the half hour by doing some fetish research online. Twenty minutes later, having discovered that 'practitioners' of the fetish often described themselves as being in an 'adult nursing relationship', Harry had definitely had a gutful. They even had their own acronym, 'ANR'. It was a weird world for sure, and Harry always seemed to end up in Strangeville. Oh, well, the bills had to be paid.

Harry's reflexes kicked in and he grabbed the Jameson bottle and his Marlboros simultaneously. He had begun medicating himself when he noticed his watch said four. He dialled Andromeda's number.

'Yes?' It was Andromeda's voice doing a rather convincing Jamaican accent.

Harry laughed. 'Nice one, Andromeda. How are you?'

'Good, Harry. Mama called to double-check your credentials.'

'She's certainly bloody careful. Her woman on the phone could have been the night receptionist at bloody Langley.'

'That was Mama, Harry. She has to run a very tight

ship there. It's a great business dollar-wise, but she has to be incredibly careful. Her clients include some very high-up people, some MPs, of course, a couple of top 200 CEOs, a movie director, very famous, and even a judge. We won't even start on the other lesser public service types. It is a long list.'

'Yeah, nothing would really surprise me. This shouldn't be any different, I guess.'

'Truth and fiction, Harry, you know it better than most.'

'Yeah. Okay, so how do I see Mama?'

Andromeda gave him an address and a six digit code for an access pad.

'You'll need to enter the code, which will unlock the outer door and let you into a sealed foyer. You'll be on camera, and Mama will be watching you. When she's ready, the intercom will buzz. You need to give a password to the very large bodyguard. He'll then open the inner door and take you on in.'

'Fuck me. Do I need the key for the nuclear launch briefcase as well?'

'I think launching a nuke would probably be easier, Harry. Anyway, your password for tonight, and only tonight, is "Shango".'

'Shango? S H A N G O?'

'Yes, spot on. The African god of thunder, Harry. And you must be there at 9 p.m. on the dot.'

'Andromeda, I haven't learnt so much new stuff in one day since I was at school.'

'Life, Harry. It should be enjoyed, in all its varieties. Taste it, and savour it.'

'Some things I sure won't be tasting on this assignment, Andromeda, let me give you the tip.'

She laughed. 'Fair enough, not my scene either. But that's the job. And if you're feeling like a bit of stress relief and something that is more up your alley, then I can let you see one of my girls, on the house.'

'Much more my style, Andromeda. I'll hold you to that offer.'

'Do so. Have fun tonight, Harry!' And she laughed again. Harry could just see the wicked smile on her face. 'Think of the money, Harry. We do. Ciao.'

Harry hung up and refilled his glass. He lit a smoke and reclined in his chair, plonking his feet on his desk. As he stared at the Cavan crystal, he turned his contemplation to his new knowledge and the evening ahead.

Twenty minutes and three cigarettes later, he snapped out of his reverie, swung his feet off the desk and decided to get active again. His last research job for the day, at least before the later plans for the evening, was to get a better eyeball on this Councillor Kasun. Now that Harry had heard about him and his hypocritical politics, as well as having the assignment on him, he'd better get more familiarity with his mug than the *SMH* photo allowed.

Harry went onto the Council's website and straightaway found photos of all the Councillors. Despite the studio photographer's best efforts on Kasun, and probably with some Photoshop work as well, there was no getting away from Kasun's flabby face, jowls dangling like some anaemic bloodhound, and the porcine stare of his eyes. Harry reflected that any woman who let him suck on her tits deserved a sodding medal, as well as every dollar she got. Harry printed off two copies of the page with the Councillor photos, and did an enlarged version of just Kasun's shot.

Harry then found the link on the site allowing viewing

of the webcast of the previous Council meeting. He had an abject lack of interest in local politics, and the egotistical pretenders it often attracted, and he'd certainly never witnessed a Council meeting before; a root canal from an octogenarian dentist with delirium tremens seemed a preferable way to spend a few hours. However, this was work, so he clicked on the webcast.

After a few seconds of the mundane formalities which were opening the meeting, Harry randomly fast forwarded. He resumed viewing as the City Mayor, Roger Bottomley, was mid-stream in droning some condescending remarks towards a female Councillor. Suddenly this other Councillor jumped to her feet and began waving her hands around and yelling at the Mayor, 'You're nothing but a fraud, Mister Mayor, a bloody fraud!'

The Mayor sneered and retorted, 'If you were actually worth anything, Councillor, I'd sue you for defamation. But that's right, you don't have a job, do you?'

Harry had no idea what had led up to this exchange, but at least it wasn't entirely boring. He looked at his photo sheet and saw that the female Councillor doing the shouting was an independent called Hannah Gorgon. Good name, thought Harry. She was short and dumpy, with long straight hair and somewhat witch-like facial features. By the way she was continuing her tirade at the Mayor, who was now sitting laughing contemptuously, Harry figured that Gorgon must have had the broomstick firmly up her arse, rather than sitting astride it.

Kasun was at the table opposite Gorgon, and he began pounding the table top yelling, 'Hear, hear!' towards Gorgon, his jowls wobbling like an angry jelly, and then turning to the Mayor and yelling 'disgrace' to complement each yell of 'fraud' from Gorgon.

Mayor Bottomley kept laughing and waving his hand dismissively at both the yelling Councillors.

Harry shook his head and clicked off the website. And this was supposed to be the grass roots of our democracy? What a complete bloody shambles.

He lit himself a smoke.

Harry was running early as usual and got the cab to drop him at Taylor Square. It was only 8.30, so he ducked into the Rainbow Plaza Hotel and ordered a double Irish whiskey on the rocks. He took his drink and headed outside to one of the tables overlooking the square so he could have a smoke and people watch. Despite all his experience he was feeling nervous about tonight's gig. As he sipped on his whiskey and drew on his smoke his nerves started to calm. Taylor Square presented its usual fascinating cross-section of inner city humanity, and Harry sat there enjoying the parade: an out of tune busker banging on an old guitar, a homeless guy fishing in the rubbish bins, a couple of junkies out of it on the grassed area, and then plenty of attractive young things dolled up and heading to bars and clubs. At ten to nine he downed the remnants of his drink, got up and headed off down Bourke Street, and then left into Linden Lane, his much anticipated destination.

He found the given address and its non-descript door with key pad buzzer on the left of the frame. He had memorized the code he'd been given and delicately pushed the six numbers, like a shy child surreptitiously prodding a present under the tree on Christmas Eve. He noticed two expensive looking surveillance cameras mounted above the door, the pair of them covering both directions up the lane. There was a deep buzz followed by a click, and he pulled on the brass handle. The door came open silently and he stepped inside. Whilst it had been dark outside, his eyes needed to adjust to the muted crimson glow inside a velvet-lined foyer, no bigger than the average bathroom, yet still containing a two-seat leather lounge and a large potted palm. The outer door clicked shut and hissed slightly as it did so, almost as if Harry had entered an airtight chamber. His nerves were taut and he was glad he'd slipped his .38 into his jacket pocket. He trusted Andromeda, but this job was so outside his comfort zone that he was still on edge.

He decided to stay on his feet. Although the lounge looked luxurious, Harry couldn't help imagining Kasun sitting on it waiting for his feed. Harry was desperate for another smoke, but thought he'd better not risk upsetting anyone at this point. The foyer was lit by two large lamps with red shades and orange globes, so the overall effect in the room was of being inside an oven. More like an antechamber to hell, thought Harry. A muted calypso was coming from somewhere although Harry couldn't see any speakers. After what seemed like an eternity, but really had only been a few minutes, Harry was startled by the buzz of the intercom. He stepped over to it, pushed the transmit button, and spoke 'Shango' into the plastic grille.

After another minute the inner door opened and Harry found himself looking straight ahead at a large metallic shirt button, about midpoint between two bulging pectoral muscles. He started to incline his head backwards, his vision travelling up to a dark chocolate tree trunk that doubled as a human neck, and then to the ceiling, it seemed, where his gaze settled on a rather handsome, but not exactly friendly, face. Perhaps it was the vicious looking scars around the jaw line that made it not so affable, but Harry wasn't going to analyse that point right now, as he was looking into the eyes of the largest black man he had ever seen in his life, either personally or on the screen. This guy was at least 220cm tall, weighing easily over 160kg, and muscled like a Nubian gladiator on steroids.

The ebony giant said nothing at all, motioning Harry into the hallway beyond the door. Harry stepped through the doorway and stood there whilst his dark, taciturn companion closed the door behind them. An index finger about the size of a black pudding pointed down the hallway, which was lit in a similar hue to the entrance foyer, and Harry deduced he was supposed to walk in the direction of the digit's indication. As he started walking he could feel the huge presence close behind him at each step. At the end of the corridor were three doors: one in front and one on either side.

As Harry reached them an enormous black hand grasped his right shoulder, not roughly, but firmly enough to constitute a silent command to be obeyed without question. Stuck in a confined space with his new companion, Harry wasn't exactly feeling in an inquisitive frame of mind anyway. As the other black dinosaur paw knocked on the door directly in front, Harry noticed the door to the right was half open. He didn't dare turn his head too much, so he had to partly rely on his peripheral vision. Nevertheless, he was able to make out what looked like a massage table, but somehow different in a way Harry couldn't pin down. Disturbingly, there were two large boxes next to the table which, from his brief sideways glance, appeared to contain nappies. The door had a sign on it saying 'Change Room'. Yeah, he really was earning his money on this assignment. As he swallowed hard he glanced sideways to his left and noted that the sign on the closed door read 'Suckling Suites'. Before he could take in any more, let alone process it, the unmistakeable Caribbean voice of Mama Jocasta invited entry. One black hand twisted the brass knob, opening the door, whilst the other paw gently propelled Harry in to the room.

Mama Jocasta's lounge-cum-office was a profusion of red, yellow and green fabrics, with a large Jamaican flag hanging on the wall behind a cedar desk.

'Well, Mr Harry, welcome to my club.'

Mama hoisted her not inconsiderable frame out of an armchair and came over to Harry, her hand outstretched. Mama was one voluptuous woman, with a bulging bosom and a round, friendly face, more milk than dark on the chocolate scale.

'Pleased to meet you, Mama,' said Harry as he shook her hand.

She waved him to another armchair. Harry could see an ashtray on the desk and thought he could detect the slightly sweet aroma of a recently smoked joint. Taking that as a tacit invitation, he pulled out his cigarette packet and raised his eyebrows at Mama.

'That's fine, Mr Harry. And what you be drinking?'

'Whiskey please, Mama.'

'No problem.' Mama padded over to a drinks cabinet and poured two drinks, one whiskey and one dark rum. Harry took the one that was offered to him and sat down in the chair. He lit himself a Marlboro.

'Thank you. Your doorman out there is a man of few words, isn't he?'

'Well, Mr Harry, he has no say in the matter. Zanza don't have no tongue.'

'What, literally?'

'He was rebel fighter in the Congo. He got caught by the government soldiers. They tortured him and cut his tongue out. They left him in the jungle to die, but he a tough one and he made it to a UN camp. The doctors from MSF fix him up and so he still alive and now he here.'

'Fuck. Well, it seems he makes his presence felt out there just fine without any words. I guess you don't have too many problems with anyone?'

'Exactly. Now, Mr Harry, we need to be talking the business. What your plan?'

'Well, I'm going to need to get some film of the Councillor doing his ... his stuff.'

Harry just couldn't bring himself to say 'breastfeeding' out loud, let alone 'suckling'.

'So, if I can have a look at the room he would use? Then I can look at options for a camera.'

'Sure. Let's go a little tour of the premises,' Mama winked at him. 'We don't be having no clients until ten o'clock tonight.'

Mama hefted herself back onto her feet, smiled at Harry – in a way which he uncomfortably interpreted as maternal – and said, 'The nervous look on your face tells me you never been in no club like this before?'

'Ah, no. Not exactly my scene, Mama.' And after this, thought Harry, even milkshakes were going to be a thing of his past.

'Well, Mr Harry, come with me and let's get you a bit more educated.'

Bloody hell, he thought, she even seemed to be enjoying herself. Think of the money, son, just keep thinking of all that lovely money.

Harry got up and followed Mama as she went to the door. As they went out of the lounge back into the corridor, Zanza was sitting on the leather couch reading a men's magazine. Rather more my style than the rest of this thought Harry. Zanza looked up and started to move his mountainous body.

'That's fine, Zanza, you stay there. Me just showing Mr Harry around.'

Zanza nodded and let his bulk settle back into the soft leather. He returned to the soft focus centrefold girl.

Mama opened the door labelled 'Suckling Suites', which led into another shorter hallway with three doors along its right side. Each door bore a brass nameplate shaped like a milk urn. They went past the first door, labelled 'The Dairy', and then Mama stopped at the second, 'The Creamery', and opened it. Inside the decor was pale blue and pink, like an infant's nursery, and there was a large, heavily cushioned chaise longue as well as a huge armchair taking up the centre of the room. The chaise had a number of pastel coloured towels stacked at the end, whilst in the armchair reposed an equally huge, brown teddy bear. If only stuffed toys could talk, thought Harry, that bear would be a goldmine. There were a number of cabinets along the wall facing the seating, on top of which were a Sony plasma television and shelf-system stereo with speakers. And there was an enveloping aroma of baby powder.

'So, Mr Harry, the man get changed back there first, and then he come in here for his feeding time.' She gave another maternal smile and Harry winced inside. 'This Councillor man, he always prefer the couch. So how you going to take pictures of him?'

'There's always a way, Mama,' said Harry as he was

scanning the room. He then stepped over to the electronic equipment. He picked up one of the speakers, inspected it carefully from all angles and then replaced it on the cabinet top. Not even a hint of dust, he noted. They certainly kept the joint clean.

'That'll work perfectly, Mama. An optical fibre lens inside the speaker with the recording device inside the cabinet underneath, all nice and discreet.'

'But he won't see it?'

'It'd take a very, very trained eye to spot the lens behind the speaker gauze. And somehow I think our Councillor will be feasting his eyes on something else.'

'Okay, Mr Harry, you the expert. The Councillor make an appointment for tomorrow night.'

'No worries, I can come back in the morning if that works for you. It'll only take me about an hour to set up the equipment and test it.'

'Okay. You make it at midday. And since I be expecting you, use the same password.'

Harry took one last look around the room, scribbled some notes in his pocketbook, and then followed Mama back into the corridor.

'I hope this going to work good, Mr Harry. We normally like to protect our customers, our business depend on discretion. But this man going to be trouble for all of us, so I hope you can make sure he disappear and shut up about it.'

'Mama, we will make this work, don't worry. And I don't think our Councillor will be even wanting to talk about it in confessional, let alone publicly. I can see myself out.'

'Okay, good night, Mr Harry. See you in the morning.'

'Good night, Mama,' said Harry, walking towards

Zanza still absorbed in his magazine on the couch. They nodded at each other and Harry walked past the silent black mountain and out into the humid Sydney night.

– 7 –

It was nearing one o'clock the next day and Harry
was sitting at the desk in Mama Jocasta's office
looking intently at a laptop screen. The install had been
straightforward, the hi-fi system proving the ideal host
for an optic parasite, and now Harry was fine tuning the
monitoring of the camera.

'All done,' he said to Mama.

Mama, who was sitting on a spare chair to the side
of the desk, moved in next to Harry, her huge chocolate
bosom pressing against Harry's arm as he manipulated the
mouse.

'Ooh, that is a good view, Mr Harry.'

'Yeah, pretty bloody good, even if I say so myself.'

Harry had spared no expense on his stock of covert
camera equipment and the image of The Creamery was
crystal clear.

'Can I ask a question, Mama?'

'Of course, Mr Harry.'

'Excuse my ignorance, but I don't get this whole thing.
How can you have women who are just lactating the whole
time, on demand?'

'Ah, Mr Harry. You need to study more history.
Women can keep lactating as long as there is suction
demand on them. In the old days there were wet

nurses. You never heard of them? Women who did the breastfeeding for the babies of other women. My girls, they all had babies at some time, but it is the clients sucking on them that keeps them milking. They not feeding their babies no more. Just the big babies in here.' Mama chuckled.

'Well, I'll be buggered. I'd never have worked that one out for myself. Thanks for sharing, Mama. As I always say, every day is a learning day.'

'My pleasure, Mr Harry. Glad to help with your education. Now, back to the job. You all good to go for the Councillor?'

'Yes, absolutely, Mama. I'll need to operate the camera from in here. What time should I come back this evening?'

'The Councillor, he come at nine o'clock. So, best if you be here before eight. Same password, Mr Harry.'

'No worries, Mama. See you then. I'm off for a much needed feed.' Harry paused. 'Rephrase that, a much needed lunch.'

Mama gave a hearty laugh and slapped Harry on the shoulder.

'See you tonight, Mr Harry. I like you, you good man.'

Harry left Club Mammary and headed into Surry Hills with a purposeful pace towards Andromeda's establishment. He had to brief her on the plan, and his idea of eating right now was anything but culinary. Andromeda had made him a generous offer, and Harry really felt like he could do with a serious relax session with that gorgeous young blonde with the rockmelon breasts. He hurried in his stride.

– 8 –

Once in the Holy Garter he again had to convince the sceptical front-of-house lady that he wasn't a local businessman dropping in for a horizontal low-cal lunch, but he really did have business with Miss Andromeda. He neglected to mention the de-stress offer.

A few minutes later he was seated in Andromeda's office, whiskey in hand, and bathed in the warm, colourful light coming through the irreverent stained glass. Harry was again delighting in the sacrilegious image. He had explained to Andromeda how the covert filming was going to work and that it was all set up, fully tested, and raring to go.

'Now we just need the Councillor to keep his appointment and I will dutifully record his entire suckling session.'

'And then how are we going to use that to silence him? If we just make it public – the simplest option – that will no doubt finish him, but it'll likely finish Mama's business, too.'

'Yeah, I know. She talked about discretion, and anyway, I was already well across that concept, being a good customer of the industry.'

Andromeda gave a knowing smile.

'Okay, granted. But where to with the film footage?'

Harry felt good inside, quietly proud of his plan.

'Well, the next time Kasun goes for his feed, rather than milk straight up he'll get a little TV show. The star on the small screen will be his good self, featuring in tonight's visit, but with a deadly serious voiceover from yours truly. That should have him running for the door and well and truly out of public office. Plus I'll be adding a little surprise touch at the end, just to seal his decision for him.'

Andromeda looked at him through the cloud of smoke between them.

'A thinking man, Harry, I do like that. And I like the plan, very much. Should do the trick nicely if all goes well. And no risk to Mama from any publicity. I knew I'd chosen well with you.'

'Thanks, Andromeda. By the time we're done, there is no chance the diligent Councillor will be able to survive in public politics, and he will know it.'

'Yes, I agree, but don't you think there's some risk that he might try to get revenge, get even for being fucked over?'

'Nothing overt or violent. These political types tend to be spineless in the real world. He might try to come up with some scheme in the future, but we can deal with that suitably in due course, if and when. I am always at your service, Andromeda.'

She smiled. 'Yes, I'm sure, and I will definitely keep that in mind.'

'Meantime, here's to the next week or so.'

Harry lifted his glass in salute and downed his whiskey.

'So is our wonderful private eye feeling a tad strained from all the hard work?' Andromeda smirked.

Harry did his best to look earnest, and wrung out.

'Well, funny you should ask, Andromeda.'

She laughed, reached to her desk and pressed a buzzer

on its side. A minute later the same young blonde with the cantaloupe chest came through a side door.

She smiled coyly at Harry.

'Harry, this is Stella. I believe you met briefly the other night?'

'Hi, sugar,' rolled sweetly off Stella's tongue.

'Hello, Stella,' replied Harry, as he reflected on the appropriateness of her name.

Andromeda, on her feet now, moved over to Stella and put her hand on her shoulder.

'Now, Stella, Harry here is a good friend of ours and has been working tremendously hard on a rather important job we need done. So, I think he could do with a couple of hours of very special treatment on the house, so he can completely unwind and relax.'

Stella nodded and grinned. 'I'm sure I can make him relax.'

'Good girl. I'll sort out a little bonus for you.'

Stella beamed at Harry, whose eyes were having trouble resisting the gravitational allure of her magnificent breasts.

'So, sugar, this time you get past the boss's office.'

'Take me away, Stella. A man can only take so much pressure and overwork.'

She laughed, as did Andromeda, who said, 'Have a good chill-out, Harry, and we'll talk soon. Keep me posted. On the job, that is.'

Harry chuckled as Stella took him by the hand and led him through the side door. He gave a parting wave and wink, theatre-style, to Andromeda.

For the next two hours, Harry thought he'd died and gone to a libertine's version of heaven. He couldn't remember a body-slide massage this damned good, and when Stella buried his face in her chasmic cleavage

Harry just wanted to fix the moment in time forever. He even managed to avoid dwelling on Club Mammary. His sole desire at that point was to be interred in that sweet melonry. After an hour of serious 'therapy' in the massage oil, Stella told him to roll on his back. She teased his scrotum with her fingertips until he was as hard as a granite obelisk, then she straddled him swiftly and lowered her delectable body onto him, enveloping his raging cock in her wet pussy. Harry groaned and closed his eyes. Stella placed her hands on his chest, the hairs matted with massage oil, and rode him like a bronco. Harry just had to lie there and take it, until he exploded and shouted her name out loud, sounding like Marlon Brando. Stella stayed on him and lowered her chest onto his. She looked him in the eye and then, much to Harry's surprise, gave him a tongue kiss to rival the sex. Then she raised her face slightly.

'How are the stress levels now, Harry?'

He smiled back at her. 'Somewhere around Buddhist monk zone, thanks to you, Stella.'

She giggled and reached over to the bedside cabinet for a packet of cigarettes, smothering Harry with her breasts as she did so. She lit two and slipped one into Harry's mouth, not showing any sign of dismounting from him. Harry admired her in a smoky silence for a couple of minutes. Then she must have read his mind.

'A whiskey, Harry?'

'Perfection just outdid itself. Yes, please.'

With that Stella slid wetly off Harry and walked over to a drinks cabinet. Harry hadn't noticed it before, being rather entranced by Stella's attributes and the promise of paradise to come, but looking at it now he was surprised. Whiskey wasn't normally on offer after a session, that's for sure.

'An unusually well-stocked bar, Stella?'

'Yeah. This is Andromeda's room for special clients, so it's all laid on here. Let's make the most of it. It's fucking great not to be on a time limit for a change.'

Harry momentarily slipped his mind from reverie to rational thought.

'So you mean we could spend the rest of the afternoon here?'

'Yep.'

'O, carry me away sweet siren! Pour those drinks, my lovely Stella. I'm not moving anywhere.'

And with that Harry settled in for the afternoon, butt naked and supremely content.

Harry had showered in the late afternoon, playfully accepting Stella's offer to wash his back, then had an early dinner at a Thai joint on Crown Street. The pub had been tempting, as usual, but he didn't want to add to the whiskies he'd had at Andromeda's, given the work ahead of him this evening. Mind you, the excellent crying tiger just wasn't the same with sparkling mineral water in place of a good shiraz.

At half past seven he paid his bill and headed off to Club Mammary. As he went in he thought he detected a hint of a smile on Zanza's dark face, but he wasn't going to assume they were on friendly terms just yet. Still, worth cultivating perhaps, as he could certainly think of future uses for Zanza's services in his line of work. He was shown straight into Mama's office where she was on the couch chatting over a coffee with another woman, whose back was to the door as Harry entered.

'Ah, Mr Harry. Good to see you. This is Dolly, she is the Councillor's favourite.'

Harry shook her hand. 'Pleased to meet you, Dolly.'

Dolly simply smiled in return. She was a solid-framed woman, in her early forties and not unattractive, with long chestnut curls tumbling over her firm, swollen breasts which were lurking beneath a jade green lace negligée. If it hadn't been for the attempt at clothing, Harry thought Dolly could have stepped straight off a Renoir canvas. For Harry this was truly turning out to be Titty Tuesday.

'I been telling Dolly about the plan, Mr Harry. She cool with it.'

'Sweet. Well, let's check the equipment with Dolly in the lounge then. You have any questions, Dolly?'

'No. Mama explained why this has to be done. So I just do my normal stuff, yeah?'

'Yep, exactly. You won't even know the camera is there. Maybe you could try and cuddle the Councillor's face towards the TV cabinet though. Any chance?'

'Easy. This one, once I've got him sucking hard, he's under my total control and completely oblivious to everything else, Harry, you've no idea.'

Damned right, thought Harry, I sure as hell don't. He again thought of medals being deserved.

Dolly left the room and Harry sat down at the desk, awakening the laptop. A couple of clicks and he was looking at Dolly in The Creamery, arranging cushions and towels on the couch. All the optical gear was functioning perfectly. Harry did a test record and playback, and satisfied himself that the digital recording side of things was hot to trot as well. All set for show time.

Harry sat back and looked to his left to the four small screens showing the CCTV camera viewpoints. The first two showed a dark and quiet Linden Lane, the third the warm glow of the empty foyer, and on the fourth Harry could see the full length of the main hallway, with Zanza on the couch in the foreground. There was still time before Kasun's appointment. Harry looked longingly at the drinks cabinet, but settled for a Marlboro instead. He was going to kill for a drink later this evening, that was for sure.

As he drew in the smoke, he suddenly thought of Tessa. He wasn't sure why, given his extreme carnal workout that afternoon. Stella had worked him over three times and left him as drained as a cabinet minister's expense account. So it wasn't like he was feeling sexually pent up at the moment, rather the opposite. Maybe because he'd been surrounded by such buxomness all day, the image of Tessa's more delicate physique was asserting itself in his mind by its sheer contrast. Plus, of course, Harry hadn't actually seen Tessa naked, and the heady lure of uncharted territory was always a big motivator for Harry. He lit another smoke and pulled out his phone. The number rang a few times before the well-bred accent announced the voicemail instructions.

'Well, my English rose, I was wondering if you'd care for a display of hot metal-working, not to mention a hot meal? Tomorrow night, if you're free, or Thursday? I know a great little French number – restaurant, that is – in the city. Text me if you're keen and I'll call you in the morning to arrange. Ciao, *bella.*'

Harry pocketed his phone, putting it on silent mode, and sat back to await Kasun's dairy call.

– 10 –

Stanislav Kasun got the taxi to drop him a couple of hundred metres further south on Bourke Street and he hauled himself onto the pavement. He was disinclined to walk at the best of times, although an evening such as this probably fell into the best category, and right now his desire to get into Club Mammary and gorge himself on those ambrosial udders had a greater sense of covetous urgency than a politician voting for a parliamentary pay rise. Tempering his craving was his preference to be able to slip discreetly into Linden Lane and into his beloved cave of maternal bosoms. Plus he didn't want any scumbag taxi driver to ever be able to sell their story to the gossip mags once he became a cabinet minister, which was only the next election away, the way things were going.

As he rolled his bulk along the street, his thoughts, as always at this particular point in his milky soirées, turned to luscious Aunty Dragana. He felt himself begin to harden, despite his discomfort with walking, at the mental image of Aunty's naked bosom. Not that he'd ever been fortunate enough to actually see Aunty naked, bosom-wise or anything at all, a fact for which he had always jealously hated that particular uncle. Nevertheless, he fantasized about gobbling on those auntly breasts more than a missionary priest longing for a naïve altar boy.

He paused at the corner of the lane, sweating profusely and breathing hard. He looked around in both directions, trying to look casual. His amateur mind satisfied that he wasn't being followed or observed, he hurried, at least as fast as a human who resembled a biped hippopotamus could, towards the door of Club Mammary. He tapped in his own access code and the door clicked. He yanked it open and secreted himself into the foyer, closing the door behind him. Taking a deep breath, he closed his eyes, both in relief at getting into the privacy of the Club, but also at the anticipation of the next couple of hours. His mouth was dry and his throat felt parched. His chest was still heaving as he gasped for breath. He was thinking of the warm, creamy slaking of his thirst when the intercom buzzed. He pressed the button and spoke his password: 'Babe'. He couldn't fathom how the madam who owned this place chose the passwords, but she had given him this one on just his second visit and it had remained unchanged. The ladies here must think he was cute, he guessed.

The inner door opened and Kasun winced as he looked up at the black beast who guarded the place. Bloody scary ape, he thought. Why these jungle bunnies had ever been let into the country dismayed Kasun. One thing was for sure: when he had sufficient influence, his rightful position of power, things would change. Seriously change. In the meantime, he swallowed his aversion to black people, and used the madam here for his own purposes. Not to satisfy his desire, of course; only white bosoms could do that. He had to be able to imagine Aunty in order to climax, and breasts the colour of coal weren't going to cut it. No, he used the black madam for another purpose entirely: to practise his slavish obsequiousness, a trait and a skill that was so far paying him handsome dividends in his political life. He'd actually run into her last visit, in the corridor before changing. And he prided himself on his performance that evening. He'd oozed his smiling charm over her, asking her about her life here in Australia and if there was anything he could do with his political connections to help out any family members back in Africa. If he could manage it with her, with her dark face that belonged in a cotton field and a distractingly enormous bosom which he definitely didn't fancy, then he figured his political masters and mentors would be a cakewalk on the greasing front.

The scary gorilla escorted him to The Creamery and closed the door behind him. Kasun felt the dark menace lift and he gazed upon the delicious Dolly and her double-D delights.

'Hello, Babe,' she sighed invitingly. 'Come and let's get you changed into something more comforting.'

Yes, thought Kasun, they obviously do find me cute. As it should be. But if only Aunty Dragana would call me 'babe' as well, how perfect life would be.

He smiled at Dolly and cooed, 'Yes, Aunty.'

Dolly, on her feet now, took him by the hand, kissed him on the forehead, and led him off to the change room.

Harry, who had been watching the proceedings intently, right from Kasun's arrival on the CCTV cameras through to his own camera in the suckling lounge, took the opportunity to have a smoke whilst they went off to get Kasun ready. The twistedly curious side of his detective nature made him half wish he had a camera in the change room.

Mama came back into the office.

'All going good, Mr Harry?'

'So far, Mama, just perfect. They've gone to get Kasun changed. How long will …'

But before Harry could finish his question, there was movement on screen.

'Ah, they're back.'

Mama came over to join Harry behind the desk, her eyes joining his on the laptop screen.

Kasun looked ridiculous, but also inanely happy if his infantile smile was anything to go by. As Dolly sat him on the couch, and he deposited a towelling bag presumably containing his clothes on the armchair, Harry took in the giant-sized diaper that was wrapped around Kasun's loins, with his gut rolls bringing a whole new dimension to the phrase 'muffin top'. He looked like a sumo wrestler in a crèche. The outfit was completed by woollen booties in pastel blue, a crocheted bonnet to match, and a bib around his neck bearing an image of Winnie-the-Pooh clutching a clay honey pot. Harry was momentarily distracted as his mind went to the locked wooden box in his wardrobe and its contents, including a well-loved and dog-eared copy of *The House at Pooh Corner*. It had been Orla's favourite bedtime read. He nodded almost imperceptibly in silent tribute and got his mind back onto the job.

For a heart-stopping few seconds it seemed as though the diaper-clad Councillor was staring directly at the concealed camera lens.

Harry held his breath. Surely he hadn't seen it.

For those moments it seemed to Harry that he and Kasun were staring each other down. Then Dolly started cooing in the Councillor's ear and he immediately turned to look at her.

Harry breathed out slowly. One of those adrenalin-inducing coincidences, nothing more. He lit another smoke.

Dolly by now had her enormous assets on full display

as the baby Kasun cuddled up to her, calling her 'Aunty' repeatedly. He started to paw her swollen breasts with his sausage-like fingers and his eyes were completely fixated on the bright red distended nipple on her left breast. Dolly cupped his jowls with her right hand and eased him maternally onto her fleshy teat.

'Here you go, Babe.'

All that came out of Kasun was a gurgled 'Mmmm' as he hungrily sucked on the swollen source of sustenance.

Harry was impressed with the quality of the image as he zoomed in on the laptop screen. Kasun's contented suckling face, with eyes closed and lips and cheeks sucking as if for life itself, was clearly visible and, more importantly, recognisable, even side on.

As the feeding continued, Dolly gradually adjusted the angle of her torso, stroking the Councillor's flabby face as she did so and cooing gently to him. Before long the camera had virtually a full face shot of Kasun, minus some obscuration by Dolly's left breast.

He came off the teat for a moment, licking his lips like a fat tabby over a saucer, and he opened his eyes, looking adoringly at Dolly. As his gaze returned to her bosom Dolly said, 'Here you go, babe,' and she squeezed her breast so that milk sprayed onto Kasun's gleeful face.

Harry, guessing that in this world that constituted the money-shot, naturally reached for a cigarette. And he couldn't go dry for a moment longer. He told Mama that he needed that whiskey, and right now. Mama obliged with a speed that belied her physique.

'It looking good, Mr Harry, very good. And Dolly do good, yes?'

'Abso-fucking-lutely, Mama. Gold medal for Dolly in my books.'

But it hadn't been the only money-shot. Harry returned his gaze to the screen just in time to see Kasun, milk running down his face, tug rapidly on his cock until he blew his load in his lap, all the while Dolly was hugging his face into her bosom.

About half an hour later, with Dolly gone from the room and having kissed Kasun goodnight, the Councillor had showered and dressed. Zanza came into the room, checked the money in the envelope, and escorted Kasun out to the foyer. Thence the Councillor and wannabe cabinet minister departed into the sultry Sydney night.

Harry looked at Mama and said, 'Well, that's curtains for the Cadbury Councillor.'

She laughed. 'Ooh, Mr Harry. You a funny man.' Mama proceeded to pour another drink for both of them as Harry packed up his gear.

'I be having one more with you, Mr Harry, then it back to business. A new client at eleven o'clock.'

'Don't tell me, Mama, a High Court judge,' Harry chuckled.

'Oh, I wish, Mr Harry. This one only from the Federal Court. Still, he be paying real good.'

'I'm sure, Mama, I'm sure.' Another thing Harry was sure of was that this place was a goldmine for extortion possibilities. Credit to Mama and her crew for their professionalism.

Mama handed Harry his whiskey.

'Thanks, Mama. This one won't even touch the sides and then I'll be gone into the night. Let me know when Kasun makes his next appointment so I can make his night for him. Cheers.' Harry raised his glass.

Mama raised hers, too. 'He usually come in once a week, and usually on Tuesday night. Occasionally he make it two times a week, but that rare. I call you as soon as I know.'

'Excellent. And the whiskey, too.' Harry downed his drink, grabbed his equipment bag and bid Mama goodnight. He tipped his forehead to Zanza as he went down the corridor. Harry was sure the big bastard did smile at him this time.

Harry headed out onto Bourke Street and grabbed a cab in the direction of his office. He needed to unload his gear, copy the footage, and call Andromeda to let her know the plan was well on track. As he turned his phone back onto active mode, he saw there was a text from Tessa telling him she loved French, food, too, and that she was free Thursday evening. Harry smiled. What a hell of a day. He started thinking about peeling Tessa's clothes off, until he caught sight of the taxi driver giving him a very strange look in the rear vision mirror.

– 11 –

Thursday morning arrived with Harry having enjoyed an uncharacteristic sleep-in, owing to no pressing work commitments and a pleasant, but not excessive, indulgence in good red wine the previous evening. He hadn't wanted to overdo it, as he had confirmed dinner arrangements with Tessa tonight and he was definitely hoping to eat her for dessert. A hangover wouldn't help his performance at all, and he was keen not to disappoint. It mattered more than when he was paying for it. In his experience, if the rampaging Kenmare tongue succeeded in bringing on a screaming orgasm on the first encounter, his women invariably came back for more. When it came to having his face buried between beautiful, soft thighs, Harry considered himself something of an artiste, not to mention a devoted connoisseur. The thought of having Tessa sitting on his face was making him hard, so he decided to get up, have a shower and conserve his libido for later. He had booked a table at one of his favourite French joints in Darlinghurst, an upstairs number called La Cuisine des Anges, where the food was divine and all the staff were actually French. In the meantime he needed to clear up his bachelor-pad apartment in the anticipation of Tessa accepting his invitation to engage in some most definitely non-angelic activities *chez* Harry.

After showering, as well as an all-too-rare smooth shave, Harry dressed, made coffee, and heated a croissant in the oven. As he sat at his small dining table having the delicious pastry with butter and strawberry jam, he looked around the apartment, making a mental note of the necessary tasks: cleaning the bathroom was clearly the main priority, followed by the kitchen. Apart from these two, a quick vacuum and removing all the empty bottles to the recycling bin in the building's garbage room should do the trick. Probably wouldn't hurt either to put away the last three months' *Penthouse* magazines which were strewn on the couch.

He had plenty of time. All afternoon in fact. He didn't need to go to the office at all, so he planned on a bit of Harry time once he had the joint looking presentable. Maybe a couple of hours reading, a rare luxury. He'd recently bought a couple of books by Carl Hiaasen, so he fancied getting stuck into one of them; the title *Striptease* had Harry interested straight up. The afternoon was his.

– 12 –

Tessa had insisted on meeting him at the restaurant, once they had established that neither of them owned a car and both lived by taxis. So 'un-Australian', yet so progressive, at least in Harry's eyes.

Harry was already standing on Victoria Road in Darlinghurst, fifteen minutes ahead of time and having a smoke, when Tessa alighted from a cab. She was early herself, so Harry hadn't even finished his cigarette.

'I really do love a woman who's punctual. Great to see you, Tessa.' Harry took her hand and kissed it.

'Well, Harry, I do love a man who anticipates the unexpected and is there waiting for the prompt woman.' She beamed at him and he laughed.

'Cool, we are off to a great start. Let's *allez manger, ma chérie.*'

'I'm ravenous. Lead on.'

Harry ushered Tessa up the stairs and they were shown to a table for two next to the windows overlooking the bustling street.

Aperitifs of pastis for Harry and Kir Royale for Tessa were followed by the signature entrée dish, the truffled gnocchi, for both of them. A bottle of Loire Valley chasselas washed down the creamy dish.

As Tessa finished licking her fork spotless, she ran her

tongue along the tines and looked at Harry.

'Absolutely delicious. That truffle could almost make a girl come.'

'Yes, and I can think of a few other things, my English rose.'

'Hold those thoughts, Harry, still two courses for the lady who is owed dinner.'

The mains arrived. Tessa had the beef fillet, done rare, whilst Harry got stuck into the confit de canard. A red from the Languedoc moistened the meat dishes perfectly.

'Glad to see you like your beef rare like the French, unlike the overcooked English efforts.'

'There's absolutely no point in eating well-done beef, Harry. May as well be chewing on an old shoe. This fillet is to die for. Try a bit?'

'Don't mind if I do.'

Tessa put a morsel of the beef, rolled in the red wine sauce, on her fork and raised it up, her hand cupped beneath it. Harry leant in and she slid the red parcel into his mouth. She smiled coyly at him as she did so.

'Oh, yes, that is bloody good, isn't it. Some duck for you?'

'Why not? Feed me.'

She gently sucked a piece of *confit* off Harry's fork and chewed slowly with her lips almost pouting at him.

'Very good, but I am glad I chose the beef. In more ways than one.'

She smiled at him as he chuckled. They continued eating. After the mains had been cleared away, it was a cheese platter plus a dessert wine, finished with a coffee each.

Throughout the meal Harry had enthralled Tessa with his investigative exploits, whilst avoiding the heavier aspects of his past, and she, in return, had enlightened him about her fashion studio and modelling agency, both of which she owned outright. And she loved to drink; Harry thought she was pretty damned close to perfect.

Harry had paid the bill and was working towards suggesting his place, when Tessa proved her utter perfection.

'Okay, Dirty Harry, I vote we jump in a cab to my place.' She grinned. 'I've got some sensational modelling portfolios that you would simply love.'

Harry fought to remain composed.

'I would be honoured to give you my professional opinion. Take me away.'

– 13 –

They got out of a cab in Pyrmont, at the base of one of the tallest apartment buildings. Tessa led Harry into the foyer and to the lifts. They got in and Tessa jabbed the button for the penthouse floor. She grinned at Harry and said nothing, just gazed into his eyes. Harry wasn't exactly overcome with words himself at this point, he just had to keep his eyes on hers, rather than roving up and down her lithe body, mentally undressing her. A few minutes later, Harry found himself standing on a balcony thirty floors up overlooking Sydney harbour, a glass of Laphroig single malt and cigarette in hand, enjoying the company of a beautiful and delightful woman who clearly was going to bed him very shortly. Sweet, Harry, so sweet. And he'd cleaned up his modest pad unnecessarily.

Tessa played with him over a drink and a cigarette, running her tongue along his lips and pressing her pelvis against the solid bulge in his trousers.

'How badly do you want me, handsome?'

'Baby, I am randier than Casanova with the keys to the convent.'

'Good. Drink up.'

They drained their glasses. She took his hand, said nothing, and walked inside, trailing Harry in her wake.

Her pace quickened as they neared the immaculate

bedroom, Tessa pushing Harry backwards into the room. Once inside the teasing turned into hungry kissing and the lustful ripping off of clothing. As Harry got down to his boxer shorts and socks, with Tessa looking delicious in a tiny black G string and similarly scant black bra, she pushed him onto the edge of the bed. His arse hit the cushioning and the mattress gave to his weight with a tidal movement. He yanked off his socks as suavely as he could, socks never being a good passionate look in his books. As Tessa coaxed him further onto the bed, Harry couldn't help laughing at the undulating terrain beneath him.

'Bugger me, Tessa, it's been at least twenty years since I've been on a water bed. I didn't know they even existed any more. I'll have to see if I can remember how to ride the rhythm on one of these babies.'

'Oh, I'm sure it'll come surging back to you. Like riding a bike, really.'

'I'll do my best to rise to the occasion.'

'Smart-arse. Now let's see what else that great kissing tongue can do for a lady in need.'

And with that, in one svelte, serpentine move, Tessa slid up Harry's body and buried his face in her crotch. Harry gurgled, ran his hands up onto Tessa's pert breasts, and amazingly quickly found the aqueous rhythm as Tessa rode his face. Evidently satisfied with the Kenmare tongue-lashing, Tessa writhed and moaned for about ten minutes, the crescendo slowly building, until she shouted and forcefully grabbed Harry's head as she orgasmed. By the time she rolled off, Harry desperately needed air – lots of it – but his respite was short-lived.

'Come on, big boy,' she commanded as she grabbed his rock-hard cock and got on her knees facing the bed-head.

Harry was still trying to regain his breath, not to mention full control of his now aching facial muscles.

'I've always thought that having a heart attack whilst doing the horizontal tango would be my choice of death. I really can't think of a better ending.'

'Just make sure you finish the job first,' teased Tessa. 'Now stop the talking and bloody take me.'

As Harry swung himself up to take hold of Tessa's enticing hips and thrust into her from behind, he found himself looking into his own face and that of Tessa. The wall at the head of the bed was entirely covered in mirrored wall tiles. As Harry plunged into Tessa's drippingly wet pussy, he found himself transfixed by the reflected image of the two of them flowing drunkenly around the mirrored squares, moving with the sexual thrusting and the rolling waves of the water beneath them. It was like watching a porn movie whilst tripping.

'That's it, my man. You got the moves. I just love to watch myself getting nailed. Fuck me hard, Harry.'

And Harry did just that.

– 14 –

Councillor Stanislav Kasun hadn't wanted to wait another week for his next dairy delight and Harry found himself back at Club Mammary on Saturday evening. He was seated behind Mama's desk, with Mama and Dolly on the nearby couch.

'Okay, ladies, here's how it goes tonight. The footage from the other night is loaded to play on the TV in the lounge. Dolly, once you've got him changed and back into the lounge, you just need to excuse yourself for a minute, and then I'll do the rest by remote control from here. Okay?'

'Yep. Sounds easy to me,' said Dolly.

'And he is the only customer at that time this evening, Mama?'

'Yes, Mr Harry. He be all alone in the premises. Only Zanza in the corridor outside.' Mama grinned.

'Yes, well I'm sure he'll find that a comfort as he departs in what I anticipate will be a great haste. I might have a small drink while we wait, Mama.'

'Of course, Mr Harry.' Mama poured Harry a whiskey.

Half an hour later the sweaty, corpulent Councillor was being shown into the lounge and Dolly, having pecked him on the cheek, took him by the hand to the change room.

Once back, Kasun in his ridiculous diaper, Dolly gave

him a cuddle and said she just had to nip to the bathroom. The Councillor settled his hungry bulk onto the couch, as Harry monitored it all on camera.

Kasun was mildly surprised when he heard the TV give out its slight electronic crackle as the screen illuminated. But his surprise turned to cold horror as he saw himself in full-feed mode on Dolly's swollen breasts, and then the shot of the milk spraying on his face. He was transfixed on the couch looking at the screen, his poisonous mind desperately trying to compute what the hell was going on. The answer arrived in a deep voice overlaid onto the footage.

'Okay, Councillor Kasun, you might think you're a player politically. But here's a new set of rules to think about,' drawled Harry.

Kasun could only sit there, mouth hanging agape, his pig-like eyes glued to the screen.

'So, Kasun, you hypocritical wanker, that motion of yours at the Council to shut down the brothels, it becomes history, ancient history, before the next Council meeting. And it stays that way, long fucking forgotten. If not, a copy of this is going straight to the Premier. You might not be flavour of the month, excuse the pun, after that.'

The Councillor, anaemic looking at the best of times, paled noticeably. Then came the knockout line.

'And along with the Premier, I think your devout sanctimonious crone of an aunty down in Canberra might also like a copy. What do you reckon, fuck-stain? Something a bit different for the Monday morning Federal Cabinet meeting, don't you think?'

Kasun was on the verge of pissing himself in sheer terror, and he certainly wasn't waiting for any more. He grabbed the bag of his clothes and launched himself at the door with incongruous agility, spluttering something about this not being the end of it 'you black bitch'.

Harry watched on the CCTV cameras as Kasun ran down the corridor, like an albino hippo on heat. This was to the obvious amusement of Zanza who had momentarily put down his gentleman's magazine. The big African, previously briefed, got up and made as if he was going after the Councillor, just for good effect. It certainly had it, since Slim turned to look as Zanza moved, and his rapid waddling went into warp-speed. Then he was out, through the glowing foyer, and into the lane.

Just for good measure, Harry had organized his mate, Trev, to be outside. Trev was sporting two Nikon digital SLRs with impressive lenses and flash guns, all to look like a tabloid journo. As Kasun emerged from the Club, Trev raised a camera and hit the trigger button, the motor drive clacking away with the accompanying flash gun display. All Trev had to say was, 'Councillor Kasun, a comment for ...'

The half-naked Kasun ran for his chubby life.

The image from the exterior CCTV cameras was absolutely exquisite for Harry and Mama watching from the office. Kasun's rapidly retreating figure resembled a fat Roman Senator wearing his toga for a loincloth, struggling to reclothe himself, and running from a huge hairy barbarian in hot pursuit, a battle-axe in one hand and a raging erection in the other.

Mama and Harry burst out laughing.

'A job well done, Mr Harry, no doubt about it.'

'Yes, Mama, I do believe that will do the trick nicely.'

Mama filled two glasses and they toasted the evening's work.

— 15 —

I t was late Monday afternoon and Harry was back at the Holy Garter, bathed in the warm light coming through the sinful stained glass, a glass of liquid sin in his hand.

'So, Miss Andromeda, did you enjoy the footage of our illustrious teat-sucking Councillor?' asked Harry, feeling justifiably smug.

'Harry, you are a true bloody professional, that's all I can say. I loved every last second of the footage. Seeing that self-righteous bastard running like a suckling pig from a Spanish barbecue kitchen, truly priceless. But tell me, who was the journo in the laneway taking pictures? Was that part of the plan?'

Harry chuckled. 'Relax. He wasn't a real journo. Just a fellow PI that I roped in for dramatic effect.'

'Sensational, Harry. I really do love your style. Now, let's have your bank account details and I'll settle the payment. The business is done.'

Andromeda sat down at her computer and beckoned Harry over. She had a banking screen open.

'What's your BSB and account number, Harry?'

Harry gave them to her and he watched as she sent a very sweet $100K to his account.

'Andromeda, I do love your style, too.' He kissed her on the cheek.

She touched his face in return. 'Harry, it's been worth every cent. I've already checked with the Council and Councillor Kasun's motion has been suddenly withdrawn, just this morning. Who would've thought?'

'Job done, then.'

'Indeed, Harry, indeed. Now, do you feel like any fringe benefits?'

Harry thought about it, but didn't need too long.

Just over a second, in fact.

'Well ... I know this is probably not quite the usual practice around here, but what's the chance of taking young Stella home for the night?'

Andromeda laughed. 'Oh, Harry, you are a man of predictable tastes.'

'Guilty as charged, your Honour.'

'Well, consider yourself sentenced to a night of hard labour with Stella.'

'Take me away. Let the punishment begin.'

Andromeda chuckled whilst Harry grinned like a feline.

Andromeda pressed the buzzer on her desk. A minute later Stella, looking lasciviously lovely in her midnight blue lingerie, appeared from the side door to the office.

When she saw Harry she smiled.

'Hi there, Harry.'

'Hi Stella, very good to see you.'

'Stella, love, go get some clothes on, there's a babe. You're going home with Harry tonight.'

Stella smirked at Harry then spoke to Andromeda. 'Do you think the big boy can take a whole night?'

'I'm quite sure you will test him to his very limits.'

'You bet I will,' said Stella as she looked back at Harry.

'Oh, yes please,' groaned Harry.

'And Stella, my babe, there is a very, very juicy bonus coming in your pay this week.'

'Thanks, boss.' Stella stepped back out of the office.

Shortly afterwards, Harry sat in the back of a cab with Stella close beside him and her hand on his leg. She dug her fingers gently into the inside of his thigh.

'I've never been home with a client for the night. Never gone beyond the one-hour session, actually. But you don't really count as a client, do you, Harry?'

'Probably not, my young Stella.'

Harry lowered his voice, even though the cab driver was more intent on chatting on his mobile to someone in a language Harry didn't recognize. He leaned his face close to Stella's ear.

'And since I'm not really a client, maybe you'd let me do things to you that your clients probably never do.'

'Harry, are we talking kinky shit?' she whispered back.

'Not in my books, babe. I am obsessed with eating pussy. I love to feel a woman come with my face buried between her legs.'

She put her right hand on Harry's face and ran her tongue down his cheek.

'Okay, you are definitely gone from the client category. So, since you are no longer the boss tonight, I am now in charge.'

'Well, ma'am, Sergeant Harry reporting for duty.'

'That's the right attitude, big boy. Now, I am ordering you, once we're at your place, to eat me until I tell you that I can't take any more.'

'At your service, ma'am.'

'Good.'

Stella slid her hand up Harry's trousers and over his now rigid cock.

'And when I'm satisfied, then this monster can be unleashed and allowed to run amok.'

She gripped his cock through the fabric and kissed him on the lips. Then she leant back and put her head on his shoulder.

'I hope it's not too far to go.'

'About two minutes away, babe.'

As Harry gazed at her bountiful cleavage, he reflected that tidying his apartment had definitely not been a wasted effort after all.

PART 4

HARRY'S WELFARE

... the set of her body dared you to touch her.
Anyone with the juices still running would want to.

- Peter Corris

'It's funny, but I'm so sure that those kisses left no
mark on me – no taint of promiscuity, I mean –
even though a man once told me in all seriousness
that he hated to think I'd been a public drinking-
glass ... I just laughed and told him to think of
me rather as a loving-cup that goes from hand to
hand but should be valued none the less.'

- F. Scott Fitzgerald

— 1 —

Tanya looked utterly superb as she strutted confidently north down Crown Street, blonde curls undulating in the breeze, ample and firm breasts asserting themselves under her low-cut pink blouse, and her perfect posterior swaying seductively with every step she took. Her delightful derrière was one that moved in all the right ways, and none of the wrong ones.

She was heading for her and Sasha's new Reservoir Street apartment, their desire to move to Surry Hills now accomplished. To an observer, Tanya's progress along the street was like a young, vivacious vixen doing a victory parade after the Great Chicken Coop Rampage, although there wasn't a single out of place feather in this scene. One of Mother Nature's truly inspired designs, Tanya's sublime backside drew more than a few admiring looks as she illuminated the drab concrete footpath. Her Levis looked like they had been airbrushed on, a look she had perfected, knowing as she did that in this life, as loaded as hers had been with shit deals, any good points needed to be exploited to the max. And in the world of carnal card hands, Tanya's body was a royal flush. And good old Fate, on that day a couple of decades ago, had clearly decided that one pristine example of perfection would not suffice, so threw in identical Sasha for good measure. Of course,

147

well-intentioned Mother Nature wasn't to know the despoiling of the young twins that would follow eleven years later, at the hands of a predatory stepfather hell-bent on satisfying his paedophilic desires.

Tanya hummed as she wafted along, her beauty glowingly enhanced by the dappled sunlight dripping through the leaves of the plane trees. She reflected that, despite the legacy of their violated childhood, she and Sasha were making a good fist of things now. They had their own place, regular and very well-paid work at the Scarlet Boudoir, and they were starting to toy with the possibility of modelling work. They shared most things as twins, and chief amongst them was an avid interest in fashion, something they had started studying at night school. They certainly had the looks, but just needed a start somewhere. All in all, Tanya was feeling pretty happy.

It was as she was approaching the corner of Albion Street that she heard the noise, unmistakeably a female crying. Not just any crying – a girl sobbing her heart out. Tanya stopped in her tracks and looked around swiftly to try and locate the source of awful anguish.

In a recessed doorway a girl was sitting on the polished granite ground, knees drawn up to her chest and her spindly arms wrapped around her legs. Her face was lowered onto her knees, but the sobbing was the dominant feature. Tanya went over and crouched down next to her. The dirty threadbare denim mini-skirt, the hot pink boob tube, and the scuffed black platform heels left Tanya with no doubt as to her line of work. Tanya reflected that this sad but real image could all too easily have been her or Sasha, if things had turned out differently. She felt an instinctive drive to bond with a kindred spirit in a hostile place. She reached out and placed her hand softly on the girl's shoulder.

'Hey.'

The girl recoiled further into the corner of the doorway and lifted her head slightly so she could look at the person capable of touching her so gently. Her eyes and face resembled a cowering puppy. Tanya thought the girl was probably only a couple of years older than her.

'I'm Tanya. What's your name?'

'Which one?' she sniffed.

'Well, at a place down the road I'm called Venus, but really I'm Tanya. You?'

Just the slightest hint of ease crept into the girl's eyes.

'I'm Lara. But it's Trixie out here.'

Lara lifted her face fully. Her shoulder-length hair was the colour of dirty sandstone and hadn't seen shampoo in many days. Her skin was sallow and uninviting, the only standout features being the cheap pink lipstick, which at least matched the grubby boob tube. There were remnants of dried semen along the left side of her lower jaw line.

'Wanna smoke, Lara?'

Lara looked eager. 'Yeah.'

Tanya took a packet of Marlboro Lights out of her handbag and gave one to Lara. She put one in her own mouth and lit them both.

Lara's eyes closed as she drew back hard on the smoke. She opened them again as she slowly exhaled.

'You wanna tell me? Some punter hurt you?'

Lara sniffed hard, sucking back a wad of phlegm. She looked at Tanya as tears rolled down her cheeks. Tanya wasn't ready for the outburst.

'They killed my baby! Those fuckers! They killed my baby boy.'

She fell into sobs again. Tanya stubbed out her half-finished cigarette and put her arm around Lara's shoulders.

'Let's go grab a coffee. You hungry?'

Tanya looked at Lara's skinny body, noticing some fairly fresh track marks on her arm, and guessed food hadn't exactly been a priority.

Lara nodded and struggled to her feet. Tanya gave her a hug and dug some tissues out of her handbag. Lara took them, blew her nose loudly and wetly, and chucked the sodden mass of tissues on the ground.

'Come on,' said Tanya, as she took Lara by the arm and stepped out onto the footpath.

The pair walked along Crown Street to the first café. They stopped in front of the counter which opened onto the street. A waiter standing in the doorway smiled at Tanya, then noticed Lara, and a worried frown crossed his brow. Tanya spotted it straightaway.

'Don't worry, mate, relax. We're getting takeaway, okay?'

The waiter reddened and scuttled back inside.

Tanya placed her order for two coffees and a bacon and egg roll with the barista and then fished out her cigarettes. She gave one to Lara and lit one herself.

As they stood on the footpath smoking and waiting for their order, an open-topped Porsche slowed to the kerb. The driver was a flabby, fifty-something bloke. He wore an open white linen shirt, revealing his dyed black chest hair, sported a pair of very expensive sunglasses, and had a receding hairline dyed from the same bottle as his chest. The car, the only remotely attractive part of the union, had slowed to a stop, and the driver leered at Tanya. She did her best to look disgusted, which wasn't difficult since she was trying to decide if the driver looked more like a really cheap advert for Schwarzkopf Men Perfect hair dye or for Ray Ban Aviator sunnies.

The driver didn't say anything at all, just took off his sunnies and raised his eyebrows inquisitively. What an arrogant wanker, thought Tanya. She took the few steps over to the car and leaned on the sill of the passenger door. Mr Slick was looking very happy with himself, and leaned back in the driver's seat, stroking the leather of the steering wheel.

'So babe, you free?'

'Listen dickwad, this isn't *Pretty Woman* and you sure as hell ain't Richard Gere, so why don't you take your tiny pecker and fuck off.'

Mr Slick looked mortified and opened his mouth, but nothing came out. Clearly the ego's speed didn't match that of the German engineering under the bonnet.

Tanya stood up and stuck her middle finger up at him.

He then managed, 'Fuck you, slut,' as he angrily threw the Porsche into first gear and pulled away from the kerb in a squeal of tyres.

A few minutes later the girls were sitting in a small park around the corner, in the shade of a large jacaranda tree, sipping on coffee and Lara devouring the hot roll like there was no tomorrow. Tanya let her eat, enjoying her own coffee and a cigarette, looking up and admiring the fluttering leaves of the tree in the sunshine, the light filtering through the feathery, deep green foliage.

She and Sasha had grown up with two lovely jacarandas in the back yard, planted by their father the day after the twins had been born. As they and the trees grew, he used to play chase with them through the carpet of purple flowers dropped by the trees each year around November.

When the stepfather later moved in he used to whinge about having to clean up the mess from the trees. Then one day he made the twins stand there and watch him chainsaw them down. Later that night he raped them both for the first time.

Lara swallowed the last mouthful of bacon and egg roll, took a big sip of coffee, and belched loudly.

'Thanks for that,' she said to Tanya. 'Any chance of another smoke?'

Tanya smiled and handed her the packet.

'Help yourself.'

'Ta.' Lara left a smear of barbecue sauce on the Marlboro packet as she extracted a cigarette. She fished a Bic lighter out of her small purse and lit up. She inhaled deeply and leant back on the bench they were sitting on.

'Wanna talk?' said Tanya.

Lara looked down and stayed silent. She opened her purse again and Tanya watched as she fished amongst the condoms, the lube sachets, and her mobile phone. A small photo emerged and she held it in front of Tanya. A cherubic face smiled innocently at Tanya.

'That's my baby. My little Beau. He was only four. And now he's gone.'

Tears started trickling down her cheeks again, cutting another channel through the encrusted semen on her jaw.

Tanya took a tissue from her bag and did her best to wipe off the residue. She put her arm around Lara's shoulders and hugged her. Lara sniffled for a few moments and spoke again.

'There were these two guys, real friendly they were, living across the hallway at my old place. They used to babysit Beau when I had to go out to work. Thought they were real good like that, bloody lifesaver for me. Anyway,

I come home one night and the cops are there, waiting for me. Only not like usual. This time they took me to the hospital, but my little Beau was already dead. Them friendly guys killed him, but they said it was an accident. Something electric I was told.'

Lara started sobbing again.

Tanya hugged her tighter.

'Hey, it's okay.'

A couple of minutes later Lara resumed between sniffles.

'So, anyway, the cops charged them an' all, manslaughter they told me. Those fuckers are going to court next month, to go to prison I think.'

Lara paused and lit another cigarette.

'But there was this cop, you know detective type cop, who was actually nice to me. Most of the pigs treat me like a piece of shit. But this detective, Brian, seemed to feel sorry for me or something, I don't know. So he told me things about what had happened that none of the other cops had told me. He said the two guys who were so friendly to me were both fucking kiddy fiddlers, can you believe that? They both been to prison. Living in the same apartment block as me. Same one where I'd been put by the social workers. Now I know why those fuckers were so friendly.'

Lara choked a little on her smoke and squeezed Tanya's hand.

'I hate to think what happened to my poor little Beau. Brian didn't say too much detail about that. He did say he couldn't figure out how social workers had put me in an apartment block next to known kiddy fiddlers. Fuck, that just shouldn't happen, should it?'

She looked pleadingly at Tanya through her tears.

'So Human Services arranged your apartment there?'

'Yeah. They'd taken out a protection order on Beau before, but then I started coping again all right. So then they gave Beau back to me from the foster family, and they set me up with the place in Dundas. It wasn't much, but it did me and Beau just fine. The social workers used to come around all the time and check that I was looking after Beau properly. I even told them I had made friends with some nice guys over the hallway and they sometimes looked after Beau. They said that it must have been a great help, especially given my work hours.'

Lara paused, and lit another cigarette from the stub of the current one.

'But how the fuck could they put me there?'

She grabbed Tanya's hand and looked desperately at her, as if expecting Tanya to be able to throw some light on her tragedy.

'Don't them and the coppers know where the fuckin' kiddy molesters live?'

Tanya winced inside. She smiled bravely at Lara. 'Well, I would've thought they'd at least know where the convicted ones are, if they're not still in prison that is.'

'If they hadn't put me there my little Beau would still be here.'

Lara broke down sobbing again and her head flopped onto Tanya's shoulder.

'So you still living there?'

'Nah. I couldn't face it after Beau had gone. Had to get out. I've been dossing at a place over on Devonshire Street, when I'm not out here. Just a room I got for myself.'

'So you okay for money to get home?'

'Yeah, I think so.' Lara started looking in her purse again.

'You sure you don't need a hand?'

Tanya was half thinking about taking Lara back to their place to clean up, but she was apprehensive about junkies. She understood, no problems and no judgement, but she and Sasha had stayed well clear of that scene, despite everything. She wanted to keep it that way, if possible. Lara relieved her of any guilt.

'No, no, all good. You've been a doll, listening to all my shit. Thank you.'

She shook her head and sniffed.

'I need to get going now.'

Lara had become a touch agitated over the last few minutes and Tanya guessed she'd be going home via her dealer. Poor girl. Junkie or not, she still felt for her.

'Lara, let me have your number. Maybe if you need someone to talk to again.'

Lara smiled. 'That'd be cool, Tanya.'

Tanya put Lara's number into her phone as she recited it.

'Okay, and I've just texted you so you've got mine, too.'

The two girls stood up, and hugged. Lara kissed Tanya on the cheek and trotted off to the footpath, hailing, amidst a screech of brakes, an unprepared taxi driver by throwing her scantily-dressed body into the roadway.

Lara climbed into the back seat of the cab. And then she was gone with a wave. Tanya waved back.

Tanya sighed and lit a smoke. Life really was full of surprises, as well as shit. She turned and resumed her longer than expected walk home.

– 2 –

The next morning Harry was sitting in his office catching up on some paperwork, giving the cobalt blue ashtray plenty of business and waiting for the clock to strike noon so he could reach for a Jameson without feeling guilty. Besides, doing his quarterly return forms for the Tax Office pretty well demanded a drink or three. Doing it sober was doing his head in.

At about half eleven, as Harry was for the third time trying to reconcile his receipts with his credit card statements, there was a light knock on the door. Harry paused and slid open his top drawer, putting his .38 snub-nose within easy reach. He certainly wasn't expecting anyone, and he'd been a bit more on guard after his last two assignments. He didn't trust senior police or politicians, and he'd done damage in both circles recently. Payback was never a too distant relative.

He peered through the dust on the glass panel (really need to clean that, Harry) and made out a distinctly feminine form in the corridor. Unlikely to be a payback avenger, at least not from his enemies.

With his left hand he pressed the newly installed button on his desk which unlocked the door and said, 'It's open. Come in.'

The handle turned and Tanya glided through the opening, a broad grin lighting up her beautiful face.

'Hi, Mr PI.'

'Well, well. The gorgeous Ms Tanya of the twins divine.'

The way 'Mr PI' had rolled off that lustrous tongue made it easy for Harry to identify the right twin, without needing to check the butt-resident scorpion. He looked past her at the still open doorway.

She looked quizzically at him.

'I just wanted to see if perfection was a single or double act today.'

She laughed. 'Just me, Harry. Sasha's on shift.'

She closed the door. Harry motioned her to the client chair.

'Come in, babe, have a seat. Smoking is allowed of course, as is drinking.' He waved casually at the ashtray and his cigarette packet.

'Bar normally opens at noon, sharp, but I could make an exception for you.'

'A bit early for me, Harry, plus I have to work later. The boss encourages us to have a drink with the clients, but she gets shitty if we turn up smelling of it.'

'Cool, well if you don't mind, I might just have a small starter. See if I can get shitty with myself. Now, to what do I owe this unexpected treat?'

Harry looked at her and admired the glowing magnificence. Her long blonde curls hung down over her shoulders and drew his eyes to her very low-cut top which was straining, hard, to contain her breasts. Clearly she had dressed to soften him up. Beneath his desk quite the opposite was occurring. He flicked his gaze to her face. She was smiling coyly.

'Well, I'd have been gutted if you didn't notice.'

'You got me there, I confess.'

Tanya lit a cigarette and sat back in the leather chair.

'I've been meaning to ask, Mr PI, why is it you call us "divine"?'

Harry chuckled.

'Well, my goddess, simply because you and Sasha are the closest to worship I am ever going to get.'

'I like that. Now, I wanted to pick your brains, Harry.'

'Tanya, babe, if you can find some wisdom in here, then I will gift wrap it for you.'

'Cool, just make sure it's with a purple ribbon. Anyway, I wanted to know about peds and the system that keeps track of them.'

'You mean the convicted ones? Or suspected ones as well?'

'Well, any of them I guess. I remember reading about some register the cops had started, or something like that.'

She dropped her eyes.

'I always remember that 'cos I thought straightaway that no fucking register would help when your own mother brought one home.' She looked back at Harry.

'Well, there is a register for convicted ones. It's run by the cops. So any ped on it has to let the cops know where they are, their job, all that stuff.'

'Right. So does anyone other than the cops get to see it?'

'Sure. Other government departments if they need to, within certain protocols. It's supposed to be there to protect children.'

'So, Human Services would be able to see it?'

Harry snorted. 'Well, yeah. They're supposed to be the main department protecting kids. Although in my experience they are frickin useless. They couldn't protect a bacon sandwich from a Jewish vegetarian on a hunger strike.'

Tanya laughed. Harry pulled a bottle of Jameson out of his bottom drawer and poured himself half a glass. He lit a smoke.

'Sure you don't want one?'

'Yeah, thanks, I'm sure. I'll take a raincheck though.'

'Cool, I'll hold you to that. Now, why the interest in the ped register?'

'Well, I met this street girl yesterday. Got talking to her 'cos she was really upset and needed a shoulder. Anyway, she tells me how her little boy was killed by these two child molesters that were living in her apartment block. Electrocuted the poor little bugger.'

Harry interrupted. 'Wait a minute, I remember a news story in the paper about a case like that. About six months or so ago, I reckon. Out near Parramatta.'

'Right? Well, these arseholes used to babysit for the girl when she went out to work.'

'I'm sure they bloody did. Scum. But I don't see why the offender register would help. She could never have found out information from it.'

'Yeah, but it was Human Services who arranged her accommodation and who were monitoring the little boy. And she'd told them about these men babysitting for her.'

'Oh, fuck. Well, they should have bloody well known.'

'Well, that's what I thought.'

'And none of that was in the paper, that's for sure.'

Tanya leaned forward and rested her forearms on the edge of the desk. It gave Harry an almost complete and perfect view of her breasts. Her locket dangled hypnotically in front of her cleavage.

'So my wonderful Mr PI, can you help this girl find out what happened?'

'Tanya, if she's a street girl I don't imagine she can afford my rates. Plus I'm guessing she probably sticks most of her money into her arms.'

'Well, yeah. But, Harry, this all sounds so fucked up.

A little boy is dead, and all because some government wankers haven't done their jobs properly.'

Harry's Celtic underdog fire was starting to smoulder, and he was thinking that with that very fat pay-packet he'd had last month from the Club Mammary job he could certainly afford a little pro-bono work, for the right cause. Tanya's voice interjected his thoughts.

'Sasha and I can pay you if that helps.'

'No bloody way, Tanya. You two need to save your dollars. Besides, I'd consider doing pretty well anything for you free of charge.'

'Oh, my Mr PI. Well, at least meet the girl. That might persuade you. Your heart is definitely in the right place, even if your dick isn't always.'

Harry laughed. 'Touché, babe.' He took a sip of his whiskey.

'All right, I'll meet this girl and then we'll see. But, Tanya, if I think there's any bullshit going on, then I'm gone. Clear?'

Tanya smiled and got up. She walked around the desk.

'There's no bullshit about her, Harry. She's just a really sad, really fucked up girl who's got nobody to stand up for her.'

Tanya bent down next to Harry, hugged him and kissed him on the cheek.

'Thank you, my dark knight.'

Harry could feel his skin start to tingle as he inhaled deeply, both to calm his accelerating pulse and to savour Tanya's delectable perfume, Guerlain's Insolence he recognized this time. And bloody magnificent.

'Okay, now that you've ensured I won't be able to stand up for the next five minutes, just remember all I'm agreeing to at the moment is to meet this girl.'

Tanya kissed him again, this time on the lips, and ran her right index finger slowly down his cheek. It stopped and rested on his chin. Her eyes were about 15cm away from his, and he felt a rivulet of sweat begin its meandering journey down his back.

'Well, Harry, I'll set up a meet and then I'm sure once you've seen her for yourself that you will want to help out. I know you're a man who likes to go all the way on his assignments.'

She grinned at him and straightened up. Harry, heady with Guerlain and blood pressure, looked at Tanya's exquisitely sculpted arse as she went back around the desk. He considered that he wouldn't be dead for quids right now. Females like Tanya made the whole shitstorm of life worth getting out of bed for.

She picked up her bag and smiled at him.

'If I can arrange it, are you free tomorrow?'

Harry took a gulp of whiskey.

'Tanya, babe, as you seem to have worked out, you and your charm could probably persuade me to say yes to riding a skateboard naked down George Street wearing a gimp mask.'

Tanya laughed.

'Thanks, Harry. But I'll stick to the visual of you riding me instead.'

'Oh, far too fucking much. Out, you!'

'Okay, don't get up, I know you can't at the moment.'

She winked at him and went out of his office, adding what he was sure was extra sway to her glorious buttocks as she walked.

Harry filled his glass and lit a smoke. He started fantasizing about bending Tanya over his desk.

— 3 —

Tanya strolled out onto George Street feeling very happy with herself. Harry would help out, she had no doubt about that. Sure, she'd known how to entice him, but he enjoyed it. And he was actually a decent guy inside. Pity her mother hadn't found a second husband more like Harry.

Tanya had developed a bit of a soft spot for Harry, despite their commercial carnal first encounters. Something about the PI was immutably masculine, without being macho. He was attractively human, totally a straight-shooter, and Tanya instinctively trusted him. That was a rare find for her, and being around Harry triggered fond memories of her decent, masculine and straight-shooting dad. She didn't care a jot for the all the pop-psychology crap about father figures. If it felt genuinely good inside, then run with it and to hell with social mores. The cheap veneer of social respectability had shrouded the repeated rapes of her and Sasha, so she hated pretence almost as much as she loathed her mother and stepfather. Tanya was certainly going to take that raincheck drink with Harry, and then she was going to have fun with him, without any customer connection. Outside of the bordello confines she was confident that there was a gentle vulnerability to her PI that she could turn into a sensual couple of hours of mutual steamy bliss. An older man friend? Well, life was full of twists and turns, you just never really knew what to expect. And that would really be one to spice up the lounge room gossip with the girls at work. She also knew Harry would give her the genuine hugs she so badly pined for.

Tanya hailed a cab heading south on George Street and hopped into the back seat. The swarthy middle-aged guy driving it had a distinct allergy to deodorant and Tanya did her best to breathe through her mouth as two beady eyes leered at her from the rear vision mirror, asking 'Where to?'

She resisted the temptation to reply, 'The nearest shower for you, mate,' and instead gave the street corner nearest the Scarlet Boudoir. The rancid driver was leering a bit too much, in fact, and a long red Metrobus had to swerve to avoid the cab as it pulled out into traffic.

Tanya got her phone out of her bag and pressed Lara's number. It rang repeatedly – no voicemail, clearly – and as Tanya was about to hang up it was answered. Lara's voice was recognisable, but only just.

'Hi ya.'

'Lara, it's Tanya. You okay?'

'Oh, yeah … I'm doing great … is that you, Tanya?'

Lara sounded as spaced out as a hippie on the other side of the looking glass.

'Lara, listen to me. I'm going to come around to see you tomorrow morning with a friend of mine.'

Lara interrupted. 'Who? What friend? Tanya, is that you?'

'Lara, listen, I've got a friend who can help find out about Beau.'

'You've found my Beau? Tanya?'

Fuck, this was hopeless, thought Tanya. Lara had obviously scored and probably wouldn't even remember the call.

'Okay, Lara, have a sleep. I'll see you tomorrow.'

Tanya hung up.

The cab pulled up on Albion Street. Tanya gave the cabbie a twenty dollar note.

'Keep the change, mate.' And buy yourself some bloody soap, she thought. In fact, it wasn't that she was feeling charitable towards the cabbie's destitute hygiene fund. Rather, she just didn't want any change from his oily and grubby looking hands. She hopped out of the cab and headed off to the Scarlet Boudoir to start her shift.

— 4 —

It was shortly after nine the next morning when Harry got out of the cab on Devonshire Street, bleary-eyed from over-indulgence the previous evening. Tanya, also a tad bleary-eyed, but from a short sleep after her late shift, was waiting outside the pub on the corner of Waterloo Street.

The air was suffocatingly close and the sky, swamped by slate grey storm clouds, felt like a lowered ceiling, creating a hint of menace in the atmosphere. Harry could sense an imminent deluge, though he hoped it would only be water raining down on him. He was packing his .38 anyway, just in case.

'Morning, Harry.' Tanya kissed him on the cheek.

Harry savoured the fresh application of Insolence.

'Morning, babe. You smell and look wonderful.' Harry grinned at her, pointed at the pub door, and said, 'So, can I buy a beautiful girl a breakfast drink?'

Tanya began to glare at him, then got it. Harry laughed and lit a smoke.

'Smart-arse,' and she poked him in the ribs, smiling and shaking her head.

Harry looked over the road at the public housing blocks, appearing even bleaker than usual in the leaden half-light.

'She live in there?' asked Harry, pointing in the general direction of the grim buildings, and hoping otherwise.

'Actually, no. She said she had a room in a place a few doors up the street, on this side. I walked past it and it looks like some sort of deros' boarding house.'

'So, is she in? And is she on planet Earth?'

'Yeah, I rang her twenty minutes ago. She's there and she doesn't sound like she's out of it at the moment. She was yesterday, so she probably hasn't scored since. It's this way.'

Tanya started up the hill and Harry fell in beside her.

'She live on her own?'

'Yeah, from what she said. Why?'

'Just like to know the numbers before I walk into a place. It always pays to be ready.'

'Ooh, my big tough Mr PI,' Tanya smirked, giving Harry another playful poke in the ribs.

'Now, now, you. Stop touching what you can't afford.'

Tanya turned, smiling, and winked at Harry. 'When I want it, my Mr PI, I'll help myself, for free.' She held his gaze for longer than was necessary and Harry was lost for words.

Half a dozen doors up the street Tanya stopped outside a dilapidated terrace house, which had clearly failed to catch the inner city gentrification virus. Harry looked at the peeling paint, historically white perhaps, which gave the place the look of an architectural leper. There were rotting timber planks sagging from the balcony, as if they were trying to lean earthwards to provide a ladder for termites, and one of the upstairs windows had a smashed pane, with cardboard held over it by packing tape. Nothing was alive in the small garden bed at the front, and piles of local newspapers and junk mail had become sodden and stuck to the front steps like papier-mâché. A few empty grog bottles added the final touch of sophistication to the front of the house. Harry ruefully pondered that in this city even this shit-box would fetch well over a million.

The front door was open, and from the street the aroma of desolate lives and desperate living seeped into the oppressive morning air and up Harry's nostrils, rendering his Marlboro inert. It was a smell he'd got well used to in the cops. That unmistakeable and unholy trinity of rancid body odour with urine, unwashed feet in their putrid cheesy socks, and many fried meals cooked in dirty pans with stale fat.

Harry turned to Tanya.

'I hope you've got the bottle of Guerlain in your bag, Tanya babe. I think we're both going to need it after this. Okay, let's do it. What number room is she in?'

'Number four'.

Harry led the way up the half dozen chipped and cracked marble steps, damaged remnants of former glory, and headed through the doorway, looking around him as he went. Tanya was close on his tail.

A faded plastic sign indicated rooms three to five were on the ground floor, further back past the staircase. They found number four. Harry stood to one side and said to Tanya, 'I'll leave the intros to you. Don't want to scare her with me knocking.'

Tanya tapped on the door and spoke through it.

'Hey, Lara, it's me, Tanya.'

There was a creaking noise like bedsprings and then some shuffling on the floor. The door opened slowly. Lara was without make-up, her face drawn and pale, with hair uncombed and badly in need of a wash. She was wearing canary yellow gym shorts and a thin white T-shirt which completely failed to hide the carmine of her nipples.

She managed a smile for Tanya, but then looked warily when she noticed Harry.

'It's okay, Lara. This is my friend I told you about. You can trust him, he's here to help you.'

Lara looked dubious.

'Okay. Come in, Tanya. But you sure about him?'

'It's cool, babe. Honestly, it's cool.'

Lara turned and walked across the room to the sagging, ragged single bed and sat down.

Harry looked around the room, thinking rather than a home it was more like a detention centre cell. The chipped and cracked plaster on the walls was stained and greyish-brown in hue. The cornice had come away and was now absent along two sides and on a third it was starting to hang down at one end, the beginning of its redundancy program. The carpet was soiled beyond any original colour and was so threadbare it resembled a large hessian sack spread over the floor. There wasn't even a window – at least most cells got one of those, even if tiny with bars. A single 40W bulb hung shadeless from the centre of the ceiling, like the hangman's final customer. It was the sole source of illumination. Harry wouldn't go so far as to think of it as light: that was too akin to the natural world and life, the opposite of this sad little corner of Miseryville. An old, chestnut brown veneer wardrobe, minus doors, was standing in one corner, like a solemn sentry at a dump. Lara's handful of clothing was either hanging on the half dozen wire hangers, or was piled on the cupboard's floor.

So this was Lara's world, Harry thought, and he started to feel glum. He thought of his bookcase at home and considered maybe Hobbes had had this image when he wrote about life being solitary, poor, nasty, brutish, and short. He looked over to Tanya for relief. She looked entirely incongruous in this half-way layover to hell, although Harry could appreciate the potential short step from her life to this one. He gazed at Tanya and thought it was rather like looking at a young Marlene Dietrich amidst the fire-bombed ruins of Dresden.

Lara picked up a cigarette packet which revealed itself to be empty. Harry saw an opportunity to curry instant favour and had his open Marlboro packet in front of her in a second. She took one eagerly and looked up at him as she slid the cigarette into her mouth. Harry thought the eyes reminded him of a beaten puppy at the RSPCA.

'Thanks, mister.'

'It's Harry.'

'Thanks, Harry. Sorry, but I don't have no chairs.' She indicated a pair of upturned milk crates.

Harry parked his behind on one whilst Tanya went and sat next to Lara on the decrepit bed.

'Lara, Harry here can help find out more about what happened to Beau.'

Lara's tears started as she drew hard on her smoke. Harry bit his tongue, aided by Tanya's steely glance in his direction. He'd only agreed to meet Lara at this point, but somehow he already felt he was being driven by a deeper force. Was it a gorgeous eighteen-year-old hooker bathed in Guerlain? Was it his Irish desire for underdog justice? Was it his urge to protect a vulnerable girl, when he'd been so unable to save his own? Who knew. Too much self-analysis for Harry's day. Tanya pressed on.

'Harry's an investigator.'

Lara started, the crushed puppy eyes looking genuinely scared, and she grabbed Tanya's hand.

'A cop?'

'No, relax. He's a private investigator. He used to be

169

a cop, a long time ago, so he knows what he's doing. But don't worry, he's not a cop now.'

Harry's eyes caught Lara's furtive glance at the bedside table. There was a saucer on it with an empty syringe and a teaspoon with the telltale caramelized stain on it. She looked nervously at Harry. Tanya spotted the look and gently stroked Lara's arm.

'Relax, Lara. Harry is so completely cool.'

Harry felt it was time to join in. The unloved puppy was getting to him.

'Lara, I couldn't give a shit about that,' waving his hand at the bedside paraphernalia. 'So like Tanya says, relax. We're here to find out about your boy. Is that him?'

Harry pointed to a small photo of a young blonde boy in a faux gilt frame with cracked glass, standing behind the opiate objects. A tear rolled down Lara's cheek.

'Yeah, that's my Beau. Was my Beau.'

She looked anxiously again at the gear on the bedside table, then looked back at Harry.

'Seriously, Lara, I really don't care. That stuff is all up to you. Personally, I reckon there'd be a whole lot less shit going on in the world if it was all just legalized.'

Tanya looked up sharply at Harry.

'You serious, Mr PI? I thought you'd be a conservative wanker on that score, being an ex-cop and all.'

Harry chuckled. 'No, babe. Not old Harry here. I've seen way too much corruption and needless crime coming from our drug laws, and still people are using whatever and whenever they want. So what's the point in keeping up the charade?'

'Mr PI, I liked you a lot yesterday. Today I like you even more,' Tanya said. She blew him a kiss.

Harry fought to get his mind back on the current task.

He turned to look at Lara, making sure he gave Tanya an appreciative smile first.

'Okay, Lara, I do want to help you find out more about Beau and those peds.'

'Okay.'

'I understand the peds were charged. Who were the cops you dealt with?'

'There was only one nice one, Brian.'

'Okay, what was his surname?'

'I'm not sure, I'm not good on last names. But I've got his card somewhere here.'

She bent down and picked up a small backpack from beside the bed. She rummaged inside it and pulled out a small bundle of business cards held together by an elastic band. She shuffled through the cards and passed one over to Harry. He leant forward and took it.

'Any chance of another smoke, Harry?'

'Sure.' Harry passed her his packet and, as she lit herself a cigarette, he looked at the card. Aside from the NSW Police logo, it gave the name of Detective Sergeant Brian Durham, Parramatta Detectives, plus phone numbers and an email address.

Harry took out his notebook and wrote the detective's details down. He handed the card back to Lara. She was still gently sobbing, pausing briefly to drag on the cigarette.

'It shouldn't have happened, Harry. Them social workers shouldn't have put me in there next to them child molesters, not with my little Beau.'

'Yeah, you're right there. That's why we want to find out a bit more.'

Tanya was smiling at him, her expression just a tad smug, like she knew she'd been spot on the mark with Harry. He winked at her.

'Harry, I'm going to stay with Lara and take her for some breakfast.'

'Sure thing, babe.'

Harry heaved himself off the milk crate. He held out his hand to Lara. She seemed more concerned with Harry's Marlboro packet, which was still in her lap.

Harry smiled at her. 'You can keep them, Lara. Well, good to meet you. I'll get to work, and Tanya will keep you posted on anything I find out.'

'Thanks, Harry. But I don't have no money to pay you with.'

'No money required, Lara. Just here to help. Tanya's my friend.'

She shook his hand and held it rather more tightly than etiquette required, almost clinging to him. Poor kid's never had anything, he thought, except the arse-end of life.

Tanya stood up and gave Harry a kiss on the cheek and a hug.

'I'll call you later,' she breathed into his ear.

'Cool. You take care.'

Harry turned and went out of the forlorn room. He headed down the corridor, seeking out the fresh air of Devonshire Street as quickly as his legs would carry him. And he needed to find a deli to get himself another packet of Marlboros.

— 5 —

The Waterworks Tavern at the bottom end of Darling Harbour after work hadn't been Harry's idea, but when he had phoned Detective Sergeant Brian Durham and suggested an afternoon coffee, he had been met by amiable, but firm, derision.

'Jesus, Harry, have you turned metrosexual or something? If that's what being a PI does to you then I don't feel quite so bitter about staying in this shitty job.'

'My apologies, Brian. So much has changed in the job since I've been out that it's hard to know what's what any more.'

'Aye, Harry, that's the ugly truth. But two things are for dead certain, and I'm not talking about taxes and nurses. One is that this lot have totally forgotten how to catch crooks, and the second is that I can still think of nothing better than a pint or three of Newcastle Brown Ale with an old mate. So, see you at the Waterworks Tavern at five this evening. Oh, and Harry, since you'll no doubt be picking my brains, it's your shout.'

'Naturally, Brian, naturally. Thanks, mate.'

The venue choice had actually suited Harry well, since it was less than ten minutes walk from his office, but he had thought it an unusual selection by Brian. Maybe he wanted to be well away from his work at Parramatta Detectives. It

173

wouldn't be helpful for him to be seen with Harry, and you never knew who was watching these days. Harry got there a few minutes early and had two pints of the warm brown nectar ready on the table as Brian walked in.

The once stocky, now rotund, Yorkshireman padded over to Harry, a broad grin on his round, ruddy face, his arm outstretched. Harry thought that might have been in readiness for the pint, but he offered his in return anyway. The pair shook hands firmly.

'Good to see you, Harry. It's been a while.'

'That's for sure. Mind you, this wasn't the sort of pub I imagined you would suggest.'

'Aye, well, not mine either on most levels, but you try finding Newcastle Brown Ale on tap. It's rarer than talent at Headquarters. I'd take a pew in a Mother Superior's bible class if the old Brown was flowing. So, Harry, how's the PI business?'

'Well, I have to say these days it's treating me pretty well. It was tough to start, but I've built a reputation now so the business comes in the door. No complaints. And, of course, I'm my own bloody boss.'

'Now that would be bloody good. I'm so sick of the dickheads running this job these days. And it just keeps getting worse. Used to be the best job around. If I was ten years younger, I'd get out. But I'm too close to being able to get out with my super, plus too old to land a gig somewhere else.'

'And obviously too ethical to try the HOD scam.'

Brian nodded and took a deep swig of his ale.

'Aye, that's one for all the bloody rorters. Hurt-on-duty my arse. Most of those wankers couldn't spell duty, let alone do any of it. Mind you, plenty of them pull it off. Grab the police pension, and then go and get a job elsewhere. Most of them are rolling in it, and they don't even have to worry about corruption allegations.'

'Not much difference, I reckon, Brian.'

'No, I tend to agree. But you watch, Harry. The government will get wise to this one some day. It's costing the taxpayers bloody millions every year. And when they do clamp down, it'll be tough for those decent coppers who do actually get badly hurt and who genuinely need the scheme.'

'Yeah. I saw a report recently in the paper that said several hundred had got out on the scheme in just the last few years.'

'The irony, Harry, is that usually in life it's the few that spoil it for the many, but in our wonderful Police Force it's all reversed. Not the only thing that's arse about, either.'

'I can't say I'm sorry to be out, even with the way it happened.'

'Blokes like you and me, Harry, we don't fit in the modern Force. Not being on the take made it hard enough in the old days, but we could still do well by just catching crooks. Nowadays, no one gives a flying rat's arse about locking up crims. Get yourself a few bits of paper that say you're qualified, kiss the right arses, and play the climbing game like you're trying to get into the last lifeboat from the Titanic and, Constable, you will go far, my son!'

Harry smiled wryly. 'Yep, the best days are definitely in the past. All this cynicism seems to be thirsty work, mate, I'll grab two more.'

'Aye, good lad.' Brian drained his pint glass noisily. 'I'll grab a table outside so we can smoke, and I'm not done with the cynicism yet, Harry, so I hope you've got a good thirst and a very pregnant wallet. After this I reckon we do The Emperor's Duck Palace, for old times' sake.'

'Hell, yes. It's a while since I did the Peking duck washed down with Tsing-tao. I'll see you outside.'

Brian was already puffing on a cigarette when Harry plonked the pints of ale on the table. He pulled out his Marlboro packet and lit one as he sat down. They chinked glasses.

Brian licked the froth off his top lip.

'Aye, that is so good. Now, Harry, before we spend the evening on war stories, what did you want to pick my brains about?'

'The Beau Jacobs case.'

'Jesus, Harry. How come you're looking at that? That's a truly toxic one.'

'Well, the mother, Lara, needed some help with it.'

'Poor bloody girl. She still alive, then? She needs a lot more help than you, Harry, no offence, lad.'

'None taken.'

'I felt sorry for her. Born badly, abused badly, and now living badly. Some of them never really have a chance. Lara's one of those poor bloody unfortunates who was branded "loser" at birth by Lady Fate and then the rest of life has treated her like one. I assume she's still on the gear and on the street?'

'Yeah. She did say you were decent to her, made a point of it. In fact the only decent bit of the whole Force, in her eyes. She'd kept your card.'

Brian shook his chubby head. 'Aye, well I felt for her. What happened to her kid was absolutely hideous.'

Brian paused and looked at Harry, meeting his eyes.

'Harry, you sure you want to be working on this case, after everything you went through?'

'Brian, mate, that's one of the reasons I do want to be doing this case. Plus, like you, I feel sorry for Lara. I don't normally work pro-bono, believe me.'

'I was wondering how she was able to afford you. Didn't think blow jobs would be currency in your world.'

Harry laughed. 'No, alas they don't pay the rent. Well, not mine anyway.'

He took a long mouthful of beer and lit another smoke.

'I remember the story in the paper when this happened a few months ago. You charged two blokes, didn't you?'

'Aye, two hard-core peds. Ronnie Teed and Jerry Aldred. Both have records as long as your arm and both have done several stretches for kiddy fiddling. Ronnie was still on parole when we grabbed them.'

'And they got charged with manslaughter?'

'Aye, that was all we could make stick as far as the DPP were concerned. They both pleaded guilty. Not surprising given what they had got away with. Scum, those two. Complete and utter fucking scum. Coming up for sentencing next month.'

'So what actually happened, Brian? I remember something about electrocution. That was why I recalled the story, it sounded totally weird.'

'Lad, truth is definitely a whole lot stranger than fiction on this one. And a whole lot uglier. The two peds were babysitting the little fella and doing who knows what. Well, the peds' story is that young Beau stopped breathing and started going blue. They couldn't find a pulse, so one of them grabs an electrical lead, rips one end off it, plugs in the other end, and tries to simulate a defibrillator. We know that bit was true because of the electrical burns on the little fella's chest. But that was all that could be proved, so manslaughter was the best the DPP would allow. The only certainty, at least documented one, from the autopsy was heart failure.' Brian was shaking his head as he gulped down some more ale.

'I'm guessing, and the old instinct hasn't deserted me yet, that there's stuff that didn't make the light of day?'

'Oh, aye. I'll never forget that fucking autopsy as long as I live. I still have sleepless nights.'

Brian again drank hard.

'The state of that little boy's anus.'

Harry held his glass in mid-air and looked at Brian.

'No DNA or anything?'

'Nope. Hence no proof. The pathologist gave me his off-the-record opinion, though. Grab us another pint first, Harry, will you? And, lad, a whiskey chaser is in order.'

Harry nodded and headed for the bar whilst Brian lit another smoke and stared at the formica table top.

A few moments later a pint of ale slid in front of him as Harry slipped back into his chair.

'Go on, then,' as they chinked glasses. 'Did it look like deliberate electrocution?'

'No. If only. No, the good doc said to me afterwards that his money was on the heart failure first.'

'What, in a four-year-old?'

'He reckoned the anal trauma would have been so severe that the kid could have gone into cardiac arrest. The sick, tragic irony is that those peds were probably trying to revive him. After they'd screwed him to death.'

'Jesus wept. There was nothing else that would stick?'

'Nope, zilch. They were smart like that, those two. Been done too many times to get caught out on forensics or DNA. The DPP reckon we were lucky to get the plea to manslaughter.'

'Been done too many times to talk as well?'

'Oh, aye. Lawyered up straightaway. Right to silence, and all that antiquated shit.'

'How times do change. And then some things don't.'

Brian slapped the table with his hand.

'Aye, in the old days we'd have given them a good tickle with the White Pages. Loosen up their conscience and their vocal chords. But not these days.'

Brian paused, then grimaced slightly.

'Oh, shit. Sorry, Harry. Forgot about your drama for a moment.'

'No, no worries, Brian. Despite losing my job, I don't have a single regret about belting that mongrel piece of shit. He deserved it, and more.'

'True. So true.'

Brian lit another smoke.

'These days, Harry, the approach is different.'

Brian sat up and tried to look prim, proper, and twenty years younger.

'We look empathetic, talk about "active listening", wave our Bachelor of Policing certificate at the crooks, and then they just go to water in front of us and confess all!'

They both started laughing. The glasses were raised.

'To the old days and golden ways,' said Harry.

'Cheers to that, and to my retirement, which can't come fast enough.'

'So what's the story with the Department of Human Services?'

'Ah, well, those inept, incompetent wankers never checked the paedophile register. They were round checking on the mother every other day, and they knew that two men across the hall were babysitting. They even spoke to them, we know that. Never occurred to the morons to check on two strange men who were so keen to babysit.'

'So how come nothing's come out about that aspect of the case?'

'Lad, this has been closed down from the very top.

I tried to push it to start with, because it was obvious Human Services was partly culpable for the little fella's death. But the shut-down came direct from the Commish's office. It seems that with all the extra funding the government gave the Department, around two billion, they really don't want any scandals raining on their parade.'

'They haven't changed much, then. So much for child protection,' snorted Harry.

'In the government scheme of things, women like Lara are worth nothing, and their kids even less. Unless they hit the paper, of course. Which is exactly why this one was shut down.'

'So nobody in Human Services was prepared to talk? No one? They are supposed to actually care about kids, after all.'

'Get real, Harry. This is about power, politics, and public service careers, not to mention the Minister, who is touted as the next Premier.'

'Sad gig for the kids, is all I can say.'

'Aye. There was one guy from Human Services, ex-copper actually, from VicPol. He was in their internal investigation unit. He tried, it seems, to expose what happened. So they upped the pressure on him until the poor bastard had a nervous breakdown, and left very quickly on medical grounds. Then suddenly this sexual harassment case against him emerged. The Department hierarchy were really pushing that one. I didn't buy it, but by the time I got to speak to this guy, he was in hospital and gibbering. He's out now, but he's a wreck and the Department have kept up the harassment case, just to make sure he's got no credibility. On the q.t. I'll slip you his details. His name's Stavros McMahon. But be careful, Harry, be very bloody careful. This case is dynamite. And the Deputy Director-General at Human Services who's taken charge of all this is the rabid Rottweiler from hell. And she's super connected. Watch yourself, lad.'

'Jesus. And I'm doing this job for free.'

Brian laughed. 'Yes, you are. And I am still thirsty. So, beer wench, hit the bar.'

'Okay, detective, on my way.'

— 6 —

With his gut bulging from plates of barbecue duck and gallons of beer, chased down with a good cabernet sauvignon, Harry had bid farewell to Brian outside the restaurant, with mutual merry assurances that they wouldn't leave it so long next time.

As he left the Mecca of Chinese culinary delights on Goulburn Street, Harry decided to go home via his office, since it was still short of half past nine. He hauled himself up the old staircase in the now deserted building and went into his office, locking the door behind him. He flicked the power switch on the computer and poured himself a modest whiskey whilst he waited for the machine to boot up. Then he sat down, lit a smoke, opened his browser and accessed his online subscription to the *Sydney Morning Herald*.

The Beau Jacobs case had been in the press only briefly all those months ago, and now Harry had a fair idea why there hadn't been much coverage. He found the newspaper story in the archive for the NSW news section. The headline was 'Dead Boy: Pair Plead Guilty'. The story was a relatively brief piece outlining the plea of guilty to manslaughter by Teed and Aldred and some scant details of the electrocution death of Beau. No suggestion of any sexual interference, although it did mention that both accused men had priors for child sex offences. Well, thought Harry, nobody was going to be able to suppress that detail once the case was in court for sentencing. And Human Services didn't even get a whisper. So, that had been well hushed up, for sure. Despite the small size of the article, there was a by-line, so Harry grabbed his notebook and jotted down the journo's name, 'Shona Taylor – Court Reporter'.

Harry then trawled for articles on the Department and the huge funding increases during the last year or two, as well as mention of the name of the Deputy D-G that Brian had given him. He didn't have to look too far before he got a story from about twelve months back, trumpeting the government's injection of two billion dollars into the Human Services budget. The Minister was quoted as saying it was 'a watershed moment for the strategic direction of child protection in NSW' and how the extra funds highlighted 'the government's ongoing unflinching commitment to children'. Then some gratuitous comment about 'sound financial management of the State's budget'. Meanwhile, the acting D-G at the time, Deputy D-G Porcia Savage, trotted out some masterful weasel words about 'structural reforms enabling protective interventions with tangible family functionality benefits for the broad spectrum of the child welfare community encompassing multicultural empowerment aspirations'. Blah, blah, fucking blah, thought Harry. The woman must have been awake all night thinking that garbage up, or perhaps it was so ingrained these days that it just flowed entirely naturally for her ilk.

Bloody government language. Before long the average punter wouldn't be able to understand it at all, but this was probably the precise reason for it, Harry reckoned. He tried to imagine sitting at a dinner party with these wankers; he'd need an interpreter, or maybe just a gun. Underneath more text in the story was a photograph of the Minister standing alongside the acting D-G, symbolically passing over a cheque for the cameras. The Minister wore the typical smarmy smile of a consummate politician, no doubt one of the contributing factors to political success, whilst Savage bore only the slightest upturn of the corners of her mouth, and even that looked like it was painful for her.

But it was the eyes that caught Harry the most. They were small in her face, piercing like two bayonets, and with a self-assured, but ice-cold, reptilian stare. Yes, thought Harry, you would indeed be a piece of work. Sometimes you could actually read a book by its cover.

Porcia Savage was relaxing imperiously behind her expansive native hardwood desk in her office at the Human Services head office building in Parramatta. As she gazed out of the top floor window she wore a self-satisfied sneer, a not infrequent expression, on her cold pallid face. She was tall and beefy, with dull peroxide blonde hair cut militarily short, to assist her blending in with the lesbian mafia that ran the Department. She resembled a Bulgarian hammer-thrower from the Iron Curtain days. Most of those who had dealt with Savage over the years tended to take away two lasting impressions, seared into their memories like a cattle brand. The first was her reptilian coldness and her utter lack of any vestige of human compassion. The second was her utter perfection in voice and expression when it came to withering arrogance and brutal condescension.

Savage picked up a large framed photo of herself from her desk, showing her receiving a departmental award a couple of years ago. She smugly mused on her Machiavellian skills. Her egotism, combined with a sociopathic ruthlessness and an arrant contempt for ethics, had meant a meteoric rise to the upper levels of the NSW public service. And she wasn't finished climbing yet. Her cronies had suggested politics as a natural progression, but Savage wasn't going there. She certainly had all the required skills when it came to double-dealing and spinning dishonesty into gospel, and she had no lack of the vulture-like appetite for sheer power. But Savage's shortfall, of which she was well aware, was that she couldn't even manage any pretence of empathy to other human beings, so the idea of having to smile to the voters and actually press the flesh was completely out of the question. The very thought actually turned her stomach. No, exerting power behind the political scenes was her forte, and she knew it. So, too, did the unfortunate souls who crossed her, and there had been many victims. Savage cherished her memories of them all.

Savage didn't really believe in friends as such, but the closest equivalent for her was the Minister for Human Communities and Youth Welfare. This relationship had significantly contributed to her career success to date, although her innate skill set had been of immense value to the Minister as well. It was, in short, a venal union which was Darwinian in its effectiveness in the world of NSW politics and public service. Savage's token husband didn't even rate in the closeness league, compared to the Minister, since it was actually just a marriage of appearance for both of them. Anyway, she went a lot further back with the Minister; they'd been at uni together in the late eighties and, very discreetly, had been fuck buddies, well before the term was even in use. And they still were, when circumstances allowed and the need for carnal release simmered over.

It was a mutually beneficial relationship that kept on giving, too. Savage's gazing out at the afternoon sunshine on the gum trees had just been a short break in her main activity of the day: packing up her office. She was getting promoted, not to the D-G's job – she wasn't ready to go yet – but something far better. She would be heading up her own brand new 'super department' in the city. The Minister had duly rewarded her for her immaculate and efficient management of the Beau Jacobs fiasco, amongst other potential scandals.

Savage reflected on the case as she pulled some reports out of her desk drawer, amongst them the final Jacobs report. That bloody case and the damned investigations manager she'd had at the time, McMahon. She'd had to weave some of her most cunning magic on that one. She should have known better than to hire an ex-cop, but she really hadn't been ready for his sanctimonious stand on ethical principles and her blood had boiled when he had suggested the Department had been negligent, if not criminally culpable. The bastard had drafted a report openly stating that the caseworkers hadn't done any checks on the sex offenders living in the same block of flats as that little druggy tramp. Didn't need the likes of her breeding anyway.

Well, she'd certainly fixed up that self-righteous McMahon; bullied him into a nervous breakdown and then buried all traces of his draft report once he was off the premises and in a psych ward. Her own final version of the report was a veritable masterpiece of spin and camouflage. The executive summary had concluded that there had been:

> ... a freakish, but totally unforeseeable combination of circumstances leading to the tragic death of a child, Beau Jacobs, at the hands of two convicted child sex offenders.

It then went on that:

> ... this Department can stand tall with everything it did to support that child during his short life and to assist a highly troubled and problematic young single mother.

Savage was particularly proud of her ultimate paragraph:

> The mother's lifestyle and erroneous choices presented risk factors for the child which were beyond the ability of any government agency to properly mitigate. The individual caseworkers showed great perseverance and commitment to a most challenging situation, were traumatized by the child's death and attendant circumstances, and deserve commendations for their dedication to duty.

And, after the report and the court outcome, with the Department in the clear, and there never having been a whisper of the truth, the Minister had personally visited Parramatta and made the commendations at a morning tea.

It was almost imperceptible, but Savage smiled just a touch as she thought back on her final twist of the knife in skewering McMahon. Finishing the prim and proper bastard off with a sexual harassment case was, in Savage's mind, nothing short of ironic genius. The alleged victim was a personal protégé of Savage's and had been eager to assist as directed. The fact that she was actually a lesbian made the whole scheme priceless. As Savage threw the report into a packing box, she considered that with the job she'd done, she well deserved to be feeling good.

– 8 –

H arry found the boarding house just off Abercrombie Street in Chippendale. He looked at the front of the old terraced building, clean and tidy if distinctly unloved: in realtor terms 'a renovator's dream project'. Harry reflected that in another few years this area would probably look like a more compressed version of Paddington. But that was in the future. Now, with the absence of any vibrant colours, it looked more like a film set from a Great Depression melodrama. Still, it was a cut above the Surry Hills hellhole he'd visited Lara in, as evidenced by the front door having to be opened by a caretaker, a large-framed man with a prematurely grey crew cut and a neatly trimmed, full, silvery moustache. The remainder of his face was regimentally clean-shaven. He had the roadmap of broken capillaries, the slightly ruddy complexion, and the faded eyes of a big drinker. But the posture was firm and upright, and he had clean breath at three in the afternoon. Along with the immaculately ironed creases, old school copper-style, down the front of his spotless, pastel blue cotton shirt, Harry saw that here was an alcoholic successfully on the wagon, not wallowing in the sauce.

He looked at Harry with a slight squint of possible recognition.

'You in the job, mate?'

Harry looked him in the eye.

'Used to be. I'd guess you were, too.'

'Yeah, in Brizzie. George Atkins.'

He held out his hand and Harry shook it. George had a vice firm grip, but was clearly practiced at restraining it. The result was an instant understanding of his strength ruled by self-control.

'Harry Kenmare. I'm a PI these days. I'm looking for a Stavros McMahon. I'm told he's living here.'

'I wouldn't call it living, Harry, but yes, he's here. Him and a squad of washed-up guys from the job. Place is owned by the police union. I run it for them.'

'Good to see somebody cares. How long has this been going? Don't remember it in my day.'

'About five or six years. I came down three years ago. Got a room here after a few weeks at various doss houses. Then I stepped up after the old caretaker passed on.'

Harry raised his eyebrows.

'Cancer. There are no happy stories in here. Endings with a remnant of dignity and some fellow humans around are the best that are hoped for in this home.'

Harry nodded with a sombre respect.

George continued, 'I hope you've not got more trouble for Stav. The bloke's in a pretty bad way already.'

'Yeah, I know. I'm trying to come up with something on the wankers that got him to this point.'

'You mean those arseholes at Human Services?'

'Yeah. Those shining lights of integrity.'

George snorted. 'The pricks are Teflon-coated, right from the Minister down. You talk to Brian Durham?'

'Yeah, I got the low-down. I know no one wants the truth out in this case.'

'Well, good luck. Stav is in room nine, upstairs and last door towards the back.'

'Thanks, George.'

'Go easy on him.'

'Will do, mate.'

They shook hands and Harry began up the stairs, with the original timber peeking through the threadbare hessian that had once been carpet. The upstairs corridor matched the downstairs, clean and unadorned, but its grey and off-white hues lit by a single uncovered 60W bulb gave it a depressing air. Harry stopped outside a jaded door with the number '9' written on it in black texta pen, over the outline and screw holes where the original plastic or metal digit had resided.

Harry took a deep breath and knocked on the greying timber. After a couple of seconds, Harry heard movement in the room and a voice spoke through the door.

'That you, George?'

'No. My name's Harry Kenmare. George said it was okay for me to come up.'

Harry heard the chain being slid into its runner and then the door opened the ten centimetres the chain would allow.

'I used to be in the job, Stavros, and now I'm a PI. I'm trying to look into this Human Services cover-up. I just want to have a chat.'

Half a sallow, unshaven face and one blood-shot eye inspected Harry through the gap, like a sad Cyclops peering through an aperture into hell. The ageing eye looked at Harry for a few seconds, before the exhausted voice joined the assessment.

'You got ID, mate?'

Harry already had his PI licence ready in his hand. He handed it into the chasm, where it was taken by a visibly shaking hand tipped with grubby, chewed fingernails.

'Stavros, you can call DS Brian Durham if you want. He'll vouch for me.'

'Mate, I don't even have a phone anymore.'

Harry thought he probably should have anticipated that, since Brian hadn't given him a number for Stavros.

'Here, you can use mine.' Harry pulled his phone off his belt.

The eye returned its doleful stare back to Harry. The unsteady hand passed the licence back.

'That's okay. You look dinkum. I don't think I've lost all my old instinct just yet. Pretty well everything else, but the old gut feeling lingers.'

The door closed a few centimetres and the chain was taken off. Stavros held the door open.

'Come in, mate. Stav. Only my mother called me Stavros.'

He held out the same wavering hand. As he stepped over the threshold into the room, Harry shook hands. The uncertain reticence was in stark contrast to the self-assured firmness downstairs.

For the second time this week, Harry breathed in the decaying bouquet of demise and misery – body odour, alcohol, stale tobacco and even staler breath. Harry considered that Stavros's teeth were probably receiving as much care and attention as his fingers. Harry had estimated Stav would be in his forties, but he looked closer to sixty.

The room was Spartan in the extreme. It was tidy, but then there wasn't enough in it to start a mess. It was almost a mirror image of Lara's forsaken cell. A steel framed single bed was against the wall away from the window with a laminate bedside stand next to it. Harry guessed that the grimy empty tumbler on it hadn't contained water overnight.

There was a matching stand next to the window with

two sun-faded, green plastic patio chairs next to it. In the far wall there was a disused fireplace with a narrow wooden mantel above it. There was a full bottle of Jim Beam on it with a half packet of plastic cups. Next was an aged wooden frame with a black and white photograph of an elderly couple in front of a whitewashed villa. The last item was a plastic A4-sized frame with a Victoria Police Commissioner's Commendation in it. On the table by the window was a half-empty bottle of Beam, one plastic cup and an ashtray with a collection of rollie stubs in it. A packet of White Ox and some Tally Ho papers were beside it, as was a dog-eared paperback copy of Camus' *The Outsider*. It was the same edition as the well-read copy on Harry's bookcase.

Stavros offered Harry a seat and then went to fetch a new plastic cup from the mantle supply.

'Drink, mate?'

Harry didn't normally touch bourbon, it didn't sit well in his gut. But he was keen to keep Stavros as relaxed as possible.

'Thanks, Stav.' Harry didn't see much point in asking about the possibility of a little ice or some Coke.

Stavros came back over, sat down in the other chair, and half-filled a plastic cup for Harry. He refilled his own, all the way.

The window was open, propped up with an old postpack tube, and Harry looked out on the concreted back yard with its old thunder-box and a pull-out washing line, a few exhausted garments hanging off it, like old rags caught on a power line. A large royal poinciana tree with its lush, green tropical foliage and flame red flowers gave the place a façade of vigour and cheerfulness. Harry got out his Marlboros and Stavros eagerly accepted one.

'This'll be nice after the rollies. Thanks.'

Stavros had a Mediterranean colouring to his skin, despite its wanness, and dark chestnut hair, now surrendering rapidly to a grey surge. But the green Celtic eyes resulted in a somewhat startling cross-cultural look. Harry guessed his mother had been Greek and had insisted on a first name to reflect that half of his heritage. He pointed to the photo on the mantel.

'Your family?'

'My grandparents on mum's side. Back in Thessaloníki.'

Stavros took a long gulp of his bourbon, whilst Harry made his tentative sip look more enthusiastic than it was. Stavros didn't seem eager to start a conversation. He was staring out the window, so Harry took the plunge.

'How long you been here, Stav?'

'Couple of months. Since I got out of the pysch ward. It's a roof.'

'Mate, I spoke to Brian Durham and I know the background to what happened.'

'So what's your interest? It's all done and dusted. The poor little kid's dead, two peds will do minimal time for manslaughter, and those arseholes at Human Services have got away with their part of it.'

'I spoke to Lara, the boy's mum. A mutual friend asked me to find out what I could.'

'Well, Brian would have told you about the cover-up. If the arseholes were half as good at child protection as they are at lying then needy kids would be doing a whole lot better.'

'You made a finding against the Department staff, didn't you? And they binned the report?'

'Yeah, that Deputy D-G, Savage, is pure evil, mate. And as for that slime bucket Minister ...'

'What exactly did you say in the report? The original one.'

Stavros put down his now empty cup and held up his right index finger. He got up and walked over to the bed, pulling a cardboard banana box out from underneath it. He came back over with a manila folder.

'Here you go, have a read.'

He sat down and poured himself another bourbon. He pointed a quivering finger at the Marlboro packet on the table.

'May I, mate?'

'Yeah, of course. Help yourself.'

Stavros did.

Harry took a more substantial slug of his drink and opened the folder. Inside was a sheaf of typed pages, stapled at the top left corner and clipped into the folder. The cover page had the Human Services logo at the top and was entitled 'Child Death Review – Beau Jacobs'. Harry started to read it, then, after the first page, he skimmed through to the conclusion section. The final paragraph said it all.

> The death of 4-year-old Beau Jacobs was a tragedy on every level. However, the fact that in all likelihood it could have been avoided elevates it from the tragic to the utterly disgraceful. As previously discussed, four of the Department's caseworkers were closely involved in this case in the field. Additionally, two managers were involved in signing off on the case progress reports. All of these personnel were well aware of the two now-charged men taking an active interest in babysitting a 4-year-old boy. That all these trained social workers and managers could not even raise a query, where even the average

person on the street would have been immediately uneasy, if not actually suspicious, beggars belief. The caseworkers failed to make even cursory enquiries about these two men, eager to babysit, and, as it turned out, both clearly recorded on the Paedophile Register. Two of the caseworkers even admitted, albeit belatedly in the enquiry when they were confronted with independent witness accounts, that they had thanked the two sex offenders for helping out the boy's mother. The fact that the caseworkers then fabricated files notes after the boy's murder in an attempt to show they did initiate the proper checks, in my view, moves their conduct from the grossly negligent into the criminally culpable domain. That they also lied to this internal enquiry simply underscores this culpability.

It is recommended that this report and all evidence gathered be referred immediately to the NSW Police for a criminal investigation.

Harry closed the folder and swallowed his remaining bourbon in one gulp.

'Fuck, no wonder they shafted you, Stav.'

Stavros was, despite the unsteady hands, almost serenely calm. Far too calm, thought Harry.

'I spent twenty-two years in the job in Melbourne, thinking justice should always prevail. I even got a commendation from the top. Call me naïve, I don't care, but that little fella deserved it to be told as it was.'

'Mate, I agree. But pigs were going to fly before they were going to let that report get out.'

'Well, what would you have had me do, Harry? What that monster Savage wanted, to ditch the evidence and rewrite the findings, to reduce it to some "procedural failure"? She's a heinous mongrel, that woman.'

'I can well imagine.' Harry pictured the photo in his mind. 'Didn't you consider going to the cops or the Ombudsman or ICAC?'

'Mate, I was going to. That's why that one copy was in my personal stuff. But then I collapsed with the breakdown and ended up in hospital. That's when the bitch saw some problems coming and so she orchestrated that ridiculous sexual harassment claim. Still being investigated, get that. And mate, you should see my supposed victim – 180cm, about 130kg, and as dyke as the Dutch waterfront. But they all got in on it so my credibility is destroyed. When I got out of hospital I tried calling the Ombo, but she'd obviously got in first. Ombo's office didn't want to know me, at least that's the impression I got. They made the right noises that they would assess my complaint, but I needed to remember that I was under investigation and it might just look like me trying to defend the harassment case. I told them not to bother getting out of their comfortable chairs and hung the fucking phone up. Then Brian Durham spoke to me and told me about the pressure from upstairs. After that the "new" report and findings came out publicly. Then I knew it was all over and I was fucked.'

Harry was still perturbed by how calm Stavros was, but he let the thought go.

'Stav, can I borrow this, please?' Harry picked up the folder off his lap. 'I want to talk to a journo I know.'

'Harry, be my guest. Nobody's going to believe it's real. And mate, I never wrote a more bloody real report in my life.'

He looked at his empty cup.

'Another, Harry?'

'Sure, Stav. One for the road. The benefit of always taking taxis, no RBTs.'

Stavros filled both cups this time.

The pair sat in silence looking out at the poinciana with its splashes of red flowers adding to the lively mirage. They drank, and thought. Thought down different avenues, but with an unspoken mutuality. A cigarette later, Harry got up.

'Stav, I've got to be making tracks. I'll see what I can do and I'll come back to see you.'

'Thanks, Harry, I appreciate it. But I won't be holding my breath.'

'You take care, mate.'

They shook hands and Harry walked out of the room with the manila folder and what he hoped was the truth. He heard the door close behind him and walked slowly down the stairs. George came out into the hallway as he came off the last step.

'How is he?'

'We talked, and drank, of course.'

George smiled, 'Of course.'

'He's pretty relaxed, all things considered, don't you think?'

'Yeah, and it's not the anti-depressants because he keeps chucking them out. This is what worries me. He's past anger, and even frustration. His fire's out, Harry.'

'What about counselling or something?'

'The only time he leaves his room is to go to the bathroom. He's given me his card and PIN, and I go out and get his bourbon and baccy. I always add in a couple of sandwiches, but they usually join the pills in the bin.'

Harry shook his head.

'All right, thanks, George. I told Stav I'd come back and see him when I'd done some more work.'

'Righto, Harry. Be seeing you then.'

They shook hands and Harry stepped out of the front door into a different shade of Chippendale grey. He missed the royal poinciana already.

— 9 —

Harry was sitting at the outdoor café in Ultimo that took up the miniature plaza cutting Macarthur Street in two. Being his usual early self he had already started a skinny white coffee and was admiring the sunlight playing through the leaves of the golden robinia trees under which the café tables were placed. The golden-green foliage was swaying in the gentle morning breeze. A tall, rangy blonde, immaculately presented in a midnight blue designer trouser suit, paused in her stride and looked at him.

'Harry?'

'Yes. You must be Shona. Either that, or my luck has taken a massive turn for the better.' He smiled at her.

She laughed. There was a hint of huskiness. She shook his outstretched hand.

The waitress came over and took Shona's order for a latte.

As she sat down, Harry was captivated by her deep blue eyes, like two glowing sapphires, set in her lean, angular face. Above her high cheekbones Harry could see a fire and a keen intelligence in her eyes – in his view essential qualities for a good journalist. He liked what he saw.

'Thanks for agreeing to meet me, Shona. Like I said on the phone, I wanted to chat about the Beau Jacobs case.'

Shona grimaced.

'A bloody grotesque case, that one. I don't think anyone who was in any way connected to it will ever forget it.'

'Yeah, I think I'm being pulled into that unfortunate club. I got the details from Brian Durham.'

She smiled. 'Ah, yes, Detective Sergeant Brian Durham. I liked him, struck me as a thoroughly decent man. And a straightshooter, no bullshit. Pity he wasn't allowed to get really stuck into that case. It seemed like there was more to it than what hit the courts.'

She looked directly at Harry. He gazed at her blonde waterfall of hair with the dappled sunlight playing on it and her azure eyes drawing him in. You could dive in to those deep blue pools and drown a very happy man, Harry thought. He decided to concentrate. The coffee arrived and Shona thanked the waitress. She looked down at the ashtray which had one of Harry's butts in it. Her hand went into her light tan leather bag. An Oroton, Harry noticed.

'I take it you don't mind if I smoke?'

'Of course not, I'll join you.'

'Excellent. Not many of us left these days.'

She lit a menthol and drew back.

'So you're a PI? And someone who knew Beau's mother asked you to dig around?'

'Yes. And I'm increasingly finding myself shovelling into a deep ditch of dung.'

'Brian told me he was under pressure to wrap it up once the two paedophiles pleaded to manslaughter. But he didn't really elaborate.'

'Do you know about the Department of Human Services involvement?'

'Well, I know that they were involved with Beau. Not exactly news given his mum was always on the street working. And I reported on the court case for the two peds. I did call the Human Services field office involved, but got the usual polite euphemism for "fuck off, journo".'

Harry chuckled. 'I bet you did. Can't comment on "operational matters".'

'Exactly. So what is your angle, Harry?'

'Well, you know there was a departmental report into the matter, given the child died under their watch?'

'Yeah. I read it, for what it was worth. Aside from being so full of weasel words as to be meaningless, it was turgid in the extreme and totally self-serving.'

'Yes, that was the official version of it.'

Shona leant in and the blue eyes locked onto Harry's like an F-16's Sidewinders.

'So there's another version?'

'Yeah. Usually the way with government reports.'

Shona grinned. 'I'd certainly agree with you there. I think they've all got diplomas in duplicity. That's how they get ahead these days.'

'Ah, so good to sit with a fellow cynic. Here, have a look at this. I'll get some more coffees.'

Harry pulled Stavros' report out of his leather zip-up document folder and handed it to Shona.

'Thanks,' she said, taking hold of it and immediately flicking to the end.

Harry beckoned the waitress and signalled for two more of the same. He lit himself a smoke as Shona read. She finished the conclusion section just as the fresh coffees were placed on the table.

'So this is what Brian Durham was alluding to when he said he had to wrap the case up. This guy McMahon, you think he's genuine?'

'Yes, I'd stake my wallet on it.'

'But this is disgusting. Government departments always put spin on things, but to perpetrate a cover-up like this one you'd have to be morally bankrupt.'

'Yep. Are you really so surprised?'

'Well, yes and no. I don't know. I know I shouldn't be, but in this case …'

She took a mouthful of coffee.

'Bloody hell, Harry. Two peds killed that little boy, and no doubt did all sorts of appalling things to him before he died. But according to this it could all have been avoided.'

She waved the report angrily in the air.

'Can you do anything with this, Shona? Or rather, will you do something with this?'

'Harry, I'm a bloody journo and this is dynamite. You really need to ask? I'd love to expose this disgrace and end a few careers.'

'Sweet. There is one hitch, though, and it's significant.'

Her eyes narrowed slightly.

'Go on then. An exposé like this on a plate would have been too good to be true.'

'Stavros McMahon is the hitch. After he wrote that they made his life a living nightmare. He had a breakdown and is, frankly, at the end of the line. His credibility will be the problem.'

'Oh, come on, Harry. Most people are hardly going to condemn the guy for having a breakdown after this case.'

'True. But there's a bigger problem for his credibility.'

'But I thought you said you'd stake money on him?'

'And I would. But that Deputy D-G, Savage, stitched Stavros up well and truly. After they put him in hospital with the breakdown, they concocted a full-on sexual harassment case, with Human Services staff lining up as witnesses against him. Anything he does or says now is going to be made out to be him making things up to try and defend himself.'

'Shit. Being the ever-sceptical journo, Harry, could there be anything in the harassment claim?'

Harry laughed.

'Sorry, it's not funny, but I bloody doubt it. The supposed victim is a lesbian, and very visibly proud of the fact. I found a photo of her online. She's not exactly a honey trap for a bloke like Stavros.'

Shona sighed out loud and drew back hard on her cigarette before crushing it in the ashtray.

'They're bloody ruthless, that coven that run Human Services. I did a bit of research on them at the time of the court case. There've been a couple of whiffs before around Savage, but she seems entirely bulletproof and untouchable, from the very top down.'

'Yeah, from everything I've heard and read she sounds like an absolute charmer.'

'Oh, yes, she'd make Myra Hindley look benign.'

Harry chuckled.

'Look, Harry, I'm certainly happy to fire some questions at the Minister's office. See what it stirs up. But from everything you've told me I don't fancy our chances.'

Harry looked across at the handsome face and decided the use of 'our' had a certain tantalization to it. He smiled at her.

'Sweet. You can keep that. It's an extra copy I ran off. Let's stay in touch.'

'Cool. I'll give you a call after I've done some mischief-making.'

She winked at him. They both stood up and shook hands. Harry wondered if her hand lingered just a touch, or perhaps it was wishful thinking and he was just overdue for a shag.

Shona turned and walked off down Macarthur Street. Harry admired the departing slender physique. No, he wasn't going to make any moves on this one. It was much better to have a friendly journo in his armoury. He looked down at his paunch and reflected that he was probably flattering himself anyway.

Harry, son, you really need to get in shape.

Mind you, Tessa was certainly keen to see him again. So he wasn't exactly lucking out with the older sophisticated ladies.

Well, not enough time at present for wining and dining, so after dinner tonight it would be off to see the girls at Puss in Boots to sate his rising appetite.

– 10 –

Later that day, Porcia Savage was just about to leave her office when her private mobile rang. It was a number very few people were aware of, and she needed to dig deep in her handbag to retrieve the phone.

'And how is my sweet little Porcy?'

The voice was at its syrupy best, like honey running down hot thighs.

'Ah, Minister. I'm very well thank you. And your good self?'

'Not too bad, considering I was in front of a House Committee all morning, but by lunch time I had them eating the very skin off the palms of my hands.'

'I'm sure you did, Minister. So empowering, isn't it?'

'Like doling out lollies in a playground. Now, Porcy, I need to see you.'

The slight emphasis on the word 'need' sent a tingle through Savage's loins.

'Of course. When would suit you, Minister?'

'This evening. Rearrange things if necessary. My partner's away until tomorrow. So let's have dinner at mine. Say around seven.'

It was a command, rather than a suggestion, but that was half the enjoyment for Savage. A bit of ministerial domination added spice to her life.

'Lovely, see you then. Bring the usual?'

'Oh, yes.'

Darkness had just fallen when Savage parked in front of the Minister's house in a leafy side street in Stanmore. As she walked up the path the front door opened and the Minister came out, closing the door, and restraining on a leash a coiffed black poodle that was eager to hit the street.

'I thought we'd take Prince for a quick walk before dinner arrives. I've ordered our usual Thai favourites, Porcy.'

Savage smiled and stepped closer. 'Thank you, Minister.'

'No touching out here, Porcy. You never know who's watching.'

Savage nodded. 'No problems.'

The pair crossed the road and entered the grassed reserve opposite, Prince stopping forward progress at the first tree for a good sniff. As a stream of hot poodle urine splattered noisily against the eucalyptus trunk, the Minister spoke in a lowered voice.

'Sorry for the walk in the park, Porcy, but you never know who's listening either. These days bloody ICAC likes to throw listening devices around like confetti. And ever since the good, former Minister for Infrastructure went down so unfairly over that planning matter and those so-called bribes, we're all being extra cautious now.'

'Understandable.'

'I get the house swept for bugs regularly, but it's still much safer out here.'

'But I thought this was a social visit.'

Savage hid her latent pang of disappointment with her reptilian smile and winked at the Minister.

'Porcy, my dear, just a quick chat out here and then it's

back inside for nothing but social. A very much overdue liaison, too.'

'Oh, yes,' sighed a relieved Savage. 'So what do you want to chat about?'

The Minister's voice dropped even lower.

'A Herald journo was on the phone this afternoon, asking questions about the Jacobs fiasco.'

'But that is all sorted, Minister, well and truly. No problems there.'

'Well, this journo says she's seen a different version of the departmental report. Could that have happened?'

'All traces of the draft report that bastard McMahon wrote have been cleansed from the system. I had an external computer expert in to do it, just to make sure. Our own people would have stuffed it up. And the expert checked that no electronic copies of the earlier draft had been downloaded or sent anywhere either.'

'So what's this bloody journo on about then? She wouldn't be stupid enough to make it up and then directly question a Minister about it.'

'Relax. The only possibility, and it is not a problem either, is that McMahon had printed off a copy before he left ...'

'How is that not a problem?' interrupted the Minister.

'Because I even arranged the properties metadata on the final report to show that McMahon had prepared that version of the document. And all appropriately backdated. The forensic expert was worth every single dollar. And with McMahon skewered courtesy of the most timely and very sordid sexual harassment case, we simply state that any other copy of the report is clearly a fabrication by McMahon to defend himself by attacking the Department. We could even release the computer details of the final report to show McMahon's authorship and really make the point.'

'Oh, I do like your style, Porcy. Always dependable and utterly efficient.'

'Trust me, Minister, no one will believe anything McMahon might come up with.'

'Excellent. Well, you organize the necessary documents from the Department's system in the morning and I'll speak to the journo in the afternoon. That should put an end to her digging around.'

The Minister's satisfied smile was clearly visible in the gloomy illumination from the sparse street lamps. Savage had to resist the temptation to touch the Minister's hand.

'It will be a pleasure, Minister.'

'Right, that's business. Now let's head back for some altogether different pleasure.'

'I'm all yours, Minister.'

'Damned right, Porcy.'

The takeaway food arrived on a garishly coloured moped, the rider having a matching loud helmet, just as they were on the Minister's front porch. The Minister paid the delivery boy and they went inside carrying several hot tubs of green curry, rice, and stir fry.

Dinner was a rapid affair, washed down with a bottle of chardonnay, lots of hand touching across the table, and Prince sitting there salivating. The eagerness of both diners for horizontal dessert resulted in a frenzied dash for the bedroom. As their backs disappeared down the hallway, a patient Prince jumped onto a chair and then onto the table. A quick sniff of the various plates and containers was followed by his muzzle descending noisily into the remaining stir fry.

Down the corridor clothes were being ripped off

speedily, tongue met tongue, and skin met skin. The pair collapsed onto the bed in a writhing mass of flesh. The Minister slid southwards without delay.

Savage whimpered as the Minister's tongue circled her love button and then set to work, combining with fingers probing her pussy.

With the unabashed feasts going on in both dining room and bedroom now, an observer in the corridor would have been bombarded with slurping in stereo.

Savage hoped the Minister's favourite dessert confection was on the menu tonight. As she lay on her back moaning in pleasure, her right hand blindly plunged into her handbag on the bedside table and plonked the large tube of requested K-Y jelly onto the bed. Several more minutes of her being teased with pussy-eating went by before she found out the Minister's intentions. The fingers slid out of her now saturated pussy, there was a generous squirting of gel, and then she felt multiple fingers working to part her lips and work their way inwards.

Savage murmured and then gasped obscene encouragement as the Minister finally eased all the way inside her. Then the increasingly purposeful thrusting had her groaning in ecstasy. The howl she emitted as she came saw a startled poodle leap from the table and seek shelter under the couch.

It was a very contented, if rather sore, Savage who rested her post-coital head on an equally sated Minister's chest fifteen minutes later, having done her part in delivering an equally loud ministerial orgasm.

'Well, Porcy, my sweet, we definitely needed that.'

'That would be a yes, Minister.'

'Now, I think we need to consider your promotion

announcement, too. Maybe we could kill two birds with one stone tomorrow.'

'Minister, you are too kind, and I am in your hands.'

'Yes, Porcy, you certainly are.' The Minister kissed her on the forehead.

The tealights flickered into darkness and the pair dropped off to sleep.

As Savage pulled away from the kerb the next morning, shortly after 7.30 a.m., in her mirror she saw a taxi pull up behind her. She'd got going just in time, it seemed. The Minister's husband got out of the cab and headed for the front door of the house.

Harry Wood

– 11 –

The next afternoon, Harry was having a post-lunch snooze reclined in his office chair when the phone rang. He came to, swung his feet off the desk and picked up his mobile. It was the journo's number. He smiled to himself.

Harry answered. 'Hi, Shona. How did you go?'

'I tell you, Harry, that bloody Minister, Gloria Steele, is slicker than a KFC grease-trap.'

Harry laughed.

'So you got a pile of spun crap?'

'You could have written the script for her, going on what you had told me before.'

'Let me guess. The report we have is all a fabrication by a disgraced former staff member who is trying any desperate measure to defend himself against a sexual harassment case?'

'Just about verbatim. She added that stooping to using the tragic death of a child was as low as anyone could ever possibly conceive of.'

'Hypocritical scum, all of them.'

'She did say more, though, about the final report.'

'Go on.' Harry lit a cigarette.

'She was quite vehement in saying that the final report, the one that went public after the court case, was actually written by McMahon.'

'Well, I don't bloody believe that for a minute.'

'No, nor do I. Aside from the background you'd given me, Steele was far too smooth when she was telling me that bit. Seemed totally prepared.'

'Still, we come back to Stavros's credibility, due to the cooked up harassment case.'

'Harry, it's worse than that. Steele said they had the computer data records to prove he was the author. And then her office emailed them to me.'

Harry sat forward. 'You're kidding?'

'No. The properties data for the final report certainly shows McMahon as the author. Is there any way this stuff could be contrived?'

Harry paused and frowned. 'There bloody has to be. I don't know offhand. Asking me about computer stuff is about as promising as asking a politician to explain ethics. But I can ask a mate of mine who's an expert on the techo side of things.'

'Okay, but even so, let's assume the data can be fabricated, and has been. Could we ever prove it?'

'Alas, Shona, no chance. If they've used someone with the skills to manipulate the data, then rest assured that all traces have been thoroughly removed as well. I really hate to concede this, but I think they've got this one sewn up tighter than a duck's arse.'

There was an audible sigh on the other end of the line.

'So is there anywhere to go now? I bloody hate giving up on this stuff. Nothing makes my blood boil more than our corrupt pollies and their public service bitches.'

'You and I both, Shona, but I can't see any avenues at the moment. I could go and speak to Stavros again, but he really is a mess and I think I got everything useful out of him last time. This is a classic case of the Establishment having the power and the means to create the history it wants. Scary, isn't it?'

'Well, yes. But it's fucking depressing, too.'

'I'm with you there.'

'All right, Harry, I'll leave it at that for the moment, unless you turn up something new. I'm not going to do a story on it. All that would do is to help shore up Steele and Savage.'

'Yeah, don't give those corrupt scum any extra publicity, that's for sure.'

'Let me know if anything else comes up. And stay in touch. Never know when we might have mutual interests again.'

Harry grinned at the possible flirtation.

'Will do, Shona. You take care.'

'Ciao, Harry.'

And with that Harry put the phone down on his desk and instinctively reached for the bottom drawer, pulling out the bottle of Jameson.

– 12 –

The following day saw a cold change roll into a grey and overcast Sydney. As Harry jumped into a cab outside his office, the wind was starting to howl and dark cloud banks were threatening from the south. Harry couldn't help thinking that the frigid, gusting air carried in the scent of an unpleasant day, like standing down wind of an abattoir. After a slow crawl along Broadway, the cab dropped Harry in Chippendale about ten minutes later.

As he walked towards the boarding house he first noticed the back of a marked police car, then he saw the white Ford Transit van double parked in front of the police car.

'No, fuck, no!'

Harry had been to enough deaths in his time to recognize a government contractor's van with his eyes shut. His pulse quickened, as did his pace. His fears were confirmed by the ashen, downcast look on the face of George, who was sitting on the top step having a smoke.

He nodded in greeting, but before Harry could make it up the path the two contractors appeared in the hallway with a wheeled stretcher bearing its shrouded, cadaverous cargo. Two young uniformed cops were close behind taking slow steps. The convoy of tragedy, thought Harry. Hell, he'd trooped along in a few of them himself back in the day. The only task he'd disliked more was having to go and do the notification to the next of kin.

George stood up to let the grim procession pass, and Harry stepped back out onto the footpath. He watched glumly as the body disappeared into the clinically clean back of the van and the gleaming white doors were closed firmly behind, like a heavy book being closed for the last time. The two attendants got into the cab, the motor started, and Stavros departed for his final road trip – to the morgue.

The cops paused briefly to shake hands with George, then they, too, headed for their car, taking no notice of Harry as they went past, carrying their evidence bags and folders.

He walked slowly up the path and greeted George as the police car moved off down the street.

'Well, Harry, it didn't exactly come as a surprise. It was more a question of when.'

'Yeah, he did have that look about him. Boxed in, beaten, and buggered. You find him?'

'Yep. Went to check on him when the bloke in the next room said Stavros hadn't been to the showers at all. He was fastidious like that, so I knew something was wrong. He'd hung himself from the curtain rail anchor with a sheet. Looks like he'd downed himself a whole bottle of courage first. The bourbon I picked up for him yesterday arvo was completely empty. And he was stone cold, so it would have been yesterday evening.'

'Poor bastard.'

'I didn't tell the uniforms this bit, but I found this on the mantelpiece before I called them.'

George pulled a folded envelope out of his back trouser pocket and passed it to Harry. As he unfolded it,

Harry saw his own name written on the front in shaky handwriting. He slipped his index finger into the unstuck gap at the top of the flap and ripped along the top edge. Inside was a piece of yellowed card, like an old library index card. Harry pulled it out.

On one side there was some writing in the same hand, albeit less shaky than his name on the envelope. It lacked any sheen to the ink, so Harry guessed it had been written a while ago.

> I have tried as best I could to be a man with ethics. That is, alas, what cost me most.
>
> - Albert Camus

Harry stared at the card for a minute, shook his head slowly, and passed it to George.

'I take it there weren't any other notes, George?'

'Nope, just this envelope for you, Harry.'

'Well, first suicide note I've seen quoting Camus. Sums it up though. Poor prick.'

'And I don't think he'll be the last either. The powers that be don't exactly hand out prizes for honesty. But some blokes like Stavros will keep trying to fight it.'

'Yeah, and lose, everything. Then some of us just get out of the fight. I'm not sure which is better. Or worse, depending on how you look at it.'

'I'd suggest a drink, Harry, but I'm not going back to my demons. I can make you a damned fine cup of tea, but you might want a stronger brew right now.'

'Yeah, George, I think so. Here's my card anyway. Feel free to stay in touch.'

Harry handed over a business card and took the Camus back.

'It'd be apt on his headstone, you know. But I can't see a burial plot somehow.'

'No, it'll be a pauper's cremation in a cardboard coffin after the autopsy. And then that'll be that.'

'Yeah, certified life extinct. No ceremony, no epitaph, no memory. It's pretty fucked, really.'

'Yeah, that's for sure.'

Harry stared down the street in the direction the morgue van had taken. George's gaze settled in the same plane. Neither of them spoke. It was the closest to a minute's silence that Stavros would ever get.

Harry finally broke the accidental tribute and turned back to face George.

'Okay, I'll be off. Be seeing you, George.'

'Feel free to drop round. Take care, mate.'

They shook hands and Harry headed back out onto the street. The nearest bar was a few minutes' walk away on Broadway and that is where Harry set off for at a determined pace, lighting himself an overdue smoke as he went.

Twenty-four hours passed and Harry was relaxing in his apartment for the afternoon. He'd had nothing left to do at his office, other than drink, and he had figured he may as well do that in the comfort of his own joint with a good book, and surrounded by his extensive collection of erotica. He'd momentarily considered a visit to the Scarlet Boudoir or Puss in Boots, but he really didn't have the energy for it at the moment. So he was lying on his couch enjoying a subdued whiskey and *The Galton Case* by Ross Macdonald, one of his favourite crime writers. Harry always found it fun to put himself in the shoes of Lew Archer, or his other hero, Philip Marlowe.

He was just reading the scene where Archer was getting a beating from thugs (he would have handled that differently, of course) when the phone rang. Harry cursed, as he had meant to turn the bloody thing off. He picked it up, saw the name on the screen, and answered it. Actually, he couldn't remember when he had last not answered a call from an attractive female.

'Shona, I didn't expect the pleasure so soon.'

'Sorry, Harry, I wish it was social, believe me. You near a TV?'

'Yeah, I'm at my place. Why?'

'The early news will be on in a few minutes. Lara

Jacobs is dead. I'm writing up the story as we speak for our edition tomorrow and the website now.'

'Fuck! No! What happened?'

'I only know what you'll see on the TV, so not much. Gotta fly though, Harry, but if I hear anything more than is news so far, I'll give you a call.'

'Cheers, Shona.'

Harry didn't get a chance to mention Stavros. He put the phone down and picked up the remote for the flat-screen.

He had to wait until after the first commercial break for the story, and even then if he'd blinked he would have missed it. Against some stock footage of Kings Cross the newsreader went through the motions.

> Police are investigating the discovery of a young woman's body in a laneway off Bayswater Road in Kings Cross. A Council street cleaner found the body shortly after sunrise this morning. Police have identified the dead woman as twenty-year-old Lara Serene Jacobs. The cause of death is not known at this stage and police will await the autopsy results. A police spokesperson said the death was being treated as suspicious. Police also said that Ms Jacobs was a known prostitute in the area.

> And now to today's sports news with Amy Phillips ...

Harry turned it off.

Poor Lara.

Thanks to the usual way the police and the media conjoined on these cases, all anyone would remember was that Lara was a sex worker. The way it came across there may as well have been a subtitle banner reading, 'The little slut got what she deserved.'

'Fuck you all!' shouted Harry at the now dark screen.

As if by some divine response, there was a flash outside and an almost immediate enormous clap of thunder. Then the rain started to sheet down.

No matter, thought Harry. I need the pub right now, big time. He felt the walls were starting to close in. All this death. He badly needed some company all of a sudden, and not of the buxom, horizontal variety.

He grabbed his jacket and an umbrella and left the solitude of his apartment. He headed straight for the Emerald Bar.

– 14 –

Liam's dependable drinking habits meant that Harry found him in the pub in his usual spot, quite well lubricated. He sat down opposite him at the small table once he'd grabbed double whiskies for two.

'Off to an early start today, Liam?'

'Here for a good time, Harry, not a long time.'

Liam gave Harry his cheekiest Celtic grin and swallowed his existing drink. He picked up the new glass and they chinked as they said 'Cheers'.

'You're looking a bit broody there, Harry?'

'Yeah. You know the dead kid case I've been on?'

'Oh, yeah, the Human Services fuck-up and cover-up. In fact, I've got a new word for it, "coverfuck". What do you think?'

Harry managed a chuckle.

'Very clever, Your Eminence. Like a "clusterfuck", but one wallowing in dishonesty and corruption?'

'Exactly.'

'The kid's mum turned up dead this morning.'

'Shit. Suspicious, I assume?'

'Twenty-years-old and found face down in a Kings Cross alleyway. Nothing natural about that.'

'Was she the girl I saw the piece about on the news?'

'That's right, Lara. And to cap off a bright and sunny

twenty-four hours, the ex-cop, Stavros, necked himself yesterday as well. Not that that came entirely as a surprise. Still ...'

'Fuck. Sorry, Harry. No wonder you look like the Grim Reaper.'

The 6 p.m. news bulletin started on the large wall-mounted plasma screen at the end of the front bar.

'Guess we'll see it on this one, too, but just before the sports again, no doubt.'

'Some people get dealt a shit hand, Harry.'

'Don't I know it. But the Establishment is full of evil scum busily rigging the deck, too.'

'So true. Survival often depends on playing the cards. But some hands are already ...'

Harry interjected suddenly and animatedly. 'Now talking of scum. There, Liam!'

Harry pointed at the TV screen and the lead story of the bulletin. The camera was doing a close up of the Minister for Human Communities and Youth Welfare, Gloria Steele, standing at a press conference outside Parliament, with Porcia Savage standing next to her.

'That's the maggot who perpetrated this coverfuck. The one on the right.'

'My, she is a hard looking giant troll, isn't she?'

Harry looked at Savage's face, the first time he'd seen a detailed close-up in live time. The short cropped peroxided hair and the evil piercing eyes were instantly recognizable from the news photo he'd seen online. But the feature that really struck him now was her mouth. Set menacingly beneath the small glacial eyes, the mouth was slightly protuberant and somewhat puckered. Given Savage's brownish skin tone, her mouth resembled an anus injected with Botox.

The Minister had her left hand on Savage's shoulder now and was in the process of announcing that Porcia Savage was the government's chosen head of the new super welfare umbrella department in NSW, the Office of Community Cohesion and Social Progress, a new government initiative delivering on one of their key election promises.

'This makes me want to vomit.' Harry's voice was rising as he addressed the screen directly. 'You corrupt cunts!'

The bar manager, Shaun, cleared his throat loudly.

Harry turned towards the bar. 'Sorry, Shaun.'

'That's not like you, Harry, and it's not even late yet.'

'Just a bit upset and very pissed off. I'll keep it down, mate.'

Harry turned back to the screen just in time for the Minister's final words:

> And for all her magnificent dedication to the
> children of New South Wales, I will be personally
> putting Ms Savage's name forward for an OAM in
> the upcoming Honour's List.

Harry shook his head and turned to Liam.

'I don't fucking believe it.'

'Harry, come on man. You know how they operate. Line the upper ranks with the most cunning, corrupt and ruthless operators they can find, and then they control the whole shebang.'

'I suppose it'd be naïvely optimistic to hope that karma will sort them out.'

'Hell, Harry, always keep hoping, mate. I've always liked to think that every dog has its day.'

'And it can't come quick enough for those two scum, the twin hounds of Lucifer.'

'Let's have a drink to the memory of the young girly, Lara, was it? She deserves someone to toast her.'

'Definitely. Then we should have one for Stavros.'

'Yes. And we won't stop there, Harry.'

Harry smiled grimly. He got up, grabbed the empty glasses, and stepped over to the bar. As he stood there waiting for the whiskies, he opened his wallet. He looked at the fading photo, discreetly kissed the end of his index finger, and touched it to Orla's pretty young face.

PART 5

HARRY'S REVENGE

People turned around to look at her. One could sense that she came from another world, a nocturnal world, and she seemed almost indecent in the harsh light of a winter's day.

- Georges Simenon

Because only when you fuck is everything that you dislike in life and everything by which you are defeated in life purely, if momentarily, revenged. Only then are you most cleanly alive and most cleanly yourself.

- Philip Roth

— 1 —

She sashayed up to him like a vixen on heat, flame red hair and eyes like molten honey. Her hand slithered up his thigh like a taxman heading for his wallet.

'Buy a girl a drink, good looking?'

She had a thirty a day voice and Harry figured 'girl' was a bit of a stretch.

Thursday afternoon had found Harry leaning on the bar at the Black Stallion in Surry Hills. He had been there for about twenty minutes, fifteen of which were down to him being early. Tanya had rung him a couple of hours previously wanting to meet up.

Harry had, as usual, been people watching as he sipped his first whiskey of the day. So he had already noticed the forty-something, predatory redhead prowling the bar before she hit him up. She was attractive, all right, with a gym-toned body fabulously shown off by her tight clothing. Well, why not? If you've got it, flaunt it, thought Harry. And, hell, in the Lycra pants she had a camel toe that would have dragged Lawrence from his duty. But she was hunter through and through. Given Harry's age she didn't exactly classify as a cougar, but Harry wasn't sure of any name for this type. Maybe hyena? They looked for older prey.

Harry looked at her face, the attractive natural contours a little tainted by over eager make-up. The smell of tobacco mingled with the sweet floral scent of her perfume, a combination that actually worked rather well for Harry. He somewhat wistfully considered that, were he at a loose end right now, he was looking at a very easy conquest indeed, although she'd probably take the victor's credit. And a redhead to boot. Harry hadn't slept with too many natural reds, only one in fact, but she had certainly lived up to the reputation as a double-comer. And, alas, he knew there was no point trying to tell her he'd like to take a raincheck, because this hyena wanted her dinner now. Oh, well, thought Harry, what might have been. He smiled as graciously as he could.

'Sorry, babe, much as I would love to, I am actually waiting for a friend. A female friend.'

'That's too bad, sugar. You don't know what you're missing.'

'Actually, I think I do.'

Her eyes narrowed slightly and her smile waned, like she was expecting an insult. Harry, on the contrary, wasn't going to forego his usual charm. After all, he might just run into her again, and burning bridges was something he'd learnt long ago not to do unless absolutely necessary.

'I reckon a good meal with charming company, back to your place, followed by truly memorable sex with a very beautiful and sophisticated woman.'

Her smile returned instantly and lit up her experienced face.

'Smooth, as well as handsome. I like that. Well, if you change your ...'

She didn't get to finish her sentence as her eyes darted over Harry's left shoulder.

Harry actually smelt Tanya's Insolence before he felt his left buttock being playfully pinched.

'Hope I'm not interrupting a precious moment, Mr PI?'

Harry smiled as he considered the immaculate timing. He enjoyed the scene as Ms Prowling Hunter looked across the twenty-five year chasm at Ms Divine Twin, then looked back at him with almost a look of admiration, tinged with envy, on her face.

'Oh, please, don't tell me. Your niece?'

The ever-naughty Tanya, as if on cue, leant in to Harry and kissed him fully on the lips.

'Great to see you, Harry.'

She looked back at the redhead and smiled, the sweet innocent smile that only a teenager could pull off.

'Definitely not his niece. Neither of us are from that sort of town.'

The wisdom that went with the older face conceded defeat in the hunt.

'Okay, pretty young thing who is not his niece. He's all yours. Sugar daddy here obviously prefers his fun on the younger side.'

She turned to Harry.

'Mind you, I'd be able to do some things to you that junior here couldn't even imagine.'

Harry got in quickly before Tanya could rise to the bait.

'Maybe, maybe not. But I'll enjoy thinking about the possibilities.'

She smiled, put her fingertips to her mouth and blew Harry a kiss.

'Well, I'll be seeing you. Harry, was it?'

'Yeah. Thanks anyway. Maybe next time.' He winked at her. He felt Tanya pinch his arse again.

'I'm Dawn. Just so you can put a name to the missed opportunity. Ciao, good looking.'

'You enjoy yourself, Dawn,' said Harry, as she turned and resumed her hungry patrol.

'Harry, what the fuck? I'm five minutes late and suddenly you're a chick magnet?'

'Actually, more like hyena prey, babe. I do seem to attract the bar flies. I think it goes with the age as well as the attitude. Now, drinks. A vodka lime as usual for you?'

'Yes please, Harry. Then let's find a table outside so we can smoke.'

Harry got two drinks and they found a table on the upstairs balcony. They both lit up as soon as they were seated.

'So, Ms Tanya, apart from understandably finding my company entirely irresistible, what was it you wanted to see me about so urgently?'

'Well, one of the girls at work told me this story which sounded like something out of Hollywood. And this girl does a few drugs, so I was a bit sceptical. But then I thought more about some of the shit you'd told me about cases you'd done. I've heard enough from you to know that anything is possible.'

'Indeed it bloody is. So what did this girl tell you? I'm still having bad dreams after Lara's case, that being the last time one of the girls told you her story.'

'Yeah, well that one was true, wasn't it? But that was no way as fucked up as this one.'

'All right, babe. Try me.'

'Okay. Em works at the Boudoir. She's a bit younger than me, a few months, only just old enough to get in for work. She's been there about three months now. Nice enough girl, but does like her eckys and that's not my scene. Though she keeps it well hidden from the boss.'

'I bet. She wouldn't keep her gig otherwise. I know your boss.'

Tanya smiled.

'Mmm, I'm sure you do.'

'Behave. And what sort of name is Em?'

'Short for Emily. Anyway, her mum's pretty drug-fucked and there's a constant string of loser boyfriends. Anyone who can score for her, basically. That's why Em got herself out of there.'

'Was she abused?'

Harry placed his hand gently on Tanya's on the table. Tanya smiled and turned her hand over so she could hold Harry's.

'She hasn't said so, but who knows. Quite fucking probably; seems to be the lot in life for some of us girls. The one thing she was saying, always, from the day she started working with us, was about how she'd left her younger sister there, Madison, or Maddie. She's only thirteen.'

'Shit. I can see where this is going.'

'You're good, Harry, but no you can't.'

'Really?' Harry raised his eyebrows at her.

Tanya lit another cigarette.

'Maddie went missing a couple of weeks ago. Then suddenly last night she shows up at Em's place. She was a mess and was hurt. Apparently one of the mother's boyfriends had suggested this youth bible camp for her. There was money involved. So the mother sent Maddie off, telling her it was to give her a holiday, but obviously it was just so the money came in for the hammer. Anyway, Maddie told Em that she'd been taken to this back of nowhere camp up in the Blue Mountains. She was kept locked in this room on her own. She was raped by several different men. A lot of it was even filmed. Then one night she got her period and managed to get one of the men to let her go to the bathroom alone to clean herself up before he had sex with her. Normally someone would take her to the toilet, but seems this guy was grossed out by the blood. So she was able to open the bathroom window and climb out. Then she ran for her life, in her underwear. Found some old clothes in a shed and somehow hitchhiked back down to Sydney and lobbed up at Em's place the next day.'

'Fuck me. Well, what about going to the cops?'

'That's just it, Harry. I wouldn't have even considered believing this until you talked to me about that cop you nearly caught. Apparently one of the men who raped Maddie at this so-called bible camp was a cop.'

'How does she know that? Surely he wasn't in uniform?'

'No. She looked in his jacket pockets when he was off having a piss and she saw a cop badge. Harry, I don't think she was supposed to get out of there alive, because she saw their faces.'

Harry's face hardened and he almost spat out his next words.

'What did this cop look like?'

'Don't know. I didn't get that much detail from Em. She was just concentrating on having her sister back, so there wasn't much else said. I haven't talked to Maddie, obviously. And, Harry, there's no fucking way she's going to the cops.'

'Do you reckon she'd talk to me?'

'Harry, apart from your irresistible charm, why do you think I called you? I can't trust anyone else, you know that. You're my go-to man.'

This time Tanya caressed Harry's hand on the table.

'All right, my divine one. Here we go again. Let's tee this up real quickly.'

'You're cool, Harry. Thank you.'

'No worries. Oh, and while I've got you here …'

Harry reached into his inside jacket pocket and produced two small gift-wrapped cubes. He passed one to Tanya.

'Happy nineteenth birthday, babe, for yesterday.'

Tanya smiled. 'Harry, you didn't need to. Your phone call was sweet enough.'

She unwrapped the little package, flicked open a red velvet box, and pulled out a pair of pearl earrings.

'Oh, Harry. They're beautiful! And my birthstone, too.'

'I know, I did my research.' Harry grinned.

Tanya almost toppled their drinks as she leant over the table and kissed Harry full on the lips. She sat back down, smiling, but with a tear meandering down her cheek.

Harry gave her the second package.

'And for Sasha, of course.'

Harry raised his glass. Tanya lifted hers and they chinked.

'Cheers. Happy birthday,' said Harry.

'Thank you, my Mr PI. You are a good man, Harry. Cheers.'

— 2 —

A cold change had blown in from the south overnight and Friday morning dawned with blustery drizzle and a drop of about ten degrees from the previous day. Harry hadn't slept much, his brain working overtime on all sorts of fantastical possibilities with this bogus bible camp. He was torn between two radically opposing emotions. One was hoping that something this depraved was merely a young runaway girl's imagination creating an avenue for attention. The other part, that of the adrenalin-addicted sleuth, was salivating at the prospect of a truly huge case to break open. Lingering at the back of this part of him was his own fantasy – that the piece of shit Detective Commander Mervyn Lowe would somehow be implicated.

Harry had put the heater on in his office when he had arrived before 8 a.m., and now, over two hours later, the air temperature was cosy without being stuffy. Tanya and the two sisters were due to come in at 10 a.m., although Harry wasn't expecting punctuality. Despite his personal obsession on this front, Harry could never bring himself to chide Tanya for her habitual tardiness. She simply had too many redeeming features.

Harry had readied his office for his youngest ever visitor. The old couch against the wall had been cleared of the stacks of papers which usually adorned it, and the decent client chair had been moved from in front of the desk over to face the couch across the low-slung coffee table. Harry didn't want the sisters having to face him across a desk. He'd also been careful to take down from the wall the police badge mounted on its timber shield, as well as a couple of framed photos of his detective days. He'd even grabbed a couple of bunches of gerberas from a corner store to brighten up the room. He hoped the cheery yellow and orange blooms in a vase on the coffee table would help put the girls at ease.

Just before 10.30, as Harry was sitting at his desk having a Marlboro and reading the *Sydney Morning Herald*, the buzzer sounded. He pressed the release button and called, 'Come in.'

The door opened and Tanya appeared, dressed down in khaki cargo pants and a black leather jacket, with just the faintest trace of burgundy lipstick and crimson blush on her cheekbones. Her curly blonde tresses were tied back in a ponytail.

'Hi, Mr PI. Sorry we're a bit late. These two weren't quite ready.'

'No worries, babe. Come on in.'

Tanya pushed the door all the way open and Harry could see the other two girls standing nervously in the corridor. Tanya turned back to them and took hold of the hand of the older one, who was about the same height as Tanya and looked about the same age, but lacking any similarity in the style stakes. The smaller and younger girl looked like a starved street urchin from a Dickens novel.

'Em, it's fine, he's a friend. A real friend.'

Emily didn't look convinced, but was tugged forward by Tanya. The younger girl, holding Emily's other hand, simply followed mechanically along. The three of them stepped into the office. Harry stood up and came around his desk.

'Have a seat on the couch, girls,' he said, trying to appear familial. 'Anyone for a Coke?'

The younger girl nodded.

As Harry went over to the bar fridge in the far corner, Emily managed, 'Me, too.'

Harry returned with two cans of Coke and handed them to the girls who were still standing, like they were hedging their bets as to whether to sit or flee. They were both looking cagily at Harry. Tanya broke the impasse by lighting a cigarette and handing the packet to the other two. She went over to Harry's desk and collected the cobalt blue ashtray as the other two girls also lit up. Tanya put the ashtray on the coffee table and slid her fine posterior onto the end of the couch. Emily looked at her and, seemingly getting whatever reassurance she needed, sat herself down. The younger girl, still holding her hand, joined her. Tanya, exhaling a cloud of smoke across the table, put her hand on Emily's right knee.

'Em, this is my very special friend Harry I told you about. He's a good man and you can trust him completely. Harry, this is Em and Madison.'

'Hi girls, pleased to meet you. Always good to meet friends of Tanya.'

Harry looked across at them. Emily was distinctly skinnier than Tanya and had a pallid complexion set with misty hazel eyes. She was a bathroom-sink blonde and the dark roots were showing along the top of her forehead. She hadn't managed any make-up, other than a smear of cherry-red lipstick. She had big breasts for her physique and Harry guessed that with make-up and lingerie she would still be a very attractive option on the menu at the

Scarlet Boudoir. But she lacked any natural beauty and the years would quickly turn the tide against her. Girls like Emily did fine until they were about twenty-five, and then it was downhill from there.

The young face next to her, which perhaps once would have been eager, was cuddling close to her shoulder. It bore plenty of colour, but not from a cosmetic counter. A deep purple blotch underlined her left eye, which was slightly less open than the right one and was very bloodshot. The right side of her lower jaw was noticeably swollen and bruised along its length, and there were some deep scratch marks and dried blood running up her right temple into her hairline. Madison was naturally fair, although her hair was tangled and matted, in need of a proper wash. She sucked on the Coke can and drew on her cigarette, whilst her limpid blue eyes never once moved off Harry. It was as though she was fixated on what this strange man's next move was going to be. Harry broke the ice with the obvious.

'How did you get the bruises, Madison?'

Her eyes remained unflinchingly on him. Silence.

'I'm here to help you, Madison. I need you to talk to me.'

'They hit me.'

'Is it still hurting?'

'Bit.'

'What about those scratches up there?'

Harry indicated his temple.

'Cut myself climbing through a fence after I got out.'

Harry looked at Emily.

'She seen a doctor?'

'Not yet. Didn't know where to go that'd be safe from them.'

Harry looked back to Madison.

'You want to tell me what happened? And then we get you to see a doctor and make sure you are safe.'

'What do you want to know?'

'Let's start with where you were. Tanya told me it was some sort of church camp.'

'Well, that's what mum told me it was going to be. Fuckin' bitch. Instead I got locked up and fucked. By different men.'

'Did you know any of them?'

'Nah.'

'How did you get there?'

'Mum's boyfriend dropped me at a house. There was another girl there, too, so I thought it was all right. She's dead now, but.'

The questions in Harry's mind were surging, but he struggled to return to his training with child interviewing; one non-leading question at a time. He'd already been a little too eager. He reached for his deepest reserves of patience.

'Do you know where the house was?'

'Nah.'

'What about getting to the camp?'

'It was dark. We stayed at the house until it was dark. Then we went in a van. Didn't see nothin'.'

'Who was the other girl?'

'Caitlin, that's what she said.'

'You said she was dead. Why did you say that?'

"Cos I saw them kill her.'

Harry was starting to wonder if this was getting too far-fetched.

'What did you see?'

'I could hear her screaming in the room next to me. There was a crack in the wall and I could peek through. This man was all in black and had a knife …'

Madison started crying and fell silent, her head down.

Harry looked at Tanya who leant across Emily and put her hand on Madison's knee.

'Hey, Maddie, it's okay. You're safe now.'

'You can take your time, Madison,' added Harry.

The young girl sniffled, wiped her eyes with her hands, and looked back up at Harry.

'He cut her across the throat and there was blood everywhere. I couldn't keep looking. Caitlin didn't scream no more. That's when I knew I had to do anything to get out.'

Harry looked into the young, quavering eyes that had seen far too much.

'Madison, can you tell me what they did to you?'

'Can I have another smoke?'

'Sure.' Harry passed over a packet and a lighter. Madison lit up.

'Let me know if you want another Coke, Madison.'

'It's cool.'

She leant in and cuddled Emily even tighter. She looked at Harry again.

'So what did they do to you?'

'The first one was on the night when we got there ...'

The non-leading questions and the compartmentalized answers went on for the next thirty minutes. By the end of it Harry had ascertained that Madison had been raped by at least four different men, in all her orifices, and most of it had been filmed. If one accepted her story, and the bit with Caitlin being murdered, then it definitely did seem that she hadn't been meant to get out of the bible camp alive. Harry went in for his personal pay dirt.

'You said one of them was a cop?'

'Yeah.'

'How do you know that?'

'After he fucked me the first time, the arsehole went to the bathroom. I looked in his jacket pockets and found a wallet with a metal badge. It was the same badge you see on the cops in the street.'

'Was there an identity card with the badge?'

'What do you mean?'

'A card with a photo and some typed details.'

'Oh, yeah. There was.'

'Did you see a name?'

'Don't remember it. I told Emily.'

Harry was getting frustrated. His private fantasy about Lowe was in the ascendant.

'Come on, Madison. You must remember the name?'

Tanya leant across the table and touched Harry on the arm.

'Ease up, Harry.'

Harry bowed his head.

'I'm sorry, Madison.'

The young face looked again at him, another tear rolling out of the corner of her unbruised eye.

'I didn't take no notice of the name. I just saw the police badge and fuckin' panicked.'

'But you saw his face?'

'Well, yeah. He was fucking me, of course I saw his face. None of the arseholes tried to hide themselves.'

'Madison, what did he look like?'

'A bloke who was holding me down and fucking me, that's what he looked like.'

Harry was going to continue with the questions, but thought better of it.

'Okay, just a minute.'

Harry got up and went to his desk. He picked up a printout and came back to the couch. He handed the paper to Madison. It didn't quite fit the rules about photo-identification, but what the hell. Pay day was coming; Harry knew it in his gut.

'Is that him?'

Madison had frozen and the Internet photo of Lowe dropped to the ground.

'Madison?'

'Yeah, that's him. How did you know?'

'Because I work to catch these people.'

Madison stared at Harry.

'Won't help Caitlin, but, will it?'

Harry winced.

'No, but it might stop more Caitlins and more Madisons.'

The girl didn't answer, reaching rather for the cigarette packet and then lighting up.

He had pretty well satisfied himself that the girl was telling a true story, but any niggling doubts were suddenly put to rest. Madison had stopped looking at Harry and was regarding the carpet as she smoked. Emily reached over to Harry with a white slip of card in her hand.

'She got this out of the wallet the cop's badge was in.'

Harry took it and turned it over. It was a business card. He stared at a police logo and the name of Detective Commander Mervyn Lowe.

Harry immediately wanted to ask more questions about which church group and locations and the like, but he knew Madison was done. It was time for a doctor, and one he could trust. Then he needed to make sure she was safe. She obviously had not been supposed to live, and some very powerful people would be wanting to find her right now.

– 3 –

Harry was sitting on a plastic chair on the back verandah of a detached house in Alexandria having a smoke and staring into the Spartan back yard, deep in thought. Anyone driving down the street would be none the wiser from outside appearances, but the former home now contained a private medical clinic for sexual assault victims. Harry hadn't known of the place himself, since it hadn't been one used by the police dealing with rape cases in his day, but Tessa had mentioned it to him when she was talking about her cousin who was a doctor.

The clinic normally only dealt with adult victims, but Harry had known right from the end of Madison's account that there was no way he could take her to a hospital or government-run clinic. There'd be too many questions and too much chance of her name showing up for anyone in government circles who might be looking for her. Lowe, for a start, and who knew what other senior public figures were involved? Madison's details going into the Health Department's computers would be a red flag for the predators out there, circling for a kill.

So Harry had rung Tessa and oozed charm, apologies, promises, and then more charm, in that order. Five minutes later, Tessa had called him back, having teed up a discreet appointment with her medico cousin, Jenny, at this clinic. The next step had been for Harry to get the girls there. He'd figured a taxi, his normal mode of transport, simply and unnecessarily increased the risks, since it meant a cabbie who might talk as well as video footage from the cab's internal camera.

Instead, he'd called Trev and asked him to bring one of his VW surveillance vans. As he manoeuvred the girls out the back fire exit of his shabby office building to the waiting Caravelle, he thought Madison was going to do a bolt when she saw the open door into the side of the van. She had frozen in her steps. Who knew what memories the waiting van must have jogged? He had considered this problem when he had called Trev, but there really wasn't any viable alternative in the circumstances. Tanya had innately anticipated the scene and Harry had marvelled as she took hold of Madison, cuddling her and whispering in her ear, as she comforted her into the back of the van. And then they set off for Alexandria.

Harry's contemplation was interrupted by Trev returning to the verandah with two mugs of instant coffee.

'Here you go, Harry.'

'Thanks, Trev.'

Harry took a sip and put the mug down.

'Gotta say, Harry, good job the girl got Lowe's business card out of his wallet. Without that I don't think I'd be too ready to believe her, even knowing what I do.'

'Not wrong, mate. But it does all fit with what we know about Lowe.'

'For sure, but the whole scene she paints sounds far-fetched.'

'Yeah, but I do believe her.'

'Okay. Now what are we going to do?'

Harry looked quizzically over at Trev.

'Well, Harry, I thought you'd probably like a wingman on this one, and given what it is, or at least what it seems, I'm in. And completely free of charge.'

'Just as well, Trev, 'cos all there is in this job is risk, a lot of hard work, and then maybe, just maybe, a payoff of immense satisfaction. But it's a bloody long shot.'

'Mate, you can count on me.'

They shook on the deal.

Harry lit another cigarette. Trev held out his hand.

'I thought you were trying to give up?'

'Some days I am, mate, but today just ain't on that roster.'

Harry laughed and handed him the packet and the lighter. Trev lit up and closed his eyes as he inhaled deeply. His face bore the satisfaction that only a smoker has with that first lungful after a few days without.

'Trev, last time you did the surveillance on Lowe, was there any indication of him being tied in with a church of any sort?'

'Not that I can remember. And I think I would have noticed any connection like that, because it would have stuck out like dog's balls.'

'True. But that sort of link would be the start point. Because we're going to have to put together a whole lot of convincing evidence before we can take this to the Feds.'

'But they saw Lowe last time, so they know he's a rock spider.'

'Yeah, but let's face it; this story is like a Hollywood thriller. It'll take more than just Madison's statement to convince those Federal boys, no matter how eager they are.'

'Well, we do have Lowe's business card, and I'm sure the good doc in there will be finding plenty of medical evidence of sexual assault.'

'True on both counts, but let me play devil's advocate. Even if the AFP lads that we worked with do believe us, they will still have to convince their bosses. You know how the brass like to stick together, and the political fallout from this is potentially massive. If you were looking for doubts here, then I'd say Madison was raped by one of her mother's loser boyfriends, and I got hold of Lowe's card in order to boost her story. See? Suddenly not so plausible.'

'Point taken. So we need to work on Lowe's sudden religious devotion.'

'What's that church that the new Commissioner and her recently promoted sycophants are involved with?'

'It's one of those happy-clappy-type ones, evangelists with electric guitars and all that shit. Damn, just trying to remember ... Second Coming, something like that?'

'Yeah, um, Coming Lord, isn't it? The Church of the Coming Lord?'

'That's it, mate. Based out in the Hills bible belt. Cherrybrook, I think. You don't reckon the Commissioner would be involved, do you? Now there would be some fallout to match Hiroshima.'

'Shit, no. Definitely not. No, I think she's just a fanatical religious type. But I could see Lowe "finding Jesus" in order to advance his own career.'

'Well, I'd better start planning some serious surveillance. Sunday might be a logical starting point.'

'Definitely. Okay, we'll nut out the details after we offload these girls.'

At that point the back door opened and the doctor came out on to the verandah.

'Well, Harry, you were right to bring Madison for help. There's clear evidence of sexual penetration, both vaginal and anal. There's still some residue that's probably semen so

247

I've done the full rape kit with the swabs. The blood tests for STDs will take a few days to come back. From a medical perspective the physical evidence is consistent with what Madison says happened to her. And she's going to need counselling, too. A lot of it. She might seem fairly calm now, but that's largely due to the after effects of shock. This is going to hit her like a sledgehammer very soon.'

'Thanks, Doc. Is there any way that can be arranged on the quiet, at least for the moment?'

'Harry, I'm not at all comfortable with this. I might be doing a favour for Tess, but you know that I have to report child abuse cases.'

'Doc, I know. And I don't want you to be in any trouble, but we just need some leeway here. You do have some time to report, don't you?'

'Well, sort of. "As soon as practicable" is what the legislation says.'

'Can you just hold off a week or two? That should give us enough time to get the evidence we need to take to the Federal Police, assuming we're going to get the evidence.'

Jenny grimaced and dropped her eyes to the old timber floorboards. Then she looked back at Harry.

'Okay, Harry. If what Madison says is true, then I certainly want to see the bastards caught. But you need to let me know as soon as you are ready, so I can do my official notification. I'm already sticking my neck out here for treating a juvenile.'

'Of course, Doc. And we'll have Madison in a safe place in the meantime. If you can arrange a counsellor then we can arrange them to meet.'

'No problems, I'll see what I can do.'

Harry shook Jenny's hand.

'Thank you, Doc. I really appreciate this.'

'Okay. The girls are ready when you guys are.'

Jenny turned and walked back into the clinic.

Harry pulled out his phone. He made a call to Sandrine, the Tunisian temptress, and turned on the charm.

'My darling Sandrine, I am in need of your specialist assistance.'

'Harry, always a pleasure to hear from you. Anything I can do, happy to help. After all you did for me with that disgusting policeman, Lowe.'

'Actually, it's sort of to do with him again, but most of the detail will need to wait for later. Meantime, I need to hide two girls.'

'Harry, you are a very interesting man. What can I do?'

Harry proceeded to give an abbreviated summary of the situation.

Fifteen minutes later they dropped Em and Madison off at an address in Surry Hills. It was a safe house used by Sandrine and other madams in the business as a refuge for sex workers being stalked or otherwise persecuted by psychologically unhinged clients. Sandrine had assured Harry the girls would be totally safe and completely undetectable there.

Next, Harry and Trev dropped Tanya off at the Scarlet Boudoir, so she could explain Em's absence. Tanya gave Harry a kiss on the cheek, leaning in the window of the front passenger door of the rather dilapidated Caravelle van, and told him to call her the next day. Harry and Trev then headed for Harry's office to plan their campaign, and raid the bottom drawer of Harry's desk.

— 4 —

The car park at the Church of the Coming Lord on a Sunday afternoon looked more like the senior officers' section at Police HQ. Harry and Trev were secreted in the back of Trev's dark grey Volkswagen Transporter, his brand new surveillance van, on a rise a couple of hundred metres away. It seemed that just about every second or third car had the giveaway extra aerial. It was still light, just after 4 p.m., and sunset would be about five. The cloudless sky meant probably another couple of hours of visibility. Trev had set up a Sony digital video camera on a mount bolted to the van floor, with its 25x zoom lens trained on the church through the van's back window. He was watching the image on his Mac laptop, whilst Harry preferred the old fashioned binoculars.

'Tell you what, Trev, this new Police Force is a far cry from the old days.'

'Not bloody wrong, Harry, but I'm not sure it's really an improvement.'

'Yeah. Same lack of talent, same egos, just different idols to worship.'

'Well, at least we know Lowe is in there. It'll be interesting to see who he talks to on the way out.'

Trev adjusted the camera lens and the image on the laptop grew larger.

'Even more interesting that he didn't park anywhere near most of the other brass.'

'Oh, well, as they say in the army, "let's hurry up and wait".'

An hour and a half later the front doors of the church burst open and the pious throng began to emerge. Harry grabbed the binoculars and focused on the crowd in the fading twilight.

'Okay, there he is. You got him, Trev?'

'Sure have, mate. And we're recording.'

Trev now controlled the camera from his keyboard, as deftly as a concert pianist, zooming in on Lowe and those heads close to him. Lowe and three other men, all middle-aged like him, were talking in a small huddled group.

'Doesn't he look like a good little boy,' said Harry.

'Doesn't he just.'

'And with all his respectable god-fearing mates clutching their bibles.'

'Well, I'm sure it's not doing his career any harm at all.'

'We'll have to see about that. I rather fancy myself as his next career event.'

Harry leant forward squeezing the binoculars to his eyes.

'Now what the fuck are they up to?'

Trev peered at the Mac screen, touching some more buttons.

'Harry, something's happening, mate. They've just swapped bibles, Lowe and the guy directly in front of him. It was smooth, but it definitely was a swap.'

'Shit, missed that. Too busy looking at the heads. Oh, now they're moving.'

Lowe and his entourage headed their separate ways into the lines of cars.

'Keep watching the bald one in the dark tweed jacket. He's the one who swapped bibles with Lowe.'

'Okay, got him. He's just unlocking that old metallic blue Commodore. You see him? It's about five cars in from the end of the row.'

'On him now. Okay, can't see the rego from here, so we'll have to grab it as he comes out. We may as well follow him since we already know where Lowe lives.'

'Sweet. You want me to drive?'

'Get her started, Harry. I'll grab a camera.'

Harry squeezed between the seats into the driver's side and fired up the van. Trev grabbed the laptop and a Pentax digital SLR and eased through into the passenger's seat. He put the laptop between his feet and readied the camera. As the blue Commodore pulled out into the road, Harry moved off at a discreet distance from its rear end. Trev was zooming in with the Pentax and clicking away.

'Cool, got the plate. Okay, let's not lose him. I know you're probably a bit out of practice on this side of things. Pretend it's one of those glamorous babes you're always chasing.'

'Smart-arse.'

They headed east in silence, the Commodore in sight, for the best part of ten minutes. Trev broke the peace.

'Mate, there's something going on with those bibles I reckon.'

'You absolutely sure they swapped?'

'I'll show you at the next lights.'

Trev reached down and retrieved the laptop. He flipped open the lid and cued up the relevant footage. As Harry pulled to a stop at the next red light, four cars behind their target, Trev pressed play and put the screen in front of Harry.

'Watch. It's very quick and very discreet, but definitely happening.'

Harry squinted at the screen.

'Shit, yes. Well spotted, mate.'

There was a beep from behind them and Harry looked up to see open tarmac in front. The target had turned onto the Pacific Highway, heading north, and Harry accelerated into the intersection to follow. Harry was pondering, brow furrowed, as he paid attention to the traffic.

'Maybe they pass messages in them?'

'Yeah, could be. Or maybe there are photos inside. I remember doing a few warrants on peds' houses back home and it was quite common to hide child porn pictures inside normal looking books.'

'True. But that'd be a bit old school now, don't you reckon?'

'Yeah, you're probably right. What the hell would it be?'

Trev hummed as he tapped his fingers on the lid of the laptop. After a few seconds, he turned to Harry and smiled.

'Mate, we need to get that bible, that's what we bloody need.'

Harry chuckled and half turned towards him.

'O, behave, Trev. You're not suggesting a bit of good old fashioned larceny, are you?'

'That's exactly what I'm suggesting.'

'All right. I'm all ears. Anything that helps to nail that prick Lowe is good with me, legal or not. So what evil plot is festering in that devious mind, Trev?'

'Well, a kindred devious spirit like you will appreciate this.'

'Fucking idiot!' shouted Harry as he swerved to avoid a car cutting in front of them without indicating. He resisted the temptation to lean on the horn as he didn't want to draw unnecessary attention.

'Sorry, mate. Do go on.'

'Well, the preferable plan is we're going to have to hope he stops somewhere before home, gets out of the car, and leaves the bible briefly. Then we get into the car, easy enough on that old model, grab the bible and get the hell out of there.'

'Yeah, but one problem there, Trev. He's going to come back to the car, see that it's only the bible missing, and get mighty suspicious about that. We don't want the balloon going up, at least not until we know what these bastards are up to.'

'Yeah, true. Just thinking that one through myself.'

Trev pulled a packet of Marlboros out of his pocket and lit two at the same time, passing one to Harry as he drew back on the other. Harry took the smoke and lowered the window slightly.

'Well, Trev, just to join you down in your felonious little sewer, as I wouldn't want you to get lonely, mate, we could actually take the bloody car.'

'Ooh, I like it! And then we should probably torch it so there's no clue left as to what, if anything, was stolen from the inside. Just another shithead juvenile car thief looking for a few more hours community service.'

'I guess it does make sense. Assuming he's a ped as well, I'm certainly not going to lose any sleep over doing the car.'

'Me neither. We just have to hope he stops before home, because he sure as hell won't leave the bible in the car then. It'll be straight inside for whatever putrid pleasure awaits amongst the prophets. And I'm not too keen on trying to do a break and enter on the house.'

'True. Bit more problematic, that one. You remember how to hotwire one of those Commodores?'

'Piece of piss, mate. Like riding a bike. Now, just don't lose him.'

It was getting dark now so Harry moved up to only two cars behind the Commodore.

They passed through Hornsby and kept heading north. Then Lady Luck smiled upon them. As they came into Asquith, the Commodore slowed, indicated left, and pulled into the car park of a supermarket.

'You little beauty,' sighed Harry.

'I think we're on a winner here, Harry. Okay, he's pulling into a spot over there. Let's hang back until he goes into the shops.'

The Commodore stopped and Mr Tweed Jacket got out, closing the door. As he walked towards the shop doors he pulled a piece of paper out of his inside jacket pocket.

'That's probably a shopping list,' said Trev.

'So he might be a little while in there.'

'Yep, and he doesn't appear to have a bible with him. All right, Harry, you sit tight here so the van doesn't get seen on any CCTV cameras at the shop doors, and then follow me out.'

Harry grinned. 'Good luck, you scumbag car thief.'

Trev smiled in return. 'All for a good cause.'

Trev grabbed a flat bladed screwdriver and some rigid packing tape and put them in his pocket. He got out of the van and walked purposefully towards the shops. He then ducked between some cars and arrived next to the Commodore's driver's door. Harry could only see Trev's head and shoulders, so missed his actual handiwork, but Trev was into the car in under ten seconds. Fifteen seconds after that the tail-lights of the Commodore lit up, followed by the reversing lights. The car started to back out of the parking spot.

'You bloody champion, Trev,' said Harry as he restarted the van. Harry let Trev leave the car park and turn south on the highway, before he moved off and followed. He caught up to the car about two hundred metres down the road. His phone rang. He answered it.

'Nice work, Trev. Definitely not your first time.'

Trev laughed. 'You don't want to know, mate. Now, I was thinking we need some nice quiet industrial zone.'

'What about that one out the back of Hornsby, on the way to Waitara?'

'Cool. See you there.'

They rang off and the two vehicles headed back into Hornsby. The light industrial area was deserted and poorly lit, ideal for the job at hand. Trev pulled over and Harry stopped behind him. Trev got out of the car and walked back to the van. He leaned on the sill of the driver's window.

'Mate, the bible's in the car, in the door pouch. I'm just going for a walk down that next side lane to make sure there are no cameras anywhere. If it's all clear, we'll take the Commodore down there. Chuck us that cap over there, Harry.'

Harry passed a dark baseball cap to Trev who slipped it on and pulled the visor well down. He strode off to the corner and disappeared down the lane. Harry was tempted to light a smoke, he was gagging for one, but thought he'd better wait. Two minutes later Trev was back.

'It's bloody perfect. No cameras on any of the premises and the only street light is out. Just let me grab the bible and anything else of interest. Mate, grab us some gloves from the centre console there.'

Harry found the forensic cotton gloves and passed them to Trev, along with two paper evidence bags.

'Mate, the fire will sort out any of your prints.'

'Yeah, but this is just on the off chance that there are any useable prints on or in the bible. You never know.'

Trev slipped on the gloves as he went back to the Commodore. He got back into the car and rummaged around. Then he went to the boot, prised it open and looked inside. He was back within three minutes, a broad grin on his face. He proffered one of the bags to Harry who peered inside it. A black leather-bound bible was in the bag.

'Fucking bingo.'

'Beautiful work. What else you got?' Trev passed the second bag to Harry.

'Rego papers from the glove box, so we've got a name and address, as I'm guessing he does own the car. Nothing else of interest, zilch in the boot.'

'Rego papers are a nice little bonus. So you want me to stay here while you do the deed?'

'Yes, mate, you keep the van running and keep an eye out. I'll just grab what I need from the back.'

Trev opened the side door of the van and climbed in. He grabbed a brown bottle of liquid, some rags, and a box of matches. Harry looked enquiringly at the bottle.

'Pure alcohol. I use it for cleaning my surveillance gear. It happens to burn beautifully, and starts gently. Arsonist's nectar. I'll be back.'

Trev gently closed the van's side door behind him, got back into the idling Commodore, and drove it around the corner into the laneway. He parked next to the dumpsters at the end of the lane and got out. He opened all the doors, to make it look like there had been multiple joyriders. After splashing the pure alcohol on the seats, the carpet, the dash and the steering wheel, he got his screwdriver out and used it to break open the petrol filler cap. He took a length of rag, soaked it in alcohol, and fed it down the petrol tank filler tube. Finished, he went back to the driver's door and pulled out the box of matches. He struck one and dropped it flaming onto the driver's seat, which immediately started to burn. He struck a second match and lit the tuft of rag hanging out of the petrol tank. Then he bolted up the laneway as fast as his middle-aged legs would carry him. He got around the corner to the Volkswagen van and jumped into the passenger seat, dropping the empty alcohol bottle at his feet. He was breathing hard, but grinning like a boarding school boy who's just seen matron's knickers.

'Let's go!'

Harry did a U-turn and they sped off up the quiet street.

Harry laughed. 'Mate, as only the bloody coppers could say, we are decamping the scene!'

Trev roared laughing, half wheezing. 'Yeah, I've always thought they must have been up all night thinking that word up.'

'Well, back at my office there is fine whiskey awaiting a couple of thirsty decamping gumshoes. Meantime, let's have a bloody smoke, I'm desperate!'

As they lit up, they heard a distinctive "kerthump" as the Commodore's petrol tank exploded.

'And there are cigars *chez moi*, too.'

Trev grinned as he blew smoke across the dashboard.

'Well, then, to your place, chariot driver! And don't spare the horses.'

The pair headed south for the city.

– 5 –

Harry plonked two Cavan crystal tumblers on his desk, grabbed the bottle of Jameson from his bottom drawer and poured two very healthy doses. The stolen bible sat on a side table with its leather cover open, revealing a cut out rectangle in the middle in which sat a 32GB USB stick. Harry had taken a video of Trev pulling the bible out of the paper evidence bag and opening it up to find the hidden item. Trev was now opening up a case of technical gear which Harry didn't recognize. He handed Trev one of the glasses.

'Thanks, Harry, I bloody need this.'

'Oh, yeah. This is going to go down better than a stripper and a sack of cash at a Cabinet meeting.'

They chinked glasses.

Trev smiled and said, 'Here's to scumbag car thieves.'

Harry chuckled. 'So what's this gear?'

'A forensic computing setup. I'm going to mirror image the USB stick and then the original gets preserved as untainted evidence. We can then work off the copy.'

'I think we should make a spare copy, too, Trev.'

'Why?'

'Call me paranoid, but just an insurance copy to go into my safe. We don't know how this is going to pan out, and I'd hate to see anything incriminating Lowe go "missing" further down the track.'

'Not paranoid, Harry, just a realist. I'll do a second copy.'

Trev drained his glass and put it on the desk.

'Another, mate?' Harry grinned as he poured.

'Do bears shit in the woods?'

Trev took another swig before putting the glass down and slipping on the cotton forensic gloves again. He took the USB stick out of its holy receptacle and plugged it into a lead coming out of one of the boxes inside the case. He then tapped some keystrokes on the keyboard of the connected laptop and turned back to Harry, taking off the gloves. He picked up his drink and lit a cigarette from Harry's packet of Marlboros on the desk.

'Okay, we'll let that run and then see what's on it.'

'And you never know your luck in the big city. There might even be usable prints on the bible pages. What do you reckon?'

'Hoping so. The leather cover's a bit too rough in texture, but I reckon a good fingerprint man might be able to do something with the pages and some ninhydrin.'

'How long will that take?' Harry pointed at the computer gear, which was making periodic electronic noises.

'Only about twenty minutes. Less if the stick isn't full.'

Trev swallowed his whiskey and put the glass down. 'Barman.'

Harry tipped his down his gullet and poured two more.

'So, Harry, assuming there is evidence on this USB ...'

Harry interrupted, laughing. 'Mate, given the means of concealment and transmission I think we can safely assume we're not about to see some reruns of *The Brady Bunch.*'

'Agreed. So what's the plan?'

'The Feds. Has to be. Same as last time we had something on Lowe. Police Internal Affairs are a waste of space and/or crooked themselves.'

'But even with them, they're still not likely to want to protect a ped in their ranks.'

'No, but the powers that be will want to protect the reputation of the Police Force.'

'They're a bit bloody late for that, aren't they?'

Harry let out a wry snort. 'Mate, the best we could hope, if it doesn't completely vanish, is for a quiet discharge of Lowe for "family reasons", or some such shit.'

'What about the Integrity Commission?'

'Nah. They're about as effective as a box of wet tissues in a wank-tank.'

'Nice, Harry, nice.'

At that point, a beep sounded from Trev's box of tricks and he turned to his MacBook Pro.

'And we're done. The contents of the USB are now on this baby, complete and unadulterated.'

'So you now make the copies?'

'That can be done anytime since it's all on the hard drive in here.' Trev tapped the laptop.

'Well, we'd better have a look, mate, but I'll pour us another Jameson first. I think we might be needing it.'

'I've got a nasty feeling you're right.'

Harry refilled both their crystal tumblers and passed Trev's back to him. Harry lit a smoke and Trev opened the video file now showing on his computer.

An image appeared on the screen, accompanied by some jumbled noises on the audio track. Trev maximized the screen and adjusted the volume setting upwards. They were looking at a dimly lit room in what looked like an old colonial era house. The skirting boards were tall and carved at the top and there were wooden picture rails around the upper parts of the walls. There was a cheap three-seater couch towards the back of the room, definitely not colonial, and this occupied the centre of the video frame. The stillness and the angle of the image indicated the camera was firmly planted on a tripod opposite the couch. Adult male voices could be heard indistinctly in the background. The sounds suddenly grew louder and amongst their deep plangent tones a child's plaintive voice could be discerned. Then, an adult male body with a towel wrapped around the waist came into view. The man's left hand was propelling forward a young girl. She was wearing just a dirty white nightie and had long blonde hair tied back in a ponytail.

'Get on the couch.' The man's voice was smooth and well-enunciated. It was unmistakably an Australian accent, but one of those plummy ones attempting to sound upper crust English. The girl was firmly shoved towards the couch and she turned as she sat, or fell, down, hands clasping her knees which were clamped together. The young, innocent face looked up.

'Jesus wept,' spat Trev. 'You okay to do this, Harry?'

'Gonna have to be, mate. This is a job that needs to be done.'

The girl was fair-skinned and no more than ten or eleven. Her eyes were puffy and fresh tears were now running down her cheeks. She was alternately sniffling and snorting as she struggled to control her breathing. There were red welts on her left cheek, as if she'd been repeatedly slapped across her face. A second male voice, less refined and still off-camera, growled, 'Take off your nightie, Skye.'

The terrified girl desperately shook her head and clutched her knees even tighter. Plummy Voice, standing near the couch, said, 'Come on, Skye. Don't make me slap you again.'

She looked up at Plummy through her watery eyes. Her face, amongst all the fear, looked hesitant, as if wondering whether compliance or pain was the better option. Or maybe she was utterly overwhelmed and confused. The decision was then made for her.

Two more male bodies, towels around their waists, entered the frame and a third voice spoke to the trembling girl.

'Take it off now.'

'Fuck, I think that's Lowe,' gasped Harry. He didn't need to wait for the proof.

Man number three stepped over to the couch and bent down to the girl. The resultant view of the head was a rear-oriented profile shot, but there was no mistaking Detective Commander Mervyn Lowe. He grabbed the girl's ponytail in his left hand, pulling her head back. With his right hand he grabbed the front of the neckline of her nightie. He gave a sudden violent tug downwards and the nightie ripped off the now almost catatonic child.

Lowe hissed to the girl, 'Next time, do as you're fucking told.'

He released her hair, stood up, and turned around. The towel around his waist couldn't hide his erection.

In the next instant, the three predators were on to the now silent girl, like jackals gorging on a downed gazelle.

Harry and Trev spent most of the next ten minutes looking into the bottoms of their glasses, which had a hefty refill halfway through. There was the occasional glance at the hideous scene and then it was back to concentrating on the whiskey and the Marlboros. On screen, the three peds moved off camera, their monstrous frenzy finished. The trio had variously grunted or groaned aloud with their orgasms, and now some lascivious mutterings of satisfaction were partly audible.

The girl had been raped in every way possible and now lay spread-eagled on the couch, looking as if she had passed out. Harry hoped it had been very early in the piece.

'We have to nail these mongrel dogs.'

'We will, if it's the last thing we ever fucking do.'

Nothing moved on the screen.

'Is that finished now?' asked Harry. 'I've had a gutful.'

'Mate, the play bar indicates we're only half-way through, unless the rest is just the camera left running with the girl passed out.'

'Let's hope so. Here, pass me your glass.'

Harry refilled both tumblers and gave Trev's back to him.

'Thanks, mate.'

They both looked back at the screen. The unconscious girl remained strewn on the couch.

'So this should be enough to take Lowe down,' said Trev.

'Reckon so.'

Before their conversation could continue, from the screen there was the sound of a door opening and a dragging noise. They turned back to the laptop.

A large, heavily-muscled male body dressed in black leather loomed into the scene. Tight leather pants and a leather sleeveless top were visible, as were numerous tattoos on both biceps and forearms. Most strikingly was an SS lightning tattoo on the right bicep, standing out on the well-defined muscles. From the man's left hand trailed a bunched bundle of heavy-duty black plastic. The girl hadn't moved. Initially, the leather-clad gorilla seemed oblivious to her. He spread out the plastic sheeting on the ground at the foot of the couch. As he bent down to do it, the back of a shaved head was in camera shot, as was a tattoo across the back of his cranium, *'Gott Mit Uns'.* Once the black sheet was laid out, Mr Third Reich stepped over to the couch and grabbed the girl's ponytail with his left hand. As he hauled her soiled little body off the couch, there was a faint opening of her eyes, but that was all to indicate she was even alive. He dragged her into the middle of the plastic, pulled a dagger from a scabbard on his belt with his right hand, and cut her throat from left to right, as routinely as if he was buttering his breakfast toast. As her blood sprayed onto the plastic sheet, he dropped her head and stepped back. He wiped the knife blade clean across her buttocks.

Neither Harry nor Trev could manage a word, let alone an expletive. Even their tumblers and cigarettes were suspended in mid-air.

The killer pulled the four corners of the plastic sheet over the top of the butchered girl and proceeded to tie her up in a dark, disposable bundle. Then he dragged her off camera and presumably out of the room. After about twenty seconds the video image went to fuzz.

Harry looked slowly over at Trev.

'And what the fuck story are we going to give to the Feds?'

Trev stood up suddenly and lurched towards the desk. He puked loudly into the wastepaper bin.

'Sorry, mate.' Trev lit a smoke, and drew back heavily whilst swishing around a mouthful of Jameson to rinse away the vomit taste.

'No worries, mate, pretty bloody close myself. I'm just

trying to fathom why they'd have left the camera running for the killing? It wouldn't interest most peds, if that's their target market.'

'No,' Trev replied, 'but it would interest certain others with more bloodthirsty cravings. There's a whole market for snuff movies, don't forget.'

'Yeah, I know that. But the risk for the peds on this one, faces and all …'

Trev interrupted. 'I reckon this is an inadvertently unedited version, been released too quickly, or maybe too eagerly. I reckon the scum running this enterprise are peddling both child porn and snuff movies. This particular one simply failed to get edited into its two respective versions.'

Harry pondered as he sipped his whiskey.

'Okay, I'll buy that hypothesis. Now, we need to sort out a story. We're going to have to visit the Feds in the morning.'

'Yep. Take it I can crash at your place? Don't think I'll be driving the van again tonight.'

'Shit yeah. Let's head there now and work on our script.'

Trev rushed for the bin and puked again.

– 6 –

The following morning Harry and Trev were standing in the foyer of the AFP Headquarters in Goulburn Street, waiting for their ten o'clock appointment. Outside, the wintry rain was making a grey part of the city even bleaker. At ten precisely, Federal Agent Tom Strong came through the security barrier and strode up to Harry.

'G'day, Harry, always glad to see you.'

'You might not be glad this time, but thanks for making the time.'

They shook hands. Tom looked at Trev, with that silent appraising look perfected by detectives the world over.

'Tom, this is Trev, a mate of mine who used to be in the job.'

Tom extended his hand, still inspecting.

'Tom Strong.'

Trev shook his hand.

'Trevor Matson. I was a Detective Sergeant in Brisbane, but don't hold that against me.'

The three laughed. Tom's expression eased from appraisal to a flicker of recognition.

'Not the Trevor Matson? The man who blew the lid off the crime stats cover-up when the Queensland government was coming into the election lead-up?'

Trev looked a little sheepish.

'Yeah, that one. I hope that's not a problem.'

'Hardly, mate. What you did took real guts. I wish I had that level of courage. Guess it screwed up your pension, though?'

'And how. But I'm doing all right down here, making ends meet and back on my feet.'

'Glad to hear it. Okay, gents, let's head upstairs. Can't wait to hear what you've got for us this time, Harry.'

Harry and Trev glanced at each other nervously as they followed Tom through the security gates and towards the lifts.

Upstairs in Tom's office coffee was made, at least the instant variety, and they sat down around Tom's desk, stacks of files all over it.

'Okay, Harry, what's the go?'

Harry swigged a mouthful of coffee, swallowed loudly and took a deep breath.

'This is fucking huge, Tom. Abso-fucking-lutely huge.'

He paused. Tom just looked at him impassively.

'We've got Lowe good and proper this time. And others.'

'I'm listening. But I hope this is not you chasing a personal vendetta, Harry, much as we know he's a ped.'

'Believe me, mate, we've got it in black and white. Well, sordid colour actually. And it's worse than rooting kids. They're killing them afterwards.'

Tom almost choked on a mouthful of Nescafé.

'Fair suck of the sav, Harry. We all know it's very rare for peds to kill their victims, too.'

'Yeah, that's right. But we all also know it does happen. The three of us in here have all seen ped snuff movies before.'

Tom pulled an ugly face, and Trev grimaced as well. Tom continued.

'Sadly, yes,' said Tom. 'So I suppose you're going to tell me you've seen a snuff movie with Lowe in it, screwing some poor kid and then killing them.'

'Apart from Lowe doing the actual killing, yes, that is exactly what I'm telling you.'

Tom Strong sat in stunned silence, looking first at Harry, then at Trev, and then back to Harry.

'Trev, the goods,' said Harry.

Trev put a large brown envelope on the desk and pulled a USB stick out of his inside coat pocket.

'The original, and I mean original, is inside a bible in that envelope. All forensically handled, at least by us two. This USB is a copy for you to view.'

Trev handed it across the desk.

'And how may I ask …'

Harry interrupted. 'We'll explain that after you've seen the footage.'

Tom looked at the USB, lying in the palm of his large, muscular hand. His face was torn between an expression of professional interest, the driving curiosity of all good detectives, and a resigned dread, as if the plastic chunk was a letter from a lawyer's office.

He looked back at Harry and Trev, saying nothing. Harry said nothing either, just motioned to Tom's computer on the right hand side of the desk. Tom looked back at the USB and then moved over to his PC. He inserted the USB and tapped the mouse.

'I hope you didn't have a big greasy breakfast,' said Trev, finally puncturing the silence. Tom looked at him a little ruefully, then back at the screen. The silence resumed until the film footage started, with its predatory and carnal soundtrack.

Fifteen minutes later, the silence again descended. No one spoke. Tom was looking decidedly queasy and staring fixedly at the screen, which had now reverted to his desktop and police badge screensaver. Harry and Trev both looked fixedly at Tom. It could have been a shot from a cinematic Mexican standoff. All that was missing was a howling wind and the tumbleweed.

Finally Tom swivelled in his chair and looked at Harry and Trev.

'I need a fucking smoke. And I was trying to give up. Fuck you, Harry.'

'Sorry, mate. But it's job on, what can I say?'

'Damn right it's job on. All right, let's go downstairs for a real coffee and a smoke. I'm sick of this swill.'

'I still remember the International Roast in our squad rooms,' lamented Harry.

'And lest we forget the ubiquitous Pablo,' added Trev.

Tom stood up. 'Yeah, well you state boys never did have our class, we even run to Gold Blend nowadays.' The three laughed.

Tom picked up the brown envelope. He went to the left of his desk and opened a filing cabinet safe. The envelope disappeared inside, the drawer closed, and Tom spun the combination wheel. The USB went into his shirt pocket. The trio then went out of the office.

Five minutes later they were huddled in the laneway next to the building with cappuccinos from the café down the street, all drawing hard on cigarettes. Harry and Trev were both silent, like two prankster schoolboys waiting for the principal's interrogation, hoping they had sufficiently colluded on their accounts. Actually, they had decided that Harry would be the sole spokesperson, to avoid any errors. Tom finally assumed the role of schoolmaster.

'All right, then, just how did you two bastards get hold of that film?'

It was a fair enough question, thought Harry. It's just that there was simply no fair answer. Harry looked directly at Tom.

'I'm not going to bullshit you, Tom.' Harry paused and had a drag on his smoke.

'It wasn't exactly legal, can we leave it at that?'

'Jesus wept, Harry. What do you expect me to …'

'Mate,' interjected Harry, 'the bloke we "obtained" this from is not likely to be reporting it missing. There might possibly be some report about his car, but, hey, that can easily disappear into the stats. Besides, the local boys aren't going to even read another incident report about a missing car, let alone get off their arses to do anything about it.'

'Granted. But, Harry, how …'

'Tom, come on, mate. You know we're not going to go into that. We got the film, and that's all there is to it. We do have the identity of the man who had the film, though, and his vehicle rego and address. Upstairs we'll give you all the background on the surveillance we did, including Lowe passing him that bible now in your safe. Even if you can't directly use the film evidence, it will give you guys everything you need to start a ball-tearer of an operation.'

'Double fuck you, Harry. This is going to cause a real shitstorm. You're really stretching the friendship here.'

Tom paused, brooding over his coffee. Then, as he pondered, and despite himself, he couldn't help the slow grin that emerged on his face.

'But this is going to be the operation of my career. I can smell it. You boys are sailing very bloody close to the wind, though. You know Lowe's got friends high up and I've got to come up with a version of how I came by this film.'

Harry frowned and pursed his lips.

'What about an anonymous informant who happened

to get it from an associate who happened to like early model Commodores. And in spite of his own delinquent habits he happens to definitely not like rock spiders. So when he saw what was on the film, he had to do his civic duty.'

'Yeah, right. That story will smell worse than a dunny in a dodgy Indian restaurant.'

'But smelly doesn't matter as long as it can't be challenged successfully.'

'This isn't the old days, Harry, please.'

'Old days, new days, right days, wrong days, whatever. This particular shitty Sydney day we've got a paedophile senior cop going for best supporting actor in a child porn snuff movie. It'll be the end of fucking days when that's acceptable or tolerated.'

Tom nodded grimly.

'Let's forget the legal and ethical ambiguities, Tom. You, me and Trev all know those arguments are for the wankers who never have to deal with the issues out here in Realworldsville.'

Tom's face showed he knew when he was beaten. He was about to open his mouth when Harry got in first.

'And don't worry about the "triple fuck you, Harry", it's a given.'

Tom smiled and shook his head.

'There are times when I feel some nostalgia for the old days, mate, for sure.'

'You're in good company there,' said Harry.

Trev nodded solemnly.

Tom looked at both of them. 'All right, let's go back upstairs and you can fill me in on the rest.'

The three sleuths, now conspirators, marched back into the police building.

– 7 –

Two mornings later Harry was parked at his desk in his office labouring through some overdue business compliance paperwork. Sipping on a flat white from the café across the street and chewing on a *pain au chocolat,* he muttered expletives to himself as he lamented how bureaucratic and over-regulated Australia had become. His mood immediately brightened as he recognized the melodically seductive knock on his office door. He didn't bother calling out, just flicked the release switch and in floated Tanya. The very beautiful Tanya, mused Harry.

'Hey, Mr PI. Imagining me naked again?'

Harry tried not to look abashed, but failed entirely, as always.

She grinned and sat down opposite him, putting her coffee on the desk. She pulled her cigarettes out of her bag and lit up.

'Good morning, my divine one. How's life?'

'Not bad, Harry, overall. Any news on the case? And don't give me any of that need to know bullshit.' She stuck her tongue out playfully.

'My Tanya, as if I would.'

'So let's hear it, otherwise I'll come around that side of the desk and tease you into a gibbering wreck.'

'Well, I might just clam up then.'

Harry could feel his loins already. This girl did it every bloody time.

Tanya's expression said she knew she had the aces. She just smiled and poked the tip of her tongue out again. Harry lit a smoke to calm his blood pressure.

'Okay. Everything is well on track. Let me fill you in.'

He then brought her up to speed on all the events leading up to the meeting with the Feds, this time not omitting the more nefarious exploits. When he had finished, Tanya beamed at him in admiration.

'I can't believe you and Trev torched the car as well. Harry, you rock. Seriously.'

Harry tried his best modest face.

'Well, when it comes to fighting the good fight, a man's gotta stand up. Anything less and you join the brigade of wimps, wankers, and bureaucrats.'

She smiled. 'And politicians?'

'I put them in with the bureaucrats. Same breed, just different method of getting there.'

'So what now?'

'Well, we just have to play the waiting game for the Feds. It won't be quick as they have a shitload of work to do on it. But rest assured, my Tanya, there's going to be a hell of a result on this one. By the way, how's Madison going? You spoken to her?'

'Yeah, I check in with her every day. She's doing all right, considering.'

'Good, good. If she needs anything else, don't hesitate to sing out.'

'Thanks, Harry, you've been great. I'll let you know if there's anything.'

She paused and lit another cigarette.

'Harry, I wanted to have a chat and get some advice from someone I trust.'

Harry blushed slightly.

'Hey, anything for you, you know that.'

Tanya dropped her eyes momentarily.

'Well, we don't have our dad and we're a bit short on solid grown-up support, you know?'

'Yeah, too true. So, gorgeous one, is there a problem? Someone giving you grief? Happy to help on that score anytime.'

She looked back up and smiled at him.

'My knight in shining armour, hey?'

Harry chuckled.

'Pretty tarnished armour, actually, but the underlying chivalry is alive and well.'

'That's good to know, my Mr PI, and I might need to call on that soon, but that's not the problem I wanted to chat about.'

She drew hard on her cigarette, and the exhaled smoke rolled over Harry like a sorceress's spell.

'Sasha and I need to figure out where we're going longer term.'

'Okay, always good thinking.' Harry momentarily reflected that he could take his own advice.

'Well, we need to broaden our horizons and get some professional skills.'

'Babe, you're not short on skills, believe me.'

'Fuck you, Harry. I need your advice, get serious.'

Her slight smile tempered the reproof.

'Sorry. Facetious is in my Irish genes.'

'Yeah, and I love that, usually. But listen to me, please.'

'Shoot.'

'Well, neither of us want to keep working on our backs for ever.'

She caught his eye.

'Or on all fours,' said Tanya.

'Touché.'

'It's fine at the moment, most of the punters are okay and the money is great. But we're not going to be doing this in ten years' time.'

'So, thoughts? Interests?'

'I think I told you once that we're both keen on fashion.'

'Yes, you did tell me. Might have been on one of those horizontal occasions.'

'Smart-arse. Well, we're putting ourselves through a TAFE diploma in fashion design, but it's a bloody hard gig to break into, job-wise. I guess I want to know your thoughts on how we should go about it, and maybe if you have any contacts.'

She looked down again.

'Sometimes I feel a bit lost and alone, except for Sasha, of course.'

A tear started to run down her cheek.

'And you, Harry.'

'I'll be here for you as long as my arse points to the ground, Tanya. You and Sasha.'

She looked up and reached her hand across the desk. Harry leant in and held it between both of his.

'Now, I may seem as close to the world of Armani and Dior as the average politician is to honesty, but I may actually be able to help on this.'

'Really?'

'Firstly, you should definitely pursue your passion, Tanya. I haven't always, and I've regretted it, every single time. Secondly, I happen to be friends with a lady in the rag trade.'

'Truly? You, Harry?'

'Indeed. Your Harry has a surprisingly wide range of contacts.'

'Friend or fuck buddy, Mr PI?'

Harry put on a look of appalled indignation.

'Oh, my! Much maligned and little understood!'

Tanya laughed, still holding Harry's hands.

'Harry, I would never malign you, and I understand you absolutely perfectly. You're a decent guy who loves good living and a lot of shagging.'

Harry withdrew his hands gently, then held them up beside his head and smiled.

'I plead guilty, your Honour.'

'So, who is your "friend"?'

'Tessa runs her own fashion house, here in Sydney.'

Tanya's eyes widened like a child being handed candyfloss at the fair for the first time.

'Cool. And do you think ...'

'Absolutely. I'm actually having a drink with her on Friday, so I will kick start your career planning then.'

'Harry, you really do rock. When do I get dinner?'

'Ah, well that could be arranged.'

'But you're obviously a man in demand.'

'For you, it can always be arranged.'

With that Tanya came around the desk and plonked herself in Harry's lap. Without a word she wrapped her arms around his neck, locked her lips onto his, and kissed him long and hard. She pulled back to take a breath, smiling at him.

'Now I know that is definitely not your Smith and Wesson I can feel.'

'No, but it's still dangerous.'

'Have you ever fucked on your own desk?'

Harry swallowed hard.

'Actually, no.'

'You mean to tell me that a man of your pussy-loving ways hasn't even christened his own workbench?'

Harry shook his head.

'No, that delicious opportunity has just never presented itself.'

'Now, I know that door is locked, so you've got precisely ten seconds to make your move or this very delicious opportunity is walking out the door, to leave you to die wondering.'

The next nine seconds were spent with Harry's psyche doing battle between the protective, advice-giving father figure, and the red-blooded Irishman looking at a stunning young woman offering him better than a lottery win. In the tenth second the struggle was won, easily, by a lustful leprechaun. Harry grabbed Tanya around her hips and placed her backside on the edge of his desk blotter. She locked onto his mouth again as he slid his hands up under her skirt and pulled her G string down. She whispered in his ear, as one of his hands cupped her left breast.

'Nothing fancy today, my Mr PI, you'll have to save your face-riding desires for another time. My schedule today dictates this really is a wham bam one.'

She ran her finger down his nose and onto his lips. Then she unbuckled his belt and unzipped his trousers. She grabbed his rock-hard penis as it burst forth from his boxer shorts and laid back across his taxation paperwork. As he stood up out of his chair, she guided him into her pussy. Harry eased into her and bent down along her body so they could kiss. The old timber desk creaked angrily as Harry pounded into Tanya, the fronts of his thighs belting onto the wooden edge. He came within two minutes, groaning Tanya's name into her ear. She squeezed her arms around his neck.

'I do like having a man inside me who cares about me, Mr PI.'

She kissed him on his forehead.

'Now consider your desk duly baptized.'

Harry straightened up, pulling Tanya with him so she was sitting on the edge of the desk again. He kissed her on her mouth.

'Sorry it was so quick, babe, I was a bit on the boil there.'

'Quick is exactly what I ordered, Harry. You can look after me properly another time. And I hope you don't have to redo too much of your paperwork.' She smiled cheekily.

'I'll just have to spill a bit of coffee to cover up the evidence.'

Tanya did Harry's trousers up and pulled her G string back on. They were both standing now and Tanya pecked Harry on the cheek.

'Thank you for your help, Mr PI. Perhaps that desk shag can be my payment for your services with this case.'

She was still smiling and she put her hand on his cheek.

'And working that out according to your hourly rates probably makes it the most expensive two minutes of sex in human history.'

'Well, I can't offhand think of a better investment right now.'

'Always the smooth one. But you still owe me a dinner, remember?'

'Babe, a pleasure in every respect. Dinner definitely. And I'll call you after I've spoken with Tessa, unless I have any news from the Feds before that.'

'Cool. By the way, does she fuck as well as I do?'

'Babe, how the hell am I supposed to answer that?'

'You can tell me over dinner, and you will.'

Tanya smiled at him and wafted to the door, grabbing her Prada bag on the way. She turned, blew Harry a kiss, and exited into the day, one which was vastly improved in Harry's view. He looked at his chaotic desk, resembling the aftermath of a bonobo colony orgy, and reached for the box of tissues. He reflected that in good old Australia, at least what was left of it, he probably wasn't going to be the first person to send semen-stained paperwork to the Tax Office.

— 8 —

'**H**arry? Tom Strong. Call me ASAP, mate.'

Harry listened to the voicemail when he emerged from his bathroom on Friday morning. Even for Harry this 'ASAP' took priority over his craving for black coffee.

'Tom, just got your message. What goes?'

'Mate, we have hit the bloody jackpot. Your friend Lowe is going down.'

'You haven't pinched him yet, have you?'

'No, mate. I promised you, strictly on the q.t. of course, we'd let you have the pleasure of spectating, and we will. Sunday morning, early, my friend. And your degenerate PI self will have to relive a good old-fashioned dawn raid.'

'Bugger, I thought I'd seen the last of those bastards. Never could sleep properly the night before.'

'Know the feeling, brother.'

'So what have you got on him?'

'Well, we got a little cunning and used young Madison as bait.'

'What the fuck? That's got ethical suicide written all over it.'

'Relax, mate. We didn't physically use her. We did a bogus call to her mother whose boyfriend is a person of interest in one of our Internet child porn operations. We've had a UC chatting with him. So our UC told the mother where Madison could be found. An address of a derelict place we used as a safe house years ago.'

'I like where this is going.'

'About an hour later the mother goes off to the shops and lover boy is straight on the phone to you know who.'

Harry whistled.

'Beautiful.'

'Lowe then rings up your bible man, gets picked up by him, and they head for the deserted house. We've got the whole lot on film.'

'But not finding anything might make them suss about the call, smell of a set-up?'

'We thought of that, mate. We put a few bits of girl's clothing in there and we got Madison to write some things in a notebook about her being raped and the house in the mountains. Left the notebook in the house, too, along with a hairbrush with some of her hair in it. Lowe will think they were just too late and she'd moved on. So, with all that and the telephone intercepts, we've got enough for a search warrant. Can't wait to see what's in Lowe's place, a regular bloody Pandora's box no doubt.'

'No doubt indeed. So what time and where?'

'Mate, you and Trev be here at 4 a.m.'

'Sweet, we'll be there.'

'By the way, you pair of pricks wouldn't happen to know anything about a burnt-out Commodore out back of Hornsby, would you?'

'What was that, Tom? You're dropping out, mate.'

Harry rubbed the mobile noisily against his stubble as he continued, 'You there, Tom? Shit reception, think I've lost you, mate.'

Harry pressed 'End Call'.

'Hear no evil, Tom.'

With a guilty smirk on his face he headed for his kitchen and some desperately needed caffeine.

– 9 –

Harry had invited Tessa to his place for their second encounter and had spent Friday afternoon tidying up his bachelor pad in anticipation. Tessa's penthouse in Pyrmont had been immaculate, not to mention expensively fitted out. Harry's modest one bedroom joint in Ultimo wasn't going to compete, despite his impressive range of literature, European movies, and his tasteful collection of bronze nudes. But he really fancied more action with Tessa, so he didn't want her running for the door calling for the health inspectors.

Harry wasn't overly sophisticated in the wooing stakes, despite his easy charm. He was more accustomed to paying a set price for a set hour, and never being disappointed. He'd picked up a couple of gentleman's magazines in the hope of a tip or two. Things other than cleaning, clearing out the empties, and putting away the *Penthouse* editions, all of which he had figured out for himself. He'd read that mood was vital, and with that in mind he'd ventured into very non-Harry territory. The lighting was now dimmed and amber-hued thanks to a coloured sarong over the standard lamp, and scented candles – cherry blossom from L'Occitane – in the lounge room and bedroom were spreading a sweet, heady smell throughout the apartment. Harry had dispensed with his usual budget aftershave and was well-splashed with the spicy aroma of Fahrenheit. He'd even had an evening shave. Tessa had commented last time on how good his smooth face had felt on her thighs. It had been duly noted.

Tessa arrived early, a wonderful trait that Harry was going to take a while to get used to, and was looking ravishing in a sleeveless short dress of burnt orange. It had black trim along the dropped neckline, leading the eye straight to the accentuated cleavage between Tessa's small, but pert, breasts.

Tessa smiled mischievously at him. 'Well, good evening private eye. How are we tonight?'

Harry inhaled deeply through his nostrils to get the full waft of her Dior perfume.

'My gorgeous English rose, I couldn't be better now. You look and smell magnificent.'

She leant in to Harry's face, her tall heels ensuring she was on eye level with him, and ever so softly pushed her pouting lips onto his. After a momentary kiss Harry stood aside and ushered her inside.

'Welcome to *chez* Harry. What can I get you?'

'Well, I guess it's customary to at least start with a drink.'

Harry laughed. 'Champagne suffice? It is French.'

'I should bloody well hope so. You're not going to be getting me naked on some sparkling pretender from Adelaide.'

Harry filled two crystal flutes, pressed the start button on the CD player, and sat down next to Tessa on the couch. They chinked glasses as Norah Jones drifted through the air. Tessa put her hand on Harry's leg.

'Come on, give me that Bogart look of yours. I love it.'

Harry tilted his head forward slightly, and looked into her eyes.

'Here's looking at you, babe.'

Tessa giggled. Then he leant in and their mouths met, their tongues quickly locking in a serpentine wrestle. A few minutes later, miraculously no champagne spilt, they came up for air.

'I've been looking forward to that all evening, as well as some real dessert,' said Tessa.

'Plenty of sweet stuff to come.'

Harry raised his glass to her. She took a sip of her drink.

'So how was your industry dinner tonight?' asked Harry.

'Boring as usual. A lot of pretension and egos trying to outdo each other. I hate them, but I have to go to keep up my contacts. A necessary evil in this trade.'

'The world seems full of egos. On the subject of contacts, I've got a couple of young lady friends who are trying to get a start in the trade. Maybe I could pick your brains later on.'

'Sure. Now get back here, mister.'

'Yes, my lady.'

Their mouths melted back together. Harry ran a finger up Tessa's thigh, slowly, but firmly. He stopped at the hemline of the dress, now sitting a mere few centimetres beneath her crotch. He pulled his face back slightly.

'The champagne is good, but I want to devour you.'

'Well, handsome, let's take the bottle to the bedroom.'

'And why didn't I think of that?'

She laughed. 'Harry, you're a bloke. There's only one thought at a time in that handsome head of yours.'

'I guess you'll have to teach me how to have sex and champagne at the same time, then.'

She stood up, her glass in one hand, the other outstretched to Harry.

'Come on then you old dog, take me to your kennel and I'll teach you a new trick or three.'

Silently, Harry stood up, took Tessa's hand and led her to his bedroom, collecting the Moët et Chandon bottle on the way.

The only light in the bedroom was flowing from the three scented candles on the native hardwood dresser. Harry put the bottle and his glass on the bedside table and moved over to Tessa, who was leaning against the dresser. She was looking at him, her tongue tip showing against her upper teeth, and her eyes burning with desire. As Harry wrapped his arms around her waist, his now rock-hard penis pressed into the firmness of her pelvis. She rubbed herself gently against him, cradling her champagne beneath their chins. As his mouth locked onto hers, one hand slowly lowered the zipper down the length of her back. Then he stood back a touch and slipped the dress down her body. Harry cupped his hands over her breasts, squeezed them ever so slightly, and then slid his hands around her back to undo the black lace bra. He couldn't find the clip and started to fumble. He looked at Tessa enquiringly, trying to mask his feeling of ineptitude.

'Told you there were new tricks to be learned. Try the front, Harry.'

The bra dropped to join the dress on the floor as she kicked off her heels. Harry didn't have any problem sliding her G string off, there being only one method for that. He ran his middle finger along her already wet pussy and she moaned, sliding her tongue along her top lip. Harry looked her in the eyes, brought his hand back up from the valley of hedonism, and put his finger into his mouth, sucking her sweet dew from it.

'Dirty boy, I like that.'

She kissed him and then backed on to the bed.

She exaggerated her English accent. 'Now get those clothes off, butler, and attend to her ladyship's needs at once.'

She lay back against the pillows and let her knees fall to their sides, spreading her thighs wide.

'Yes, my lady. Forthwith,' said Harry attempting a poor English accent in return, but sounding more Irish. He was ripping his clothes off at breakneck speed, like he was the late guest at a Roman orgy. He hopped on one leg and then the other as he removed his socks.

Tessa stifled a laugh.

'When you're ready, Jeeves, her ladyship's needs start here and then progress slowly upwards.' She circled her right index finger in the air, mesmerizing Harry, and then pointed to her glistening pussy.

The now naked Harry plunged headlong onto the bed. Any thoughts of slowly licking his way up the inside of her thighs had been exiled by an invasion of primal lust. He plunged his face into her crotch. As his tongue started to massage her clitoris and play with her labia, she began to moan loudly, her hands sliding onto the back of his head. She didn't need to, of course; Harry had no intention of leaving his duty station until his face ached and she was entirely satisfied.

Half an hour later, both glazed with their intermingled sweat and smelling like a pair of rutting polecats, they lay on the bed drawing on cigarettes and sipping refilled champagne glasses.

'In one way it's a pity you're not still a cop.'

'Why so?' Harry turned his face to look at her and frowned.

'Because you'd still have your handcuffs, and that's something on my bucket list.' She turned and grinned at him. Harry chuckled.

'No problems. If you want that, I will duly obtain some for next time.'

The aristocratic voice returned. 'Is the butler being presumptuous?'

'Was her ladyship completely satisfied with the service?'

She laughed. 'Touché. You bet she was.'

They chinked glasses and drank.

'So, my English rose, I am very curious to know what exactly it is that appeals to you about me?'

'You mean apart from that incredible tongue?'

Harry laughed.

'The Kenmare tongue is a given. And you clearly enjoyed that. Seriously, though, I'm keen to know what grabs you.'

'Actually, that's easy, Harry. You've got real ethical principles, and you live by them.'

'My techniques aren't always purely ethical, alas.'

'I mean ethical on the fundamental principles. You Aquarian, you. Most women wouldn't even understand, but that's what turns me on.'

'Fuck, that's a first for me.'

'Like I said, most women wouldn't be capable of appreciating it. Too fixated on money and status, and captivated by egocentric male bullshit.'

'Won't argue there, I've met more than my fair share. So can Jeeves now be presumptuous and ask about seeing you again?'

'Absolutely. I'm away for the next ten days. Buying trip around Asia. Maybe dinner when I get back. And you can tell me about your "young lady friends".'

Harry didn't take the bait.

'It's a date.'

Harry swung himself off the bed.

'More champagne, your ladyship?'

'Ooh, more service all round, thank you, Jeeves.'

A naked Harry walked on air as he headed to the fridge for a second bottle of Moët.

The cool and eerie grey light of dawn was just seeping over Sydney at six on Sunday morning. If any Eric Road resident in leafy, peaceful Artarmon had been up for an early jog or dog walk, they would have found themselves to be front row spectators of a scene straight from television. Eight black-clad and heavily armed officers from the AFP's Specialist Response Group were bearing down silently on Detective Commander Lowe's town house. They'd been deployed as Lowe was armed with his police-issue Glock, and who knew how he'd react to this unconventional wake-up call; they weren't going to be knocking politely on the door. Behind them was the team of detectives and forensic officers waiting for Lowe and the house to be secured by the tactical squad. Whilst there weren't any local spectators, there were some blow-ins.

Harry and Trev were watching the show unfold from the warm and slightly cosy confines of a white plumber's van with one-way rear windows parked in the visitor's area of the town house complex. The alleged tradesmen were two of the AFP's surveillance crew, and they had had a digital video camera running since arriving an hour earlier to confirm the presence of Lowe's car. Then the tactical team were given the green light. It was complete silence in the back of the van. A notepad was used for any essential communication, those were the rules when in close proximity to a target like this. Wouldn't do to have any nosey passers-by wondering why there was a plumber's union meeting in the back of a closed up van before sunrise.

Harry was restless and pumped with adrenalin, almost as if he was going in the door himself. He actually wished he was. To see that first look on Lowe's face, that would be priceless. However, he was grateful just to be here to see Lowe get dragged away. And he was busting for a smoke. He concentrated on the ninja-like figures fifty metres away.

As the first discernible orange glow crept above the rooflines, the idyllic suburban peace was shattered. There was the slightest arm signal from the tactical team leader and then the largest ninja, looking more like a large black bear, pile drove the metal battering ram into Lowe's front door. His considerable bulk followed the ram inside as the timber door crashed open. The other black figures stormed in, Heckler and Koch G36 assault rifles up to their shoulders, barrel torches on. The shouts of 'Police! Police!' were the only noise following the splintering surrender of the door. Harry had to get his hanky out to wipe the sweat from his forehead. There were some muffled noises from inside the house, faintly detectable from where the van was.

Less than five minutes later, the senior ninja appeared at the destroyed doorway and gave the thumbs up to the waiting detectives. Then the suits headed in the door, followed by the forensic white coveralls. Harry smiled as he thought the scene could almost have been a fancy dress theme night at the Inferno Club on Oxford Street. Not that he'd ever been there, of course. He just had it on good authority.

'Okay, gents, silent mode completed,' said the AFP team leader in the van. 'They're going to be a while in there, so if you blokes want to stretch your legs and have a smoke, now's the time. But don't take too long.'

'Roger that, mate, and cheers,' said Harry. 'Want us out through the driver's door, or this side one?'

'Use the front door.'

Harry climbed over the driver's seat and opened the door. He sucked in the fresh morning air, just a hint of lavender from the neat garden beds, and clambered out of the van. Trev followed him. They took a few steps to get behind the van and then lit up.

'I can't bloody wait to see Lowe getting hauled out of there,' said Harry.

'Yep. A great way to start the day. And I bet they find a swag of kiddy porn.'

'For sure. And from what we've seen I reckon a fair bit of it'll be locally produced.'

The pair smoked a second cigarette, with one of the Feds joining them. Within ten minutes the three of them slipped back into the van. Now all they had to do was wait.

Half an hour passed and Harry was fighting down his impatience when he felt his iPhone vibrate on his belt with a message.

> Hi Mr PI. No ur busy now but need ur help this arvo. Call when u can. T x

Harry smiled at the kiss, thinking of his desk a few days previously, but was intrigued by whatever Tanya needed his help with. Calling her would have to wait, though.

'They're coming out,' said one of the Feds.

Harry and Trev looked out through one of the rear windows. Tom Strong led the column of bodies emerging from Lowe's front door. Behind him, two forensic officers carried out some plastic evidence bags, a collection of video tapes, DVDs and computer discs clearly visible.

'Looks like a good haul,' said Trev.

'Couldn't happen to a nicer bloke,' said Harry.

And then the scene they had been really waiting for: from the front door emerged another detective, holding the upper arm of a handcuffed Mervyn Lowe. Harry looked at the grubby white T-shirt, faded jeans, and trainers. Well, arsehole, you don't look much like the cocky Detective Commander now, thought Harry.

Lowe was screaming at them, 'This is all a set-up. I'm innocent.' He was pushed into the back of an unmarked AFP Ford Falcon and the escorting officer got in beside him. Tom Strong waited at the open front passenger door, talking to the lead forensic officer. Three other sets of white coveralls came out of Lowe's house with several more bulging evidence bags, as well as a computer box and a laptop. Tom strong got into his car and his driver started it up. They moved past the surveillance van out onto the quiet street with the forensic van and another car following. Two uniformed officers were left at the smashed front door to await the repair company. One of the Feds turned to Harry.

'Where can we drop you blokes?'

'George Street around Chinatown would be great.'

'No probs.'

The other Fed started the van and they drove out onto the street. As they were cruising down the Pacific Highway towards the city, Harry pulled out his phone and tapped on Tanya's number.

'Hi Mr PI. How did it go?'

'Absolutely beautiful. He's in custody and on his way to a very shitty future.'

Trev smirked.

'Now, babe, what can I do for you this arvo? I hope you're not having any trouble?'

'Sasha is. She's got this freak stalking her.'

'Well, I'm sure I could help with that. A bit of Harry's touch, maybe?'

'Sash and I are going to see a band at the Muso Bar in Annandale this arvo, and Sash reckons this freak will turn up. What are the chances of a hunky Harry bodyguard?'

'Of course, babe. But I'll look a bit out of place, won't I?'

'No, there are always older people watching the bands there, too.'

'Well, thank you for saying "older" instead of "old".'

Tanya laughed. 'Can you meet us there at four? Out the front?'

'No probs, babe. And I'll bring Trev. Us oldies need to stick together. Safety in numbers, all that shit.'

'Thank you so much, my Harry. See you then. And a hug and a kiss from both of us.'

Tanya rang off as Harry was saying, 'Yes, please.'

'Trev, when was the last time you saw some live rock music?'

'Mate, a long bloody time ago somewhere in Brizzie I reckon.'

'Heard of the Muso Bar since you been down here?'

'Read about it, not been there.'

'Well, you and I are going there this arvo to see a band.'

'Mate, you never cease to amaze me. What's on?'

'We might have a little bit of old-fashioned biffo, mate.' And Harry filled Trev in on the details.

— 11 —

Harry and Trev hopped out of the cab on Parramatta Road in Annandale, opposite the pub. The live music was thumping out as they crossed the road. Harry being his more-than-punctual self meant they were ten minutes early for the twins. Harry offered his cigarette packet to Trev.

'May as well have a smoke while we wait. Won't be able to in there. Won't be able to bloody hear ourselves think, either.'

Trev laughed. 'No shit, Sherlock. Reckon this stalker bloke will show up? Or are the girls just a bit paranoid?'

'Apparently he posted on Facebook that he was coming and he was "looking forward to rocking with his fantasy chick", meaning Sasha. It was the bit about "riding her like his dream bitch" that really freaked her out.'

'Bloody Facebook. Remember that young girl in Melbourne who got stabbed to death and stuck in the wheelie bin? That fucker got hold of her on Facebook, I think.'

'She was only early twenties from memory, and a lovely looking kid. Bloody tragic.'

There was a pause. Trev broke their moment of reflection.

'So how did this bloke find out Sasha was coming here if she hasn't had any contact with him?'

'Another girl announced the gig on her page, some shit like that. It's all a bit beyond me, but the threat sounded clear enough. That sure doesn't change with the technology.'

'And here they are,' said Trev.

Harry turned as Tanya and Sasha walked up to them. The girls were dressed to match, long black leather boots, short black skirts, tight-fitting magenta T-shirts, and short-cut leather jackets. The only discernible difference was the colour of their small Mulberry bags, black for Tanya and burgundy for Sasha. They were both wearing the pearl earrings.

'Well, don't you two ladies look dressed to kill,' Harry said as he gave them both a kiss on the cheek. 'And "guess who's dying", to borrow from the great Roxy Music.'

Trev rolled his eyes and groaned. 'Lame, mate.'

Harry smirked. 'Trev, you've met Tanya before. This is Sasha, the other half of this double dose of perfection I'm always rabbiting on about.'

Trev shook their hands. Tanya pulled out her cigarettes and took two out. She passed one to Sasha.

'Let's have a quickie before we go in, we've got time.'

'Now just because I was a bit fast last time, babe …'

Tanya laughed. 'Yeah, Harry. A fast man, but a good one.'

The girls lit up.

Sasha turned to Harry. 'Thank you so much for the earrings, I love them.'

She kissed him on the cheek.

'My pleasure, gorgeous girl.'

'And thanks for doing this, Harry. That creep has got me worried.'

'Trev and I, we'll look after you. If he does turn up I

can assure you that by the time we've finished with him, you'll be the last thing on his mind.'

Tanya touched Harry's forearm.

'I do like a hard man.'

Trev groaned again. 'I've found myself on the set of a B-grade sitcom.'

Harry laughed and the girls smiled.

'You got that photo I emailed you?' asked Tanya.

'Yep, we've both got a copy. That's his Facebook picture I assume?'

'Yeah, the most recent one.'

'Good. Well, we'll head on in and park ourselves at the bar. If we walk in with you we'll look like a right pair of old sugar daddies.'

The girls laughed. Tanya poked Harry playfully in the chest.

'Actually, Harry, the main conversation would be in admiration at just how far above your weight you were punching.'

Trev jumped in. 'I like that idea, a bit of a touch up for the old ego.'

'I'll massage your ego at the bar, mate,' said Harry. 'Let's go. We'll be watching you, girls.'

'Thanks, guys,' said the twins.

Harry and Trev went up the steps into the hotel entrance, paid the admission fee, and headed into the riotous chamber. Harry leant close into Trev's ear. 'Beer, mate?'

'Yeah, whatever's on tap and local.'

Harry stepped up to the bar and ordered two Carlton draughts. The beers were handed over and the pair turned, leant their backs against the edge of the bar and sipped from their schooners, quietly scanning the room.

The music stopped as the band on the northern stage finished their last number to applause and cheers from the youngish audience. Another band was setting up on the southern podium. Harry looked at the tall singer with shoulder-length blond hair testing his microphone. 'One, two, one two.'

The banner hoisted up behind the band's drummer bore the name 'Snaketide'.

'Is that the band the girls are here for?' asked Trev.

'Yep. And enter the most gorgeous women of the day.'

More than a few heads turned as Tanya and Sasha imposed their raunchy beauty on the seedy and rundown interior of the pub. They ignored Harry and Trev and ordered themselves Vodka Cruisers from the barman. They took their drinks over to the other side of the room and stood at a tall table just as the blond singer's unmistakeably English accent blasted over the sound system.

'How you punters doing tonight?' There were whoops from the crowd. 'We're Snaketide.'

And with that the guitars and drums fired up and the first number began, to enthusiastic shouting and whistling from the audience, including the twins. Harry noticed that the crowd had swelled quite suddenly and it was getting hard to keep a visual on the girls. Trev tapped Harry on the shoulder and yelled in his ear.

'Mate, I think that's him over there, about three metres to the right of the girls, holding the smartphone up.'

Harry turned and focused on the man. He got close to Trev's ear.

'Yeah, that's him.' Harry was looking at the palm-sized photo in his hand. 'And the arsehole is photographing the girls, not the band.'

The first number finished, the singer roused up the crowd with gusto.

'This one's "Overdrive",' he roared.

The next song began booming out from the speakers. Their target meanwhile started moving through the crowd towards the door.

The music rolled on:

Caveman in me is in ... overdrive
Move a little closer and hang on tight ...

Trev yelled, 'Toilet, I reckon. He won't be leaving yet, not with Sasha still here.'

Harry grinned and yelled back, 'Yeah, I'm busting, too.'

The two sleuths drained their nearly empty glasses, plonked them down on the bar, and walked out into the foyer. The target was just heading up the corridor towards the bathrooms.

Harry quickly scanned the area, but there was no one around at all. The only nearby person was the girl who had taken their admission fees, and she had her back to foyer, completely engrossed in watching the band.

The music continued in the background:

Feeding my desires in your perfumed skin
Take me for a ride and red light on ...

The pair walked up the corridor and approached the door to the men's room, into which their man had disappeared. Still no one around. Harry noticed two wires hanging from a wall mounting below the cornice, which would have held a CCTV camera in its prime. He pointed it out to get Trev's attention.

'Even rundown fleapits have their good sides.'

'Sweet, you gotta win some.'

With that Harry led the way into the toilets. Their prey was standing at the urinal swaying slightly and pissing hard. Trev leaned his shoulder against the inside of the door, ensuring it was going to stay closed to anyone else. The creep finished his piss and went over to a basin, completely focused on his smartphone. He seemed oblivious to Harry bearing down on him. Harry stood at the next basin and turned on the tap. He looked over at the phone and saw a photo of the twins. Then the photo switched to a video, again of the twins, with the music loud in the background and the girls moving their lithe bodies to the rhythm.

Harry leant over. 'Oh, yeah, they're hot those two, aren't they?'

Creep didn't look up, just tapped the image of Sasha dancing.

'Yeah, mate. And I am going to fuck this one, real hard. She won't ever forget me. And then I'll do her twin sister.'

'Is that right?'

'Damn right. Those sluts are mine.'

'Those "sluts" happen to be my nieces, "mate".' Harry turned to face the guy, who now finally looked up from his phone.

'Yeah, righto. Why don't you fuck off, "uncle".'

He moved to go around Harry, but Harry pushed him back. The surprise of the physical contact made the creep drop his phone.

'Fuck you, old man. Tell you what, as I'm fucking doing her I'll tell her that "uncle" sends his love.'

'Bad, bad move, fella,' was just audible from Trev.

Harry stared at the creep, who was just beginning to bend down to pick up his phone. Harry's vision was suddenly and fleetingly interrupted with a flash of a little girl's brutalized and lifeless body. His Orla. Some man, some predator. Taking her, using and abusing her. Killing her. Then his focus zoomed back to the here and now: the present predator. Mr Creep never saw it coming. In one rapid and fluid movement Harry placed his hands on the back of the lowering head in front of him and brought his right knee up like a torpedo into the stalker's face. There was a sickening crunch as his nose was smashed, and he shrieked in pain. He dropped to his knees, bringing his hands up to his face as the blood started to flow. Harry swiftly dragged him into the first cubicle and grabbed him by the throat, pulling him upwards and squeezing hard with his left hand.

'If you ever, ever go near those girls again I will hunt you down and fucking kill you. Understand, arsehole?'

Mr Creep's swelling lips moved slightly amidst the blood, but 'Fuck you' was just audible.

'Another inspired move,' said Trev, still providing the human door jam.

'Oh, "fuck me", is that right?' said Harry, as he drove his right fist hard into the guy's solar plexus, causing him to collapse onto his knees again, gasping in pain and this time fighting for air. Harry then grabbed his hair and plunged his head into the toilet bowl, managing to jam it right down to the water line. Mr Creep had been having enough trouble drawing breath before this latest move, but as his face went into the water his arms started to flail about.

'Remember, fucker, I will hunt you down, and rip your fucking throat out.'

With that, Harry then kept his left hand hard on the back of the semi-submerged head, reached up with his right hand and flushed the toilet. The arms flailed some more, but less animatedly. Then the body slumped as Mr Creep passed out. Harry let go of him and he fell over next to the bowl.

Harry pulled the wallet out of the guy's back jeans pocket, opened it and removed the drivers licence. Then he dropped the wallet in the bowl to let the water take care of any prints. He stepped back and let the door of the cubicle swing closed.

'Never know when we might need his address,' said Harry as he pocketed the licence.

'Don't forget the phone over there,' added Trev.

Harry picked up the phone and the two of them walked out, back down the corridor, and out of the hotel. No one saw them leave.

Tanya's phone flashed a message a few minutes later.

Job done. C U over road after band. H x

– 12 –

The bright morning sunlight wasn't doing much to warm up the Silverwater Correctional Complex, thanks to a howling southerly coming in from the alpine snowfields. In any event, the collected hearts inside the razor wire perimeter, whether dressed in green or blue, would have needed a lot more than sunlight to lift their temperatures: maybe a nuclear firestorm. Two of the very coldest hearts in those confines that wintry morning were residing in very different parts of the prison.

Inmate 588323, better known to the world as the suspended from duty Detective Commander Mervyn Lowe, was brooding in his cell in the segregation wing of the remand section of the complex. This wing, known colloquially as Fraggle Rock, had eleven guests. There were several men of various ages awaiting trial for child sex offences, one man in his twenties still trying to get bail for a string of bestiality charges, one ex-cop due to go to trial for drug trafficking and money laundering, and then Lowe.

Mervyn Lowe was methodically going over in his fetid mind the way forward for him. He was going to beat this, he was sure. He'd been smart enough to refuse to answer any questions in his police interview. Instead, he'd relied on his lawyer, provided as a matter of urgency

304

by the church, repeatedly telling the Federal Agents that, 'My client has been advised not to answer your questions. He will defend himself in the courts.' God bless that right to silence. It had been a long and one-sided electronic interview at AFP headquarters. He had fought to keep his reactions under control as various video clips were played to him. However, he hadn't been able to completely stifle a slight gasp when the footage of Skye's rape was played. In all the other videos, his head was never visible, so he could deny he was there easily. But why had he been so careless on that one, to bend down and talk to the girl? He should have controlled his anger with that one. And why the fuck hadn't those incompetent morons edited it, as was the arrangement?

There were only two options, really. One was to deny it was him, and say it was someone who closely resembled him. Two was to say it had been digitally manipulated to frame him. Yes, he liked number two. It would segue nicely with his explanation for all the child porn found in his house. That had all been planted there, of course. That would give him the avenue to blame that fucker Harry Kenmare, who he was quite sure had something to do with his arrest. He just didn't know exactly what the connection was, and it was eating at him like a lion chewing on a zebra's carcass. Still, with a bit more massaging and some creative input from his lawyer, who had kept his face out of all the videos, a story that Kenmare was on a vendetta for his getting thrown out of the Force would provide a solid motive for him trying to frame him. All going well, at the scheduled bail hearing in two days he would be out of here, and Fraggle Rock could go fuck itself. His lawyer had assured him his church friends were not deserting him and the surety money had been duly raised.

In the meantime, he could sit this place out. Being in Fraggle Rock, he was safe. None of the peds would touch him, the animal fucker didn't go near anyone else at all, and the other cop, an ex-Fed, had shown no interest in speaking to him. When he had arrived from the court the Prison Superintendent had actually come down to Admissions for a chat. He'd told him that he'd be completely safe in the segregation unit, as it was just for peds and ex-cops. The Super had then smiled and told him that perhaps wearing both hats, Lowe was a 'bit over qualified', laughed, and then walked off. Prick, thought Lowe, and added the Super to his list of accounts to settle after he was free.

A few hundred metres away, inmate 133412, also known as Nolan 'The Boot' Kelly, was pacing the exercise yard adjoining the high security wing. Kelly's footwear moniker didn't, as many assumed, arise from any primal penchant for kicking the shit out of his victims. Rather, his predilection was to abduct his victims, always bank managers, stuff them in the boot of whichever car he had stolen for the heist in question, and then drive to their bank and force them to hand over large sums of cash. Next he'd leave the bound and gagged bank johnnies in the boot of the car, now dumped in some quiet bush area on Sydney's outskirts. Then his finale would be to set the vehicle alight before being picked up by an associate and driven away. In all, Kelly had barbecued four bank managers before his capture, and he was now doing four life sentences.

Kelly's home life hadn't exactly been an oil painting of suburban domestic bliss, with alcohol, drugs, and violence removing the need for any reality TV shows. Whilst he would be considered a bad apple in almost all facets, like a lot of hard-core crims, Kelly felt from the bottom of his dark, grey heart that all rock spiders should be put down. He'd actually always thought this, but since his eleven-year-old boy had run away from the happy home for the sixth time, only to be taken in by a kindly older gent who was rather tactile in his attentions, Kelly was adamant on hunting down paedophiles. Young Caleb had finally turned up in Nepean Hospital, gibbering unintelligibly for several days. The doctors had said it would take a lot more than a few days for his anal injuries to heal. Kelly hadn't been able to visit his boy, due to the limited lifestyle of being in remand at the time, bail refused.

Caleb's mother, Noreen, hadn't come near Kelly for over three years, ever since he'd broken her jaw. Well, he reckoned, the slag deserved it. He'd come home after one of his roasting robberies to find Noreen enjoying a mouthful of his cousin's dick. But Kelly considered himself a fair man; the cousin got a broken jaw as well.

So Noreen turned up on visiting day, telling Kelly that whilst she hated him and he deserved to rot in prison, she thought he had a right to know what had happened to their son. Caleb had eventually started to make sense and told the doctors about a group of men who had repeatedly raped him at some house, he didn't know where, until he managed to run away. Caleb hadn't wanted to talk to the police; he was his father's son in that regard.

Visiting day two weeks later brought Noreen back again, even more distressed than the first visit. As she relayed it, Caleb had, the day before, walked out of the hospital, up the road to Kingswood railway station, and then off the platform in front of the 4.15 afternoon express service for the city. The train driver never had a chance to stop in time, and Caleb's misery was permanently ended under the metal train wheels.

According to Noreen the cops who came to tell her and take her to the morgue in Glebe to identify the various bits that had been Caleb, hadn't exactly been sympathetic, knowing the dead boy's lineage. But it was her overhearing a cop at the morgue saying to a colleague that the boy's death would at least save the taxpayers the cost of a prison cell later in life that had really made Kelly's blood boil. It was just as well he was in solitary lockdown at that time, because after that visit he had been desperate to beat the living shit out of someone. Anyone, in fact. Those 'fucking pig bastards' was his recurring thought every day since as he paced his cell or the dust of the exercise yard.

Now, six months later, Lowe's arrest and charging had been all over the news, but the media hadn't been filled in on where Lowe went after bail was refused. But the word had travelled like wildfire around Silverwater. A paedophile pig, my holy fucking grail, thought Kelly, as he squeezed his hands around a bar of his cell, like it was a human neck, until his knuckles were white.

Kelly thought about as highly of the prison guards as he did the cops, but at least some of these screws could be bought easily. Plenty of the money from Kelly's last robbery before his capture was still held by an associate, and so Kelly was able to arrange payments when he needed to. He'd quickly worked out which of his captors were either bent or vulnerable. Two of the guards in the block had chronic gambling problems, one was a coke addict, and one wanted cash to pay for his demanding girlfriend's breast enhancements. All in all, Kelly had managed to get two mobile phones, six SIM cards, some good quality porn, and a steady supply of weed.

So which of the bent screws would he approach now? Officer Doyle, otherwise known as 'Mr Silicon

Tits', would do the trick nicely. Doyle had let slip that he needed another five grand pronto as his girlfriend was getting very toey for her new breasts. Kelly called through the bars to the guard, also crooked, on duty down the corridor. The guard walked down.

'What do you want, Kelly?'

'Officer, can you let Officer Doyle know I want to speak to him. Something I heard he might be interested in.'

'Yeah, righto, Kelly. I'll tell him on the change over.'

Kelly went and lay down on his bed. Doyle's tart would be getting her swollen rack quicker than she expected.

Later that afternoon, Lowe had just finished a visit with his devout lawyer and was being escorted back from the visiting section. The prison guard opened a door and motioned Lowe through. He hesitated.

'But this isn't the same way I came up.'

'No, mate. We're mixing your movements around for security, so none of this lot can figure out where you might be,' replied Officer Doyle.

Lowe nodded and went through the door. Three corridors and five doors later, Lowe didn't have a clue where he was. The lack of any windows in this custodial labyrinth made orientation impossible. They arrived at yet another door and the guard took hold of his key.

'Here you go, Lowe. Home, sweet home.'

As the door opened and Lowe was hit by daylight, a hand between his shoulder blades propelled him through the opening. The door slammed shut behind him. Lowe felt panic rising. This wasn't Fraggle Rock's exercise yard. It was much bigger, and there were a lot of prisoners walking around. Quite a few had turned to look at him. He turned and started thumping on the firmly closed door, shouting for help.

Lowe never saw Kelly approach; he was far too intent on pleading with the uncooperative door. He banged on the metal aperture with increasing desperation, his normally controlled and controlling voice rising in a panicked crescendo.

A hand grabbed Lowe's hair and a rough unshaven face came up next to his. As he was dragged away from the door, screaming, the last words he heard were, 'Hello, cunt.'

Kelly lifted the boning knife, stolen from the kitchen and sharpened in the workshop by an inmate who owed Kelly a favour. He held it momentarily in front of Lowe's face, just long enough to let him process what was about to happen. Then Kelly roared, 'Die, Fucker!' With that he plunged the knife into Lowe's throat. Blood started spraying everywhere as Kelly dragged the steel blade right around Lowe's throat and neck. As Lowe's body collapsed, Kelly went down over him, still gripping his hair and now sawing at the spinal column with the knife. Blood was running like Niagara Falls and Kelly was looking like an abattoir worker. Other inmates were whistling and cheering. Then the alarms sounded. With one final violent hack, Kelly lifted Lowe's head clear from the now prostrate body and stood up tall. He held the trophied head up, blood pouring down from it, and raised his free hand, fist clenched around the knife, in a power salute.

The cheering rose to a climax. Then there were three loud bangs as guards fired tear gas grenades into the enclosure. Prisoners started running for the exit doors from the yard. Through another door burst a team from the Special Operations Group, dressed in black with matching helmets and gas masks, waving long metal riot batons.

Kelly stood his ground, holding up his carnal prize. The now dripping blood and the swirling white cloud of gas merged into one around him, creating a visceral red haze, amongst which Kelly looked like some primeval predator. Into this vision of hell charged the black uniforms, and Kelly eventually went down under a hail of baton blows, but still clutching Lowe's head. Nobody noticed in the orgy of sanctioned violence, but Nolan Kelly was grinning from ear to ear as he lost consciousness.

– 13 –

PAEDO COP EXECUTED:
JUNGLE JUSTICE RULES!

This *Daily Telegraph* front page would be a souvenir worth framing, was Harry's first thought as he handed over the coins for a rag he didn't normally touch. His second thought was that the paper would get away with this pre-trial assertion of guilt as the dead, may they rest in peace, couldn't sue for defamation. As Harry sat at his desk, feet up, having his first morning coffee and his third morning cigarette, he savoured the headline on his desk. 'Every dog has its day' had always been one of the cop proverbs Harry had subscribed to, especially when injustices prevailed. Lowe had been the most heinous of all mongrel curs. Thanks to another hound from hell, 'The Boot' Kelly, Lowe had had a very dramatic and infinitely fitting last day on the planet, pondered Harry.

But life was also a clashing contradiction of ugliness and beauty. At a particular point in time yesterday his nemesis Lowe's lifeblood had been seeping into the dirt of the Silverwater exercise yard. At the same particular point in time, in a far more civilized part of town, red wine was flowing down the throats of three very beautiful women. A trio of exquisite ladies, and Harry had slept with all three of them. He smiled as he reminisced. He had put Tessa in touch with the twins, and it seemed the ladies' lunch yesterday had been a great success. Tanya and Sasha would be starting part-time paid traineeships with Tessa's fashion house next month. All in all, Harry felt pretty damned good right now.

But then his mobile phone rang.

Twenty minutes later Harry was sitting in Tom Steele's office at AFP Headquarters.

'I was in two minds whether to call you or not, Harry. But then I figured you deserved the option ...'

'What do you mean "option"?' interrupted Harry.

During the phone call, Tom had simply said he wanted to see Harry ASAP, so Harry was feeling a bit disconcerted right now.

'The team has been going through all the shit we seized from Lowe's place. There's a video with a young girl in it ...'

Tom was struggling.

Harry was starting to feel a sick dread in his stomach.

Tom swallowed audibly.

'We've been cross-referencing the seized material with old case file material from the state boys. We're not completely sure, Harry, but we think the girl is Orla.'

Harry had an appalling vision of his Orla and Lowe. He dry retched. Tom seemed to read his mind.

'Lowe's not in the film, mate. One of his associates is, though, so we think Lowe had the film as part of his child porn collection.'

'I want to see her.'

'I'm only going to let you see if it is her, Harry. I'm not letting you watch it all. I've lifted a short from it.'

'But ...'

'No "buts", mate. I've got two daughters and I wouldn't want to see it all if it was one of my girls.'

Harry looked at Tom in a sad silence.

'Shall I?' Tom pointed at the flat screen monitor on his desk, angled so they could both see it.

Harry nodded and turned slowly to the screen. A video frame opened to show a naked girl on a bed. The bed was pushed into a corner and the girl was huddling in it. Her terrified eyes were staring at the camera and tears were running down her cheeks.

Harry reached forward and two of his fingers touched the young face on the screen. He started crying. He tried to talk, but nothing would come out, except a bubble of dribble. His fingers ran down the screen a few centimetres, coming to rest on the gold shamrock pendant hanging down Orla's immature bosom. The short video clip ended.

Harry slumped back in his chair and closed his eyes. His voice returned.

'The pendant was a Christmas present just after she turned nine. It was supposed to bring her luck. Two weeks later she disappeared.'

'I'm sorry, mate.'

Harry was now staring at his hands clenched together in his lap. He remained silent. A couple of minutes later Tom broke it.

'Mate, I'll keep you posted. There's a joint task force running with the state boys and we're making good progress. We will catch the fuckers who took Orla from you.'

Harry stood up.

'Thanks, mate.'

Harry's face had hardened and a savage storm was brewing behind his eyes.

'Can I call anyone for you?' offered Tom.
'No, she's right, mate. I'll take care of … myself.'
'Harry, if you want some help …'
'Thanks, Tom, I will take care of it myself.'
They shook hands.
Harry turned and trudged out the door.

— 14 —

Tanya was lying on her couch watching her third episode of *Twilight* for the afternoon of her day off. She looked at her phone which had just bleeped with a message.

Hi babe. At my local. Need u. Hx

Tanya smiled to herself. Bloody Harry. Obviously had got off to an early start at the pub and was now feeling randy. Well, why not, she had nothing planned this evening. And he could shout her a slap up dinner first, she was starving, and some champagne. Yes, go hard girl. She texted him back and went to her room to get changed.

Half an hour later she walked into the Emerald Bar. She bought a vodka, lime and soda, and looked around.

'Is Harry here?' she asked the bar manager.

'Out in the beer garden. And not his normal self, I have to say,' Shaun replied.

'His mate Liam's not here?'

'No. Liam's away. Couple of weeks of sunshine up at Port Douglas.'

'Half his luck. Thanks.'

Tanya picked up her glass and walked through to the beer garden. Harry was sitting over in the far corner, a bottle of Beaujolais on the table, and he was smoking. He looked up as Tanya approached.

'Mr PI, that's a very sad face.'

As she got to the table she could see he had been crying. She put her glass down and crouched next to him, taking hold of one of his hands.

'Hey, Harry, what's wrong?'

Then she saw a photo on the table in front of Harry, positioned between the wine bottle and his Marlboro packet. It was the same photo she had caught sight of in his wallet before.

'Your daughter?'

Harry nodded.

'I saw Orla today.'

Tanya was confused.

'But I thought she was ...'

'Yeah, but the Feds found a film in Lowe's place.'

'Oh, fuck.'

Tanya sat herself on Harry's lap and hugged his head to her chest. Harry started sobbing. Tanya held him tight.

Finally, he lifted his head a fraction.

'Talk to me, Harry.'

He proceeded to tell her about Orla, and the film, and the connection to Lowe and the church paedophile group.

'I'm going to hunt the fucking scum down, babe. I'll get my own justice for Orla.'

Tanya nodded and held him tight. She kissed his forehead.

'I think, Mr PI, it's about time you had an assistant. Sounds like you're going to need one.'

'What? I thought you were all set to work in fashion with Tessa.'

'Yeah, absolutely. But that's only part-time to start,

and it doesn't have to be my only interest going on, does it? I rather fancy this detective shit, having got to know you. And fuck knows, your office is screaming out for a feminine touch.'

Harry looked at her.

'And you just know I would be good at it, Harry.'

He couldn't argue that point.

'Okay, we can talk about that. Right now I need an assistant who gives lots of hugs.'

Tanya kissed him on the lips this time, and then enveloped his face between her breasts, hugging him hard.

Harry closed his eyes, breathing in the Gaultier that was starting to make his sadness less so. Life from here was going to be somewhat different. It was going to revolve around Tanya, a beautiful assistant-to-be and sometime lover; around Tessa, now a good friend and also sometime lover; and around avenging the death of his beautiful daughter, Orla, a girl he loved and would always love in a totally irreplaceable way.

He figured his world was going to change irrevocably, but gorgeous women were still going to dominate.

After all, this was Harry's world.

EPIGRAPH SOURCES

PART 1 - page 1:

1. Raymond Chandler © 1949.
   The Little Sister, p.296.   (Edition – Penguin 2010).

2. Gabriel Garcia Marquez   © 2005.
   Memories of my Melancholy Whores, p.30.
   (Edition – Jonathan Cape 2005).

PART 2 - page 25:

3. Ross Macdonald   © 1954.
   Find A Victim, p.24.   (Edition – Vintage
   Crime/Black Lizard 2001)

4. Michel Houellebecq   © 2001.
   Platform, p.319.   (Edition – Vintage 2003).

PART 3 - page 75:

5. Dashiell Hammett   © 1924.
   'The House on Turk Street', in *The Continental Op*,
   p.101.   (Edition – Vintage Crime/Black Lizard 1992).

6. Graham Greene © 1978.
   The Human Factor, p.43. (Edition – Penguin 1978).

PART 4 - page 145:

7. Peter Corris © 1981.
   White Meat, p.51. (Edition Fawcett Gold Medal 1981).

8. F. Scott Fitzgerald © 1922.
   The character Gloria in *The Beautiful and
   Damned,* p.152. (Edition – Penguin 1986).

PART 5 - page 227:

9. Georges Simenon © 1954.
   Inspector Maigret and the Strangled Stripper,
   p.22. (Edition – Curtis Books 1973).

10. Philip Roth © 2001.
    The Dying Animal, p.69. (Edition – Vintage 2002).

GLOSSARY

For all my readers who are not familiar with the local vernacular, here is a helpful list of the abbreviations and Australian slang and colloquialisms used throughout the text. Some non-Australian ones are included.

ABBREVIATIONS:

AFP	Australian Federal Police
BSB	Bank State Branch number
D	slang for 'detective'
DPP	Director of Public Prosecutions
HOD	hurt-on-duty (a police injury scheme)
IA	(Police) Internal Affairs
ICAC	Independent Commission Against Corruption
MSF	Médecins Sans Frontières (an international NGO)
NSW	New South Wales

OAM	Order of Australia (an award in the Australian honours system)
OIC	Officer-in-Charge (of a police unit)
PIC	Police Integrity Commission (external to the police)
RBT	random breath test
RSPCA	Royal Society for the Prevention of Cruelty to Animals
SMH	*Sydney Morning Herald*
TAFE	Technical and Further Education
UC	undercover police operative
UN	United Nations
VB	Victoria Bitter (an Australian beer brand)
VicPol	Victoria Police

COLLOQUIALISMS:
(In the sense they are used in this text.)

arvo	afternoon
baccy	tobacco

biffo	fist-fight, punch-up
bogan	red-neck, rough-neck
Brizzie	Brisbane (capital of Queensland)
deli	delicatessen (corner store, convenience store)
dero	tramp, itinerant
dinkum	the real thing, genuine
doss house	lodging house, somewhere to sleep
dossing	lodging, crashing somewhere to sleep
dunny	toilet
eckys	ecstasy tablets (the drug MDMA)
fair suck of the sav	fair go, fair chance
Feds	Australian Federal Police
ped	paedophile
pineapples	Australian $50 notes (yellow in colour)
piss	alcohol

Plastic Fantastics	derogatory term for the Australian Federal Police, used by the state police forces
rego	registration number (of a car)
rock spider	paedophile, child molester
root	sexual intercourse
rort	trick, deception
rorter	someone who pulls off a rort
sav	short for 'sauvignon', in wine terms
schooner	a beer glass (in NSW 425ml, or 15oz)
sledging	throwing insults
super	short for 'superannuation', an Australian pension system
thunder-box	an outdoor toilet

ACKNOWLEDGEMENTS

Back in 2005 I had to do a 500 word creative writing piece for a university subject I was studying. And that could have been the end of it ...

Instead I have now written and published my first novel. Those original 500 words which gave rise to the idea of *Harry's World* remain, with only slight editing, in the first part of the novel, *Harry's Tribulations*.

Aside from taking ten years on and off to get to print, I want to thank a number of people who in various important ways have contributed to the book you are now reading ...

For boundless encouragement and support my heartfelt thanks to my partner Ruth and my sister Katie, the latter also keeping my French usage in line.

To my writers' group since 2012, Janine Hewitt and Nigel Bartlett, who have given many hours of careful feedback on all the draft material, and we have enjoyed some lively and productive discussions along the way.

To my friends Richard Purcell and Graeme Dunne for their reading, feedback and encouragement.

To my friend Myles Ward-Thornton, lead singer of the band Snaketide, for the song lyrics in *Harry's Revenge,* and for his encouragement and inspiration in the creative space.

And for the professional expertise and services provided during the latter stages of the project …

Claire Chaffey for her editing advice and proofreading.

Luke Beeton at Sailor Studio for the cover design.

Stephen Hill at Dylunio for logo and stationery design.

Ruth Chambers at Effective Marketing Strategies (EMS) for the marketing plan and implementation.